# Shaken

A TWISTED FOX NOVEL

## CHARITY FERRELL

# Archer

"YOU SELFISH BASTARD!" He charges toward me, his face darkened with fury.

The commotion around us—people crying, asking questions, breaking down—fades away.

I stay in place, unmoving, while waiting for the assault I deserve. The crack of my jaw is all I hear before the pain strikes, and I stumble back, wiping the blood from my lip with the side of my clenched fist.

Straightening myself, I prepare for the next blow.

It connects with my nose.

I don't fight back.

I deserve this.

I am a selfish bastard.

The old proverb, *One night can change your life*, is on the mark.

My life has changed.

*Fuck the lifestyles of the rich.*

*I'm out.*

# CHAPTER ONE

# Georgia

CALL me the queen of embarrassing moments.

Tripping up the stairs and face-planting at my high school graduation.

Side-swiping a car during my driver's test.

Today's embarrassment winner of the week is …

*Drumroll, please.*

Getting stood up for a date.

Even worse, while waiting on my date, the guy I'd dumped six months ago arrived with his. Lucky asshole's date actually showed, and I provided them with free entertainment as they witnessed my disaster.

*It's what you deserve for swiping right on a dude with a mirror selfie as his profile pic, Georgia.*

In my defense, it was margarita night, and I was third-wheeling it when said swiping ensued.

To recover from the mortification, I drive to my happy place —the coffee shop. Iced coffee never fails to pull me out of the *I'll be single for the rest of my life* funk.

"Jackpot." I smile when I spot an empty space before abruptly stopping. "You've got to be kidding me."

Parked next to the only available spot is a car—foreign,

expensive, one of those you see in the movies with rich-people problems.

*Parked* is an understatement.

I pull into the sliver of a space, and like the mature and not-at-all-annoyed woman I am, I give the foreign-car-driving asshole no room to open their door. With a shrug, I step out of my car—American, cheap, one of those that always breaks down in the movies—and stroll into the coffee shop.

Fifteen minutes later, I'm walking back through the parking lot and fueling myself with cold-brew deliciousness. My sipping stops when I notice a man standing behind my car. Shoving my sunglasses down my nose, I take a better look.

"Siri, find me a tow company in the area."

*The hell?*

I scramble toward him, waving my arm in the air, and shriek, "Whoa! Don't call a tow truck!"

*Is that even legal?*

Lord knows I can't afford it if he does. I can barely afford my iced-coffee dependency.

When he turns, my breathing stalls, and I freeze. Momentarily, my car being towed becomes an afterthought.

The man is gorgeous.

*GQ* cover-worthy.

Looking every shade of pissed off.

The sight of him is stronger than any caffeine shot.

His sexy ruggedness—tall and built like a linebacker, broad shoulders, and muscle-bound biceps—is such a contrast to my small frame. Stubbled hair and scruff, trimmed to the jawline, scatters along the slope of his cheeks and down his neck. His hair, a shade matching the drink in my cup, is thick and hits the nape of his neck.

He's clean-cut *but not* clean-cut.

Fighting not to fit the profile of a wealthy man.

A man who gives no fucks … which unfortunately also applies to his parking.

He glowers as I make my way to him, and I keep a short distance between us.

"This your car?" His voice matches his appearance—cold and sharp, like a knife slicing through ice.

"Yes," I answer.

He stares, waiting for me to elaborate.

I take a loud slurp of my coffee before saying, "Please, put your phone away. No need to call a tow company."

"Did you just get your driver's license?" Authority fills his tone, as if he were scolding a child, when he signals to my park job. "Who parks like that? Do you need a booster seat to see over the steering wheel?"

*Rude.*

Short jokes are so grade school.

"The better question is who parks *like that*?" I scowl and gesture to his car. "You took a spot and a half. Not cool."

The collar of his simple white V-neck tee stretches out when he tugs on it. "That was the only available spot when I got here—"

"That means you can park however you want?"

"If you'd let me finish. When I got here, the car on the opposite side of me was parked like shit. A motorcycle was in your spot, so the way I parked provided plenty of room for the both of us." He holds up the coffee cup in his hand. "I planned to run in and out, but when I *ran out*, your car was in my way."

"I planned to run in and out, too, but when I *ran out*, I had to deal with you."

"Move it or get towed." He impatiently waves his phone in the air. "I have shit to do."

"You can't tow my car. It's not even legal."

"Call it a citizen's tow."

"Call it *you're an asshole.*"

The frustration on his face grows. "Move your car. Nothing gets towed. Easy fix."

"You're an ass."

"Never said I was nice."

"Fine, whatever." I narrow my eyes while stalking toward him.

The faster I'm away from this asshole, the better. As I circle him, his slate-gray eyes meet mine, and I trip.

"Holy shit!" I yelp, pushing out my hands to save myself from face-planting. That save results in me losing my coffee.

"What the hell?"

I gulp and peek up at him while on my hands and knees. Coffee drips down his shirt, shaping into a forever stain. My cup is empty and upside down at his feet.

Scratch my earlier statement.

This is the embarrassment winner of my week.

Hell, the embarrassment winner of my year.

"I'm so sorry," I rush out.

He doesn't offer a helping hand as I lift myself and dust off my scraped-up knees.

When I go to pick up the cup, he retreats a step, worried I'll bring him more damage, and stops me. "Just go."

"I'm *sorry*," I repeat, stressing the last word.

He pulls at his shirt, inspecting the stain, and shakes his head. "Make it up to me by getting in your car and leaving."

My remorse spills into anger. "You know what? I take my apology back. I'm not sorry, you jerk."

"Cool," he deadpans, my insult bouncing off him like rubber. "Now, move."

"Asshole." I walk around him, sans tripping this time, and get into my car.

Curses fly from my mouth when I slam the door, crank up the radio, and flip him off as I pull out of my spot. I drive around the building and wait for him to leave before taking his old spot.

"Here we go. Coffee, round two," I mutter.

My phone rings when I kill the ignition, and Lola's name flashes across the screen over a selfie of us.

"You won't believe this," I say, answering my best friend's call before retelling her the coffee nightmare.

"Swear to God, this stuff only happens to you." She laughs. "And what a dick."

"Tell me about it." My head throbs from the lack of caffeine and the mess of today.

"You know, I have a hunch you'll run into each other again."

I snort. "Okay, Miss Cleo. That'd better not happen, or you'll be bailing me out of jail for purposely spilling coffee on him next time."

Queen of Intuition is Lola's nickname. I swear, the girl was a fortune-teller in her past life.

The hairs on the back of my neck stand at her remark.

*Do I want to see him again?*

My heart races at the thought.

# CHAPTER TWO

# Archer

Two Weeks Later

"TELL the attorney to score a better deal," I demand. "It's a bullshit plea."

"Archer." My mother's voice carries through my car's Bluetooth speakers. "Katherine works for the finest firm in the state. Trust me, she's doing her best."

"She can do better." *She has to do better.* "We're paying her a shit-ton of money to get him out of this."

"To get *them* out of this."

I snarl and tighten my grip on the steering wheel. "No, to get *him* out. I don't care about anyone else."

At the same time as my gaze returns to the road, the driver in front of me slams on their brakes. I ram my foot onto my brake pedal, hard enough that I'm waiting for my foot to hit the concrete, but I'm too slow.

"Motherfucker," I hiss when I jerk forward and rear-end the car. "Let me call you back."

I end the call and glance in my rearview mirror. When I see the car behind me is pulled to the side of the road, damage-free, a rush of relief hits me. Moments later, they pull back onto the street and drive past me. One less collision for me to deal with.

I swerve to the side of the road, my jaw clenching, and shift my car into park. The car I hit does the same.

An accident isn't what I need today.

Or any damn day.

I'm already dealing with enough wreckage.

I snatch my Italian leather wallet from the cupholder, stretch out of my car, and straighten myself. As much as I love my Aston Martin, they make them for tiny fuckers, not dudes hitting the six-six mark.

I glimpse at my newly purchased and shipped-from-England DBS Superleggera, and I grit my teeth. It'll cost a pretty penny to repair. My gaze flicks to the car I hit. There isn't much damage. It's at least a decade old and worth a few grand at most. I'll throw cash at the problem for a simple fix.

"You've got to be kidding me," I hiss when the driver steps out of the car.

The sour look coming from her confirms she remembers me. I slip my hands into my pockets and stroll toward the brat who blocked me in at the coffee shop a few weeks ago. If this encounter is like our last, it won't be as easy as I hoped. No doubt this chick is about to add more stress to my day.

"Just perfect," she yells, throwing up her arms. "It's the Prick Parker. Not only do you suck at parking but you're also a terrible driver."

She straightens her shoulders when I reach her. The woman might grate on my nerves, but she's drop-dead gorgeous. Every physical feature of hers matches her spitfire personality. Random pieces of her caramel-colored hair are braided, tumbling across her sun-kissed shoulders, and she's wearing short-shorts that show off her toned legs.

She has the face of trouble, of fun, of happiness.

She's a shot of serotonin in a crop top.

The opposite of me.

The type of person I steer clear of.

While she's a dose of pleasure, I'm a cocktail of misery.

My attention falls to her plump lips, and I lick my own, curious how she tastes.

Probably sweet.

Like a sugary doughnut or a juicy strawberry.

I shake my head to murder those thoughts. "Don't you know you're not supposed to slam on your brakes out of nowhere?"

"Don't you know there's a three-second distance rule?" She smirks, pleased with her comeback.

*That smart-ass mouth.*

Had this been years ago, I would've loved it.

Would've wanted to fuck it.

But I'm not that man anymore.

"I didn't expect you to stop for no damn reason."

"There was a reason."

"Which was?"

"A chipmunk ran in front of me."

"A chipmunk?"

"Yes!" she shrieks. "A chipmunk! Furry little thing." She lowers her hand until it's nearly touching the ground. "About yea high."

I stare at her, working my jaw.

"Oh!" she scoffs. "You'd rather me murder Alvin the Chipmunk? You truly are a heartless, shitty parker of a man."

"No, I don't want you to murder a damn whatever chipmunk." I scrub a hand over my face as cars pass us, surveying my situation with their nosy eyes. "Look, I'm in a rush. There's hardly any damage to your car—"

"Whoa." She gestures to her bumper, now renovated with a minor dent and scratches. "That *is* more than hardly any damage."

I rub my hands together. "I'll tell you what. We'll call it even."

"Excuse me? What do you mean, *call it even?*"

"You ruined my shirt during our last little run-in, and I didn't make you pay for it." I shrug. "Tit for tat."

Her jaw drops. "You think a ruined shirt is equivalent to car damage?"

"When the shirt most likely cost more than the car, yes."

"Wow," she calls out as if she were in front of an audience, and her mouth forms an *O*. "Alexa, show me the definition of a rich, arrogant prick."

It was a low blow.

Cunning.

Bragging about my wealth isn't a hobby of mine, but if it makes someone hate me, I'll boast away. Throughout the years, I've learned the easiest approach for convincing people to leave you alone is for them to dread your presence. No one wants to hang out with the brooding bastard.

She holds her chin high, awaiting my next move, for me to solve the problem for us. I have no issues with paying for the damages. Hell, I'll buy her a new car if she wants. The issue is compensating her while also maintaining a low profile.

"How about this?" I say, and her gaze meets mine in expectation. "Let's exchange information and not worry about a police report."

Another police report with my family's name added to the stack is the last thing we need.

She skeptically stares at me, and her words come out slow. "You're admitting it's your fault, correct?"

A rumble shoots through my skull. "Sure, it can be my fault."

"But it was your fault."

"That's what I said, sure."

"*Sure* isn't you accepting responsibility."

"Jesus, fuck." I rub the back of my starting-to-sweat neck. "It was my fault. You happy? You want me to get it tattooed on me?"

"That'd actually be kind of hot." She smiles in amusement. "Will you put my name next to it ... or possibly my face? I once dated this frat boy—" She pauses, holding up a finger. "Correction: not *dated*. We talked, went to a few parties together, you know—"

"No, I don't know," I talk over her. "Nor do I care or understand how the fuck that pertains to our situation."

"My point is, he said I have a face made for art." She uses her full palm and circles her face through the air.

"Again, I have no idea how this pertains to me hitting your car." I shake my head. "I'll pay for the damages. Don't worry about mine."

"I'm not worried about paying for yours since it was *your fault.*"

I cock my head to the side when I catch a hint of her perfume. Never in my thirty years have I met someone who smelled like cotton candy, like a damn carnival snack. Not even when I was the age of a kid who was excited to attend a carnival.

Like everything else, it suits her.

Gives way to her personality.

Has me wanting to get to know her more than I should.

To kill that, I open my wallet and riffle through the business cards until finding the one I need.

"Here's my info." I offer her the card. "Call this number. My assistant will get you taken care of."

She snatches the card from my hand and holds it in the air, reading it as if it were toxic. "A card? How do I even know this is you?" She points at my wallet. "Can I see your driver's license? Proof of insurance? You could run off, and I'd never see you again."

"Trust me, your damages will be paid." I grab the card, pull a pen from my pocket, and write my license plate number on the back. "I won't run off."

I turn around without giving her a chance to ask more questions.

"What the hell is happening?" she mutters.

I get into my car, and this time, I'm the one leaving her.

# CHAPTER THREE

## Georgia

I FOCUS on his license plate number when he pulls away.

Homeboy isn't leaving me high and dry with a banged-up car.

It matches.

*Who knows their license plate number by heart?*

Hell, half the time, I forget my birthday.

I sigh and lean back against my car.

*Why do I always need a moment to refresh, to regain my thoughts, when he's around?*

I play with the card in my hand. Expensive card stock. The name *Chase Smith* written in gold.

He didn't look like a Chase Smith.

Didn't put off a Chase Smith vibe.

The name is too simple.

Generic.

No offense to any Chase Smiths out there.

He was right about the damages being minimal, but I don't have the cash for even minimal repairs. When I get back into my car, I crank up the air-conditioning and make myself comfortable for some stalking.

I Google Chase Smith.

The results pop up with a list of generic Chase Smiths.

Frat boys.

Guys with fishing poles thrown over their shoulders.

Family men.

None of them the grumpy, handsome, *has a stick up his ass* man who keeps ruining my days.

I bet he doesn't use social media.

He doesn't seem like the type to post selfies or double-tap memes.

Not that he'd have many followers or likes with that stank attitude of his.

*Damn you, Lola.*

*Jinxing me with the* you'll run into each other again *shit.*

I call the number on the card to make sure I don't need to call the cops and report a hit-and-run accident. Rather, a *hit, stop, hand card, and run* situation.

"Hello, this is Kiki," a woman answers in a chirpy voice. "How may I help you?"

"Hi, this is Georgia Fox. Your boss, Chase Smith, hit my car and said to call this number."

"Ah, yes, he told me to expect your call." She proceeds to give me all the information I need.

---

TWO DAYS LATER, Kiki—a woman close to my mother's age with bright red hair and dark sunglasses—shows up at my door.

"From Chase," she says, handing over a thick white envelope and leaving.

*It keeps getting weirder with this guy.*

When I open it, I nearly faint.

It's cash.

I count the bills.

Fifteen thousand dollars.

Way more money than the damages would cost.

Way more than my car is worth.

*Who is this man?*

*Is he into illegal shit?*

*A Mafia dude?*

I pull out my phone to do the thousandth search of this mystery man.

*Chase Smith, Mafia.*

Nothing.

*Chase Smith …*

*I want to know more about you.*

## CHAPTER FOUR

# Archer

3 Weeks Later

*FUCK THIS DAY.*

*And fuck tomorrow too.*

I signal to the bartender for another shot.

He delivers.

*This one's to failure.*

I knock it back.

Ask for another.

*This one's for defeat.*

Another.

*This one's for Lincoln.*

Tonight, I've chosen to test my alcohol tolerance at Bailey's, a hole-in-the-wall dive bar. Over the past few months, I've become a regular here, spending more time in the run-down bar than my home, even though my penthouse holds a superior liquor collection.

You don't come to places like Bailey's for the liquor selection.

Or the customer service.

Or the decor.

You come when you've stopped caring.

Sometimes, you're so down on life that you want to pop a squat on a broken stool and drink cheap booze.

Bailey's provides privacy from my life without complete isolation.

The only person I had left in this shithole life is in prison now.

No matter how big of a dick I was to my brother, Lincoln, he never let me push him away. Now, it's me, the outcast of the family, drinking alone in a bar that reeks of mold and desperation.

As if the bartender, Ted, can read my mind, he slides another drink to me. My gaze lifts as I grab the glass, and my attention drifts to the opposite end of the bar. Every hair on my body stands when I see her. She drapes her purse over the ripped barstool and runs her hands down her patterned dress, smoothing out the wrinkles. When she slumps onto the stool, her posture mimics mine.

*Why is she here?*

Reasons swirl through my mind so fast that it's hard to keep up.

*It's not her.*

*She doesn't belong in a place like this.*

Man, this cheap shit knocks you on your ass.

I wipe my eyes with the heels of my hands, expecting to find an empty stool when I drag them away, but disbelief clouds my drunken brain.

*It's her.*

Ted approaches her with a smile—one too friendly for my liking—and she delivers a forced one in return while speaking to him. I edge closer, hoping to eavesdrop on their conversation, but there's too much chaos—people yelling over the loud music and glasses being moved around. He taps the bar, pulls away, and starts on her drink.

It's a struggle to make out her features underneath the faint, sorry excuse for a light shining above her. Even though I've consumed enough booze to stock a small distillery, my throat turns dry as I observe her. The distance separating us doesn't conceal her pain.

She's hunched over in defeat and flicking at the chipped wood on the bar.

The glow she carried before has faded.

Vulnerability owning its place.

The feisty, spot-blocking, chipmunk-saving, pain-in-the-ass woman is heartbroken.

She roughly snatches her phone sitting next to her, powers it off, and shoves it into her bag.

*Georgia.*

Kiki gave me her name.

Weeks have passed since I rear-ended her, but she's loitered my thoughts, surfacing when I grab a coffee or take the road where I hit her. There was a powerful urge to learn more about her during our encounters. Every time, *Want to grab a coffee to replace the one you spilled,* was at the tip of my tongue, but I bit into it, puncturing the idea.

It would've been selfish.

A woman like her doesn't belong with a man like me. She doesn't deserve to have her time wasted.

I'd never be what she wanted.

What she needed.

I'd siphon any bliss from her life.

To avoid that, I stepped aside and had Kiki handle the situation. I instructed her to pay Georgia more than what the car was worth, more than what the repairs would cost, and in cash, so not a penny could be traced back to me.

The Feds like manipulating shit.

I drink her in, swallowing a view that hits me harder than any drink behind the bar.

Someone did what I'd refused to.

Broke her.

*I want to kick his ass.*

I slug down my shot, killing it at the same time Ted drops hers off, and revel in the slow burn slipping down my throat. When I stand, my heart punches my chest in warning.

*If you carry out this plan, it will change your night.*

I make a beeline toward her, the alcohol controlling my every move and coaxing my drunken mind into thinking this is a good idea. Thankfully, there are open seats around her. The stool's legs scrape as I yank it out and sit next to her.

That sweet cotton-candy scent assaults me, adding to my intoxication, and I can almost taste the spun sugar.

She peeks over at me and downs her drink, and her tone is harsh when she speaks, "Are you serious right now?"

*Not the response I was hoping for.*

*The response I should've expected, though.*

Instead of answering, I lift two fingers in the air—a signal for Ted—and he comes over.

Gesturing to her, I say, "This one's on me."

She draws in a breath, contemplating whether to play this game, and focuses on Ted. "I'll have a Manhattan, please."

"Hennessy good?" he asks.

She nods.

*Hennessy?*

I took her for more of a margarita or lemon-drop drinker, sure as hell not cognac.

Ted's attention slides to me. "You?"

"I'll also have Hennessy." I rub my hands together. "Straight. On the rocks."

He tips his head down. "On it."

As soon as Ted's out of earshot, she turns and glowers at me. "Are you stalking me?"

"I was here first," I reply, fixing my stare on her. "The better question is, are *you* stalking me?"

She rolls her eyes. "You wish."

There's that attitude.

It isn't as snarky or as hateful as before but still lurks inside.

The pain in her eyes confirms the woman I dealt with before isn't coming out tonight. Like me, tonight's drinks aren't for entertainment. They're to evade our reality.

I clear my throat, my eyes not leaving her. "First, let's start with what my stalker's name is."

Her jaw falls slack. "I'm *not* your stalker."

"Okay, what's my *not*-stalker's name?"

She can't know I asked Kiki about her.

She glares at me in suspicion. "Georgia."

"Okay, Georgia. Want to tell me why it looks like someone told you Taylor Swift quit making music?"

"It's personal." She clips a curly tendril of her long hair behind her ear. "Want to tell me why you look like a depressed dick?"

"It's personal." I pay a quick glance to Ted when he drops off our drinks.

She flips her hair over her shoulder, exposing the curve of her neck, before grabbing her drink and taking a sip.

*What I'd do to run my lips over her soft skin, up the side of her neck, while whispering every way I wanted to pleasure her.*

"You came to me, so you wanted conversation." When she plucks the cherry from the glass and plays with the stem in her mouth, my cock stirs. "What do you want to talk about? Chipmunks? Spilled coffee?"

"I figured you could use some company."

I should've thought this through before approaching her. Per my grandfather's advice, you always have a plan before undertaking a task. Going in blind only leads you into walls.

She signals to her face. "This face screams, *Give me company?*"

"Yes, it's interesting."

The crowd, the TVs, the hustle and bustle fade as I fixate on her. A sense of unworthiness hits me at seeing her so up close, so vulnerable, as if it's something I don't deserve. Even with her swollen eyes—my guess, a result from crying—and the mascara caked along the bottoms, she's gorgeous. Her effort of wiping off the makeup shows, but she didn't catch every inch.

I pinch the bridge of my nose to stop myself from reaching out and running a hand over her cheek, rubbing away the spots she missed and erasing the evidence of her pain.

"Interesting?" she fires back.

"It interested me enough to come over and be your company tonight." I grab my glass and take a slow draw of the cognac.

"There are plenty of other options for company." She does a circling motion around the room. "Other women. Go give them company because, forewarning, I won't be a good time."

*And I look like I will?*

"I'd rather have a drink with someone who's had as shitty of a day as I have, who isn't here for a good time, and who can sit with me in silence yet throw out a few comments here and there."

"And I seem like that someone?"

Gripping my glass, I raise it to my lips, but instead of taking a drink, I tip it in her direction. "I don't know. Are you?"

"So …" She taps her nails—colored designs on each one—against her glass before placing it on the bar. "You want to sit here in silence?"

"Silence. Small talk. Whatever."

"All right then. I guess we'll sit here and *whatever*."

I take a sip of my drink, the rich, spicy liquid coating my tongue, and stare while attempting not to make it obvious. She shifts her attention forward, and when her lower lip trembles, it crushes my soul.

She doesn't deserve sadness.

Pain.

People like me? We do.

I hardly know her, but I'd gladly rip away her pain and attach it to mine.

"You sure you don't want to talk about it?" I ask.

*Let me fix this for you.*

She shakes her head, releasing a sharp laugh. "Not interested in becoming the *crying drunk in the corner* cliché."

"I won't let you cry. Promise."

She scoffs.

I scoot closer, erasing the distance between us, and press my hand to my chest. "I'm an asshole, remember? You're too cool to cry in front of an asshole."

She releases a heavy sigh and hesitates. A wave of silence passes, and I nurse my drink while waiting. As badly as I want to beg her to spill her guts, I stop myself from asking.

It's her story. If she needs to take all night, so be it.

It's not like I have anywhere to be.

"It's daddy issues," she finally whispers. "No one wants to hear about a woman's daddy issues."

*She's right. Generally, people don't.*

*But tonight, for some weird-ass reason, I want to hear hers.*

"Daddy issues away." I slide my glass over, and it bumps against hers. "Look at it this way. I'm the best person to talk to. You'll never see me again. Unleash your bullshit on me, and I'll scrape an inch of the pain off your heart. It'll be our little secret —a secret no one in your life will know."

She downs her drink, and without thinking, I reach down to relax her bouncing knee, my hand resting along the bare skin underneath the hem of her dress. My head spins as I realize what I did, and I peek up at her. There's no reaction to my touch—no flinch, no side-eye—as if it were where it belonged.

"I'll need another drink for this." She holds up the glass. "An extra shot of truth serum."

Following her lead, I finish my drink, call Ted over, and order us another round. Not a word is muttered while we wait for the delivery of our *truth serum*. She doesn't give Ted the chance to set her drink down before she grabs it straight from his hand and knocks it back like a pro.

Ted shrugs, hands over my drink, and wanders off to take an order.

She points at me with the empty glass. "Don't say I didn't warn you."

"Lay it on me." I squeeze her knee, giving her the green light to start.

Her gaze drops to her lap, to my hand, and I wait for her to shove it away. Instead, she relaxes.

"My father left us when I was a baby," she begins. "Six months ago, I tracked him down, and today, I mustered the courage to visit him." She grimaces. "It was stupid to think he'd want to meet me, but he seemed like a decent man on social media. Married, tagged in pictures with his children."

A sniffle leaves her before she inhales a deep breath, and I give her knee another reassuring squeeze.

"I felt like a lost puppy who had found its way home when I showed up on his doorstep, but as soon as I introduced myself, the excitement, the hope, it died. That's when I realized I was the puppy no one wanted in their home. I was sent on my way, shown I wasn't welcome. He'd changed into the family man he needed to be but for another family."

My stomach knots at the thought of humiliation and rejection that raw.

The horror of being turned away as if you were nothing.

"I'm sorry." Before I can stop it, I rip myself open as deep as she did. "My father went to prison today." My tone is lower than hers. "And he took my brother down with him."

Her mouth drops open, shock flashing in her eyes.

I relax in the chair. "It appears we both have daddy issues."

"Your father ..." She clears her throat, searching for the right words. "He's in prison? For what?"

"Embezzlement." I pull my hand away from her leg and scratch my cheek. "Money laundering."

"I'm, uh ... sorry about that."

"I'm sorry about your shit."

I hold out my empty glass. She does the same, and we clink them together.

"To fucked-up fathers."

"Hear, hear."

Silence makes a reappearance.

"Can we talk about something else?" she asks. "I could use the distraction."

"We can talk about anything you want." The liquor is changing me into a different man—one open to speaking about his problems and hearing another's. "You decide."

*Who is this guy?*

Maybe it's the Hennessy.

The day.

The woman next to me.

She peeks over at me. "I don't know. Puppies, sports—which I know jack shit about, FYI—the Pope. Anything but my problems."

All those subjects sound like a damn bore. I fix my gaze on her, drinking in the view, and can't stop myself from saying, "Can we talk about how beautiful you are?"

*Fuck!*

*Douchebag alert.*

I'm *that* guy now.

The one who uses a cheesy-ass pickup line.

Not that I'm trying to pick her up.

"What?" she stutters, gawking at me.

"Just needed to get that out there." I shrug—an attempt to put off a give-no-fucks attitude.

When my gaze drops to her lips, she licks them.

"Thank you." She displays a hint of a smile, and I pride myself on providing some light in her darkness. "Tell me more about you, Chase Smith. Are you married? Dating anyone?"

I cringe when she says Chase. "Nope and nope."

She turns, settles her elbow on the bar, and leans against it, granting me her full attention. "Why not?"

"Shit doesn't always work out." *That's an understatement.*

She nods in agreement.

"What about you?"

"Single as a dollar bill. No hubby. No kids. I do, however, have a pet rock."

"Why single?"

"Shit doesn't always work out." She smirks.

"I like this game."

"What game?"

"Using each other's answers against one another."

"I must say, it's better than confessing daddy issues."

I smile.

She smiles back.

We order another round.

Drink and make small talk.

I find my hand back on her thigh.

As the night grows later, she leans into me.

When a laugh escapes her, I mentally pat myself on the back.

It's not much, but it's something.

Something other than sadness.

"You want to get out of here?" she asks all of a sudden.

I still, my hand tightening around the neck of my beer bottle.

I moved on to beer to save myself from getting too shit-faced.

Somehow, my goal tonight has shifted.

Because of her.

"Never mind." Her voice is unsteady as she flicks her hand through the air. "I swear, that isn't something I ask on the regular. I've never even had a one-night stand. I can count the men I've slept with on one hand—"

Unable to stop myself—and rougher than I should—I grip the curve of her neck and bring my lips to her ear. "How drunk are you?"

She shivers, goose bumps spreading over her soft skin, when I loosen my hold and trail my fingers along her neck. She lifts her chin, heat creeping up it, and allows me easier access. I tip my head down and replace my fingers with my lips.

My tongue brushes her neck when she says, "Tipsy, not drunk."

Her voice is clear.

No slur.

My cock stirs as I croak out, "Your place or mine?"

"Yours."

This is where I usually say I don't do sleepovers at my house.

I don't.

Instead, I press one last kiss to her neck before drawing back.

I pay our tab, and her hand finds mine as I lead us outside. The destination: my place. The short drive to my penthouse seems ten times longer, and unable to restrain myself, I slip my hand under her dress. She gasps, parting her legs, and I skim a single finger along the lace of her panties.

Back and forth, not going any further.

She whimpers, "More."

My thumb moves to her clit.

She's soaked.

So wet that I can feel it through the lace.

It's a struggle to hold back from plunging a finger inside her. The Uber driver eyes us suspiciously, as if he knows we're up to something. As soon as we arrive at my building, I grab her hand and lead her into the elevator.

When we walk into my penthouse, I briefly hear her say, "Nice place," before I slam my mouth onto hers.

I kiss her hard, tasting the alcohol on her lips, hitting me stronger than the Hennessy.

*Fuck.*

Fucking her will be the best antidote to my hell.

No alcohol will beat this.

No drug.

She's the one thing I never knew I needed.

Her kiss sets me on fire.

It's passionate.

Hot.

Our tongues meet, as if drawing the pain out of each other. Our mouths don't separate as I lead her to my bedroom. As soon as the light flicks on, I strip her, fling her dress across the room, and pull down the duvet on my bed. Grabbing her hips, I toss her onto the bed, and she lands on her back.

She holds herself up on her elbows.

I stand at the foot, stroking my chin, and admire her naked body.

The way her breasts bounce as her breathing turns heavier.

Her hard pink nipples.

Her smooth legs slightly parted as she waits for me.

My bed has never looked so damn tempting.

She gasps as I climb between her legs.

She moans when I take the first taste of her.

Licking my way up her slit before sucking on her clit.

*So damn delicious.*

I lick, slip my tongue in, add fingers until she's writhing underneath me.

As soon as she gets off, I frantically unbuckle my pants. She moves just as hurriedly, pushing them down, and I pull my shirt over my head. Seconds after, I slide the condom on and thrust inside her.

"Chase," she moans.

I freeze, squeezing my eyes shut, and she stares up at me in question.

*Don't call me that.*

*Moan another name.*

To stop myself from admitting my truth, I shove my face into her neck, tasting her sweet skin, and fuck her gently.

We're strangers in the missionary position, but it's like she fits me.

Gets me.

She begs for more.

I fuck her harder.

I savor her.

Her name leaves my lips as I explode into the condom.

Then round two starts.

When we're sweaty and all orgasmed out, I pull her into my side, drape my arm along her waist, and mold her body into mine.

I don't ask her to leave.

Don't kick her out of my bed.

What a damn mistake that is.

# CHAPTER FIVE

## Georgia

I'VE NEVER WOKEN up in a stranger's bed before.

Although is he considered a stranger if I let him bang my brains out last night?

The bright sunlight streaming through the wall of windows assaults my eyes, and I throw my arm over my face to block the rays. Giving myself a moment to adjust to the light, I move my arm, stretch out my body, and yawn.

My thighs ache.

My legs are sore.

My mouth is dry.

I shift in the crisp sheets.

Sheets that don't belong to me.

In a bed that doesn't belong to me.

It's *his* bed.

In *his* room.

My heart pounds at the memories of what happened in this bed last night.

I'd stopped at the bar yesterday to avoid going home and sulking in an empty apartment. My plan was to have a drink to settle my nerves, leave, and watch murder mysteries until passing out.

When Chase sat next to me, like a broken knight in shining armor, my night changed for the better. My view of him before —the arrogant ass—had dissolved, making me see him in a better light.

He made me feel wanted.

Needed.

Gave me more orgasms last night than I could count.

Blame it on my daddy issues, but on the day I felt the most discarded, he was there to collect the pieces and put me back together.

My stomach sinks when I glance around the empty room, and I shift my attention to the adjoined bathroom. The light is off, and I gulp at the silence hanging in the air.

"Hello?" I call out, my voice raspy and timid as if I were in a horror movie, heard a bump in the night, and Jason was coming to slaughter me.

Silence.

I clutch my arms against my chest as my heart batters against it.

*Did he leave?*

Reasons for the stillness rush through my mind.

*He's waiting for me to leave.*

*He grabbed breakfast.*

*He bailed.*

*He's already been slaughtered by Jason.*

Hell, at this point, I'd rather hear a chain saw than this silence.

*Bring out the killer, please and thank you.*

Let him murder my humiliation if this guy hit it and quit it.

Chase hadn't exactly been open to conversation during our first two run-ins. As I relaxed in his arms last night, I convinced myself what we'd shared—the drinks, secrets, and sex—made up for his previous asshole behavior.

"Hello?" I call out again.

No response.

*My naivety strikes again.*

I drop my hands to my stomach as the urge to vomit last night's drinks and this morning's embarrassment seep up my throat. I do another once-over of the room and form the sign of a cross when I spot my phone on the nightstand. The chill of the room hits me when I reach out and grab the phone. Unlocking it, I hit Lola's name. My best friend is a pro in these situations.

"Lola," I hiss when she answers, gripping the phone tight against my cheek.

"Oh my God, Georgia," she groans. "It's eight in the morning. This'd better be an emergency and not you asking me to yoga again. Spoiler alert: not happening. Call Grace."

"I'm stuck at a guy's house," I rush out before she hangs up.

"What?" Her sleepy tone becomes alert.

"I'm stuck at a guy's house."

"How'd you get stuck at his house? Are you being held hostage? Do I need to call 911 ... or send ransom money?"

"No," I groan. "I had sex with him last night."

"Good girl." She whistles. "It's about time you got laid."

"Not good, considering he's gone." It's a struggle to keep my voice low.

"Gone? Like, gone from the house or just the bedroom?"

"The bedroom."

"You haven't looked anywhere else?"

"I don't hear any noise."

"Hmm ..."

"Tell me what to do."

"Have you slept with him before?"

"Nope. It was the first and *only* time." I rub at the throbbing temples. "He bought me a drink, and next thing I knew, we were having sex." More memories of that night hurl through my brain, intensifying my headache.

She laughs. "I hate when that happens."

"Enough small talk. *What do I do?*"

"Are you naked?"

Stupidly, I pull down the white sheet and check. "Yes."

"Get up and find your clothes."

I jump out of bed, the sheet still in tow to cover myself, and start gathering my clothes scattered throughout the room. I'm light-headed as I slide on my wrinkled dress, slip my panties up my legs, and shove my feet into my sandals.

"Done," I say.

"Step one, complete." Humor fills her voice. "Now, go look for any signs of life—outside, in the kitchen, in an office. Just because he's not in the bedroom doesn't mean he bailed."

Her words don't give me hope. When I pad out of the bedroom, I grab my bag that was drunkenly dropped to the floor when he dragged me to his bedroom. My sandals squeak against the marble floor as I move through the home, eyeing the wall of windows and modern furniture. As I hit the kitchen, I spot a box of doughnuts and two coffee cups on the counter.

"Breakfast is on the counter," I say.

"That's a nice turn of events," she replies. "Maybe he isn't a runner."

As I grow closer, I notice a note and cash next to the food. As I read it, I cover my mouth and gag.

*Here's money for a cab or Uber.*
*You can see yourself out.*
*Don't worry about locking up.*

*What the actual fuck?*

As if yesterday's rejection hadn't shred my heart enough, this guy tattered what I'd had left.

I pull in a breath to stop myself from crying. "He left a note."

"A note?" Lola asks. "Like a love note?"

My hands are shaking when I read it to her.

"Code red. Time to run. Take the coffee, snag a doughnut, and fuck him—differently than you did last night."

For a moment, I debate on staying—lounging around his lavish home until he returns, so I can call him out. I can take a bath in the massive whirlpool, drink the overpriced alcohol on the bar cart ... or pour it all down the drain in spite.

Or rob him. I'm sure I could find a pretty Rolex or piggy bank around this place. He deserves some good thievery. Unfortunately, unlike the man I slept with last night, I'm a decent person with morals.

Those morals could be somewhat questionable after last night.

I went home with a man who I'd previously Googled to see if he was in the Mafia.

With a doughnut in my mouth, I rummage through my purse for a pen. I fail but find something better. A rush of satisfaction shoots through me when I march to his bathroom and write, *Your dick is small,* in red lipstick across his mirror.

---

A LOUD YAWN escapes me when I fall in a creaky chair at my brother, Cohen's, kitchen table.

After leaving Chase's this morning, I took an Uber, the driver judging me for my walk-of-shame outfit, and picked up my car from Bailey's.

A bar I'll never return to.

I held my chin high during the drive to my apartment, showered, popped a few painkillers, and napped before coming to Cohen's.

Cohen isn't just my older brother; he's my entire family, bunched into one person. He stepped into the role of parenthood, playing the mother and the father, when ours wouldn't. He was my parent, big brother, provider, friend, babysitter, and also authoritarian. Had he not stepped up, my childhood years would've most likely been spent in the system, jumping from foster home to foster home.

"I need to tell you something." I pop one of Noah's fruit snacks in my mouth before gagging. "I'm also requesting you don't buy sugar-free fruit snacks again. Gross."

He peers over at me while washing a Ninja Turtle cup in the sink. "What's up?"

"I found Dad." My attention slides from him to the wall as guilt surfaces over hiding this from him.

The cup slips from his hand, falling into the sink, and the water sprays his shirt.

He quickly turns off the faucet, grabs a towel, and dries his hands. "Okay?"

"And I might've gone to see him yesterday."

"Jesus Christ, Georgia. Why didn't you tell me?"

"You would've said it was a stupid idea."

"From how you look, it was."

"Rude," I grumble, failing to meet his eyes.

Crossing his arms, he rests his back against the counter. "What happened?"

"He has a new family." I rub at my eyes—an attempt to stop the tears from surfacing. "A woman answered the door, looking like she wanted to kill me. My guess is, she thought I was his mistress. He knew who I was as soon as he saw me. When I blurted out that I was his daughter, the woman nearly fainted. She had no idea he'd had a family before her. He showed me the door and demanded I never come back."

He blows out a ragged breath. "I'm sorry, sis."

I shrug, and my voice cracks. "That chapter is closed now. No more what-ifs, you know? I wish I'd been like you and not cared about him."

As he stares at me, I take in the similarities he has to our father—tall, brown hair, sharp jaw. "Dad left when you were a baby. You never knew him, so no one can blame you for being curious. I never cared because I was seven when he bailed and knew what kind of person he was." He motions for me to stand. "Come here."

There's a sense of comfort, of security, when he wraps me into a tight hug. I cry into the shoulder of the only man who's never broken my heart.

"Screw anyone who doesn't want us in their lives," I mutter.

He squeezes me tighter. "Yeah, fuck them."

*Fuck POS fathers.*

*Fuck men who ditch you.*

*Fuck Chase Smith.*

---

I'M my heart's worst enemy.

No doubt if it could choose a different chest of residence, it'd pack up and haul ass.

My brain, on the other hand, is *my* worst enemy.

When I return home from Cohen's, I come up with the brilliant idea to call Chase. The problem is, I don't know *his* number.

What I do know is *his assistant's* number.

She answers on the second ring, "Hello, this is Kiki."

*No going back now.*

"Hey, Kiki," I say. "It's Georgia. I'm the woman—"

"I know who you are, honey," she interrupts. It's not a rude interruption yet also not friendly. More of a *why are you calling* tone. "What can I help you with?"

*Here goes.*

"Can you give me Chase's number?"

"Why?"

"I need to ask him a question."

"I'm sure I can answer that question."

"Not exactly."

"Let me put you on hold for a moment."

The line turns quiet, and I pull my phone away, checking to see she didn't hang up on me.

A few minutes later, she's back. "I'm sorry, Georgia. He's busy at the moment."

I need to talk to him, to know why he did what he did. Even if it's an answer I don't want to hear, one that'd break my heart, it's what I want.

"I can wait."

"Honey, you'll be waiting forever then."

"What?"

She sighs. "Listen, don't pursue him. Nothing will come of it. Arch—I mean, Chase will not take or return any of your calls."

Short, simple, no bullshit in her tone.

"All right," I say softly.

We end the call.

Briefly, I debate on driving to his house but stop myself.

*For someone who doesn't want to talk to a hookup, why did he take me to his house?*

I need to listen to her. To my gut. To Lola when she told me never to speak to him again. I need to remember every time he showed me his true colors—from threatening to tow my car to leaving me.

He's someone I never want to have a conversation with again.

# CHAPTER SIX

## Archer

One Month Later

"A BAR?" The question falls from my mother's lips in disdain.

I nod. "A bar."

"Archer, darling," she says slowly, "why don't you wait until Lincoln is released before doing anything drastic?"

"This isn't drastic."

"Starting a business out of the blue is drastic."

"Out of the blue?" I shake my head, clearing my throat to create the perfect sternness in my voice. "After grandfather's death, I wanted out but stayed for the family. It's not happening again."

She can push and plead all she wants, but this time, there's no changing my mind. No more arguing, no more working at a job I hate, no more stomach sinking in guilt when I take the elevator to the top floor at Callahan Holdings.

No. Fucking. More.

"You'll ruin the family's legacy," she argues.

"Blame that on Dad. Not me."

That *legacy* was trashed by Warren Callahan II when he pleaded guilty for breaking the law.

Since childbirth, my life plan has been to work for my family's empire. Callahan Holdings was founded by my grandfather decades ago. He purchased real estate— predominately farmland—dirt cheap and cashed out when it was commercialized. Callahan Holdings owns shopping centers, office buildings, and businesses out the ass. After my grandfather's passing, my dad promoted himself to president. I declined the VP position, and my younger brother, Lincoln, took the job. I became the chief operations officer—the smallest role I could take—but I quit when I discovered my father's fraudulence.

Knowing this would be her reaction, I waited to break the news to her until I was certain of the decision. For years, I've been questioned why I bartend. I don't need the money, but it's not what bartending is about for me. It's a therapy, slinging drinks and being in the zone. When I'm there, I'm not in my head, tormenting myself with regrets of my actions. Which is why, the day after Lincoln was sentenced, I decided I was not just returning to bartending; I was going to open a bar.

It's for my sanity, not the money. Even after quitting my job, I have enough in savings and from my inheritance to never have to work another day in my life.

"You're doing this because of him," she says.

We both flinch at her statement … at the mention of my grandfather.

It's harsh and terrible timing, yet it's true.

I shut my eyes, her remark a verbal punch to my gut.

"Sorry," she whispers, backing up and sitting on a barstool behind my twelve-foot kitchen island. "If this makes you happy, that's all I care about, but—"

"How'd I know there'd be a but?"

Josephine Callahan isn't one who loses easily. "As your mother, I believe you'll regret this decision." When she places her hand to her chest over her heart, her sparkling ten-carat wedding ring is on display. "Everyone knows your grandfather expected you to take over the company when he retired."

I grit my teeth, the headache resurfacing—the same one that always comes when he's brought up. "Had he been able to see into the future, he wouldn't have."

"Honey, it was an accident," she stresses, her face softening. "Stop punishing yourself."

"Accident or not, it's on me."

My penthouse falls silent, and I sigh at the deep sadness on my mother's face. She's had a rough year, losing my brother and my father to correctional facilities. She's been left with the negative son who wants nothing to do with the lifestyle she lives.

She perks up on her stool, always one to mask her emotions. "Don't forget your grandparents' party is tonight."

*Party.*

My mouth turns sour at the word. "You know I don't go to parties." Those days are over.

"It's not *any* party, Archer. It's a small social gathering to celebrate their fiftieth anniversary. They'll be delighted if you show."

Small social gathering, my ass.

My grandmother doesn't do *small*. She's the queen of over-the-top parties. For my fifth birthday, she rented out an entire amusement park. My mother wasn't born a Callahan; she married into the name, but she was born into wealth by her parents.

My phone ringing stops this dreadful conversation, and I swipe it off the counter. My friend Cohen's name flashes across the screen.

"I need to take this." I hold up the phone and walk toward my office while answering, "Hey."

"Hey, man," he replies. "Barbecue tonight at my place. Come through."

I met Cohen when we bartended together. A few weeks ago, I called and asked if he'd be interested in starting a bar together.

"Nah, I'll have to pass."

"Come on," he groans around a chuckle. "For years, you've passed on all my invites. You're coming. We can talk business."

I rack my brain, searching for an excuse.

Excuses are a part-time gig for me.

I'm a fucking pro at making them.

Although a barbecue sounds better than my grandparents' party.

Looks like I'm choosing the lesser of the two evils.

"Sure, I'll be there."

I end the call, return to the kitchen, and tell my mother I can't attend *her* party because I have a business dinner.

# CHAPTER SEVEN

## Georgia

"THE HUNGOVER GEORGIA LOOK IS SERVING," Lola says, snapping her fingers from side to side in front of my face.

We're in Cohen's backyard for one of his barbecues. It's something he regularly throws together to catch up with his friends. Being a single father of a four-year-old boy, his schedule is hectic, and it's not like he can barhop to have drinks with the guys. His friends, Finn and Silas, are here and so are Lola and Grace, my besties.

I'm sitting at the table with the girls, Cohen is manning the grill a few feet away while talking to Silas, and Finn is pushing Noah, my nephew, on the tire swing Cohen recently hung from one of the massive trees.

Shuddering, I scrunch up my nose, remembering why I look like hell. "The hungover Georgia is tired and dehydrated—the aftermath of her dullsville date last night."

Lola waggles her finger toward me. "I told you an accountant named Bill would be a snooze fest, but *no one* listens to Lola unless it's advice on what liquors mix well together or if they need guidance on escaping a one-night-stand morning gone wrong." She shoots me a pointed look, and I flip her off.

I gesture to Grace next to me. "Blame it on her! She set me up."

"We all know Grace is ..." Lola pauses and gives Grace an apologetic smile. "No offense, babe, but you're a terrible matchmaker. Your ex was *a priest*."

"Wrong," Grace argues. "He was *in line* to become a priest but relinquished the idea when he discovered sex was better than celibacy." She rolls her eyes. "Unfortunately, that sex wasn't *with me*, his girlfriend."

"Rat bastard," Lola mutters, dragging a hand through her straight jet-black hair.

Five minutes into my date last night, I realized it was a bad idea.

What did I think was a good idea?

Ordering one too many cocktails.

If the guy isn't providing decent conversation, it's time booze tapped in.

It's not Grace's fault.

While I like nice guys, I don't do *puppy nice*.

I need a man who challenges me, and that wasn't Bill.

Boring Bill talked about his mother and went into full-blown details about his lactose intolerance after I ordered cheesecake, and the way he fumbled with his fork while eating convinced me he'd be fumbling to find my clit.

Typically, I'm not so hard on men.

Maybe it's me still being caught up on Chase.

He didn't struggle with finding my clit.

I grab my water bottle and take a long drink—an attempt to wash away thoughts of him.

I swore off men after the Chase incident, and even though it wasn't a *breakup*, I did the whole *change your hair* thing. I'm now a blonde.

New hair.

Not new me because I can't get that *rat bastard* out of my head. I was stupid enough to believe a man who parked like a selfish idiot wouldn't smash and dash. My dumbass should've asked more questions, delved deeper into his asshole of a soul before taking a trip to his bed.

"You're thinking of him, aren't you?" Lola asks, interrupting my thoughts.

*That damn intuition of hers.*

Grace glances at me. "Thinking of who?"

Lola smirks. "Her one-night-stand runner."

"Oh," Grace says, her green eyes widening. "The coffee jerk."

"The guy who rear-ended her twice," Lola confirms with a nod.

I flip her off again.

They know about my Chase nightmare—how I stupidly went home with him without even questioning if he was a serial killer.

Lola laughs. "We do need to give homeboy some credit for the coffee and doughnuts. He provided … what do they call it? A continental breakfast?"

"Funny," I grumble.

"Have you tried reaching out again?" Grace asks.

I shake my head. Kiki made it clear it'd be a waste of my time.

"I'm officially swearing off men," I say, slumping in my chair.

"What about the guy coming tonight?" Grace smiles. "The one Cohen is opening a bar with. Maybe he's single."

"I'm swearing off *all men*," I clarify.

A smile tugs at my lips. Not because of the man possibly being single but for my brother. Owning a bar is his dream, and it's finally coming true. The other day during Taco Tuesday, Cohen mentioned he was in talks of starting a bar with a guy he used to work with. Said guy is coming to today's barbecue.

"Archer Callahan will make a great business partner," Lola states matter-of-factly. "A great man to date? Definitely not."

"What do you know about him?" Grace asks.

"He's cool and wealthy as fuck, and he has bar experience," Lola replies. "Hell, he has straight-up business experience, given his family. The Callahans own half the commercial real estate in Iowa."

"The Callahans?" I cut in. "My brother is going into business with a Callahan?"

Lola nods. "You didn't know that?"

I shake my head. "At least I know Cohen will be in good hands."

Like nearly everyone else, I've heard of the Callahan family, but I don't know much about them.

Grace tilts her head to the side. "If he's so wealthy, why doesn't he work for his family?"

"Do you guys not watch the news?" Lola replies.

"Too busy," I say while Grace mutters, "I have homework to grade instead."

Lola leans in, ready to spill the tea. "His family was busted for doing shady shit. Archer's father was laundering money through the company, hiding funds overseas—all those white-collar crimes you see in the movies. The word is, Archer knew something sketchy was happening and quit—probably not wanting to star in the male reality show version of *Orange Is the New Black*. Feds went to town on his family's assets, and everything came crashing down. Archer and his mother were the only ones left unscathed."

I suck in a long breath—hyper-focusing on her words. The story, it's so familiar to what happened to Chase's family.

Surely, it couldn't be him, right?

People go to prison all the time.

I'm sure shit like that happens on the regular.

I gulp. "How do you know all this?"

"His father collects … well, *collected* expensive liquor and was a regular customer at the distribution company I work for. They tend to send me to their high-profile clients since I'm a kick-ass saleswoman." She winks, swiping fake dirt off her shoulder. "Dude was nice, enjoyed flaunting his riches … and hiding it apparently."

As if with perfect timing, Cohen yells, "Archer, my man! You came."

"Speak of the devil," Lola says, pointing over my shoulder.

My heart races when I turn in my chair to find Chase strolling through the backyard. I hold in a breath and wait in anticipation for another man to come into view.

For *Archer* to come into view.

Maybe he and Chase are friends.

"Archer finally shows his fucking face," I hear Silas call out behind me.

*This motherfucker.*

Asshole gave me the wrong name.

Archer the asshole.

Seems fitting.

I turn to face my friends and lower my voice, "That's Archer Callahan?"

*Say no. Please say no.*

Lola nods. "Sure is."

I grip Grace's arm in panic. "That's *him.*"

Grace blinks at me. "Who's him?"

"The guy I slept with," I hiss. "That's him!"

"What?" Lola shrieks. "You fucked Archer Callahan?"

# CHAPTER EIGHT

## Archer

THIS IS A FUCKING SHITSHOW.

When I scan Cohen's backyard and see *her*, a deep chill climbs up my spine, and I contemplate leaving.

She might've dyed her hair blond, but there's no doubt it's her.

Georgia.

The woman I should've never sat next to at the bar.

The woman I should've never touched.

The woman whose face still haunts my thoughts.

*Why is she here?*

*Who is she to Cohen?*

*Jesus, fuck, please don't be his girlfriend … or someone related to him.*

Our eyes meet, and hers are darkened with resentment as she glowers at me. I wait on her next move before making my own.

*Will she rat me out?*

*Smack me in the face?*

She tightens her hand around the armrest of the chair but doesn't stand or make a move in my direction. After a good thirty seconds, I realize me standing there, staring at her, will only draw questions. I smash our eye contact, shove my hands into my pockets, and walk toward Cohen. With each step, I pray she's some random person to him.

Cohen turns down the grill's temperature when I reach him and circles it, and we share a one-armed bro hug.

"You fucker," Silas says, shaking his head. "I had twenty bucks on you not showing."

Cohen holds out his hand, and Silas pulls out his wallet before slapping a twenty into it.

*I can't believe those fuckers bet on whether I'd come.*

Actually, I can.

"You know the guys," Cohen says, and I spot Finn and Noah playing in the background.

Finn and Silas worked with us at a club a few years ago, and Noah tagged along with Cohen when he stopped by to pick up checks, drop off paperwork, do manager shit.

Cohen shifts and points at the table I'm avoiding. "This is my sister, Georgia."

*His sister.*

*Of course it's his goddamn sister.*

It couldn't have been his sister's *friend* or a neighbor.

No, it had to be my future business partner's sister.

Sure, he's mentioned having a sister a few times, but I never knew her name or what she looked like.

"Georgia, this is Archer," Cohen continues, clueless that his introduction is mentally knocking me on my ass.

*No need for the intro, bro.*

*We're already acquainted.*

I've touched her, kissed her, been inside her.

Knowing it'd look suspicious as fuck if I ignored his greeting, I slowly drag my attention back to Georgia. The phoniest smile I've ever seen is plastered on her face. I have to give her props; she's doing a kick-ass job at hiding her dislike for me. I swallow rapidly, waiting for her to rat my ass out.

Instead, she clears her throat before saying, "Hi," in a flat voice.

Her eyes refuse to meet mine.

She's looking straight through me.

I'm curious if Cohen is picking up on the tension, but he's smiling without one concern on his face. Her friends are a different story. Their attention bounces back and forth between Georgia and me, as if we're tonight's entertainment.

"Grace," the strawberry-blonde says with a polite smile.

"Lola," says the other—no polite smile from her. More of a scowl.

I recognize Lola. She's shown up at my father's office countless times to sell him overpriced liquor. I was convinced he was buying it because he liked to look at her, not for the product.

I tip my head in their direction. "Hey."

"I like your name," Georgia says. "It's *so* original. I would've pegged you for a Chase." She glances at Lola. "Doesn't he look like a Chase?"

Lola nods. "Come to think of it, you're absolutely right. You have Chase written all over you."

Cohen, finally realizing this isn't happy-go-lucky, shoots Georgia a *what the fuck* look.

"Beer?" he asks, changing the subject.

I nod. "Sure."

*How about something stronger?*

*Something potent enough to wipe out the memory of how I spent a night fucking your little sister.*

I spare another glance to Georgia as Cohen opens a red Coleman cooler.

Her glare is cold, and she mouths the words, "*I hate you.*"

A Corona is shoved in my hand, stealing my attention from her, and I don't reply. I pop open the cap and take a long draw, and on my next peek at her, she looks as if she wants to chop off my dick and fry it on the grill.

Not that I blame her.

Sleeping with her was destructive.

It proved I was who I'd been labeled.

Selfish. Heartless. Asshole.

When I led Georgia into my bedroom, when I tasted her, when I thrust inside her, I didn't plan on bailing. The alcohol had swayed me into believing I was a better person that night, but then the reality of the next morning proved I had been wrong. Ditching her was a dick move, but it was the only choice I had.

I'd never let her in.

Never let *anyone in.*

It was better to end it that morning than to lead her on further.

Cohen returns to the grill, and when he opens it, my stomach growls at the sight of grilled chicken and steaks. I make small talk with Silas and Cohen—mostly them speaking and me inputting random comments every few minutes. Crossing my arms, I attempt to listen to the women, who are now huddled around the table, whispering. Randomly, one of them throws a dirty look in my direction, and I catch Lola subtly flipping me off.

"Food is ready!" Cohen yells. "Let's eat!"

"About damn time," Silas says, rubbing his stomach.

Noah and Finn come barreling toward us.

"Dad! Don't forget I want my burger cut into tiny little pieces," Noah shouts.

Cohen ruffles his hand through his son's hair. "I got you, buddy."

Georgia and Grace run into the house while Lola starts ripping open bags of chips. She pours them into brightly colored bowls.

Finn rubs his hands together. "I'm starving."

We make our plates and take our seats around the table. I wait until Georgia plops down in the chair she sat in earlier and take the one farthest from her. Sipping on my beer and eating chicken, I listen to them make small talk.

I blankly stare ahead as the group chats around me.

Act like I give no fucks.

It's who I am—a master of pretending and concealing my true self.

I'm a complex man—a once-heavily-sought-after book whose pages are torn, now shoved into the back shelf of the library.

Georgia, on the other hand?

She's so damn transparent—as easily read as a children's book not thrown in the back corner.

They've invited me to their infamous barbecues for years, but I always decline—until now that is. Sure, on a few occasions, they've managed to drag me to a sports bar, where I could input a few words while watching a game, but it's where I usually draw the line. Something personal like this—where it can lead to one-on-one talks and deep conversations—I steer clear of.

Then the shit with my family happened, and my life became consumed with attorney meetings and court dates. I couldn't go out because people would ask me endless questions:

*Did you know they were breaking the law?*

*Where's the money?*

*Are you going to prison?*

*Will you be poor?*

It's why I gave Georgia a fake name—something I do frequently. I know when someone recognizes me, and Georgia definitely didn't. After people find out who you are, they try to take advantage of the situation—ask for more money, sue, sell it to the papers.

Georgia is as quiet as I am. She picks at her food, hardly eating it, and forces a few laughs here and there.

My presence here has ruined her day, making me feel like an even bigger asshole.

COHEN SMACKS his palm on the table. "All right, let's talk business."

We're seated by ourselves while everyone else is playing cornhole.

On our slow nights, he talked about his life, how he'd raised his little sister after their father bailed and their mother was in a constant state of fucked up. We threw around the idea of starting our own bars, but doing it together was never a conversation. Our situations were different. Cohen had to work to start a bar, had to acquire the funds. That's not an easy feat for a single father.

When my family's fraud hit the news, I quit bartending because of the questions from drunken patrons who knew about my family. I wasn't sure what Cohen's response would be when I called him. Lucky for me, he was thrilled with the idea.

We've yet to talk specifics, but I want to open as soon as possible.

Hell, specifics might never be discussed if my sleeping with Georgia comes to light.

"You been doing okay?" Cohen asks.

"Happy the headache is over, not happy with the results," I answer.

He nods and sips on his beer.

His response is why I like Cohen. After that statement, people would normally give me advice on what to do—whether it be their opinions, questions, or what I might want to hear to get on my good side.

Cohen is cool, quiet, and not in people's business. He can be the face of the bar, *the boss*, and I'll sit in the corner, silently playing the bartender role.

I trust him, and that's one of the biggest things that matters to me.

"Are they filing an appeal?"

"That's the plan."

He claps my shoulder. "You know we got your back if you need anything."

*"We got your back."*

I've had friends for years, friends I've grown up with, cousins from my mother's side, and none of them have reached out to me. None of them have made it clear that no matter what happened, they were there.

"The bar will help take my mind off the bullshit," I reply.

"You sure you're ready for this ride?" Cohen asks. "I know you're feeling some type of way because of the sentencing, but I'm in this for the long haul, man. I don't want this to be a gig to temporarily take your mind off your problems, and then in a few years, when the dust has settled with your family's legal issues, you decide you want out. This is my dream, man, and I won't lose it."

"I'm one hundred percent in," I reply. "It's what I need to keep my sanity."

He's unhappy with my answer.

"I'll put it in our contract if that'll make you feel better. No backing out for seven years, and if I want to leave, you can buy me out for cheap. This is more for my sanity than for money."

"Sounds good, man. I talked to my bank about getting a loan, and I have money saved, but—"

"Whatever else you need, I'll cover."

He shakes his head. "Nah, you don't need to do that."

"I know, and that's why I am."

He holds out his knuckles. "Let's do it then."

Guilt surfaces for not telling him about Georgia and me.

I brush it off and fist-bump him, like the dick that I am. "Let's do this."

---

AFTER THE BEER, I opt for water.

I'll be leaving soon and dipping into something stronger

when I get home. Until then, I need to find out where Georgia's head is. The last thing I want is to start the process with Cohen and then him bail as the ball starts rolling because he found out I'd slept with his sister. If Georgia tells him about my actions the morning after, he'll be done with my ass.

When Georgia walks inside the empty house, I follow her—thankful to finally get her alone while also hoping no one notices me on her trail. She's stayed with her friends the entire time I've been here, so this is my first open opportunity.

She whips around when the back door slams shut behind me, and we land in the kitchen. "Why are you following me?"

I scratch my cheek, searching for the right words. "This is a fucked-up situation."

She tilts her head to the side and pouts her lips. "Agreed."

"What do you want to do? Tell him? Act like what we did never happened?"

Her expression turns flat. "What did we do?" She coldly laughs and opens the fridge, turning around with a bottle of water in her hand. "You're a fucking asshole."

"We slept together. It was a one-time thing. It happens all the time."

You would've thought my response was a slap to her face because she retreats a step.

"Happens all the time? Maybe for you but not for me." Horror is on her face when she slams her water on the table. "Oh my God. How much *all the time* do you do it?"

"That's not what I meant." I backtrack. "I'm saying that people have sex and never talk again or act like it never happened all the time."

"If only we could be in the category of never talking again. You might as well have thrown my clothes out and told me to kick rocks." She grimaces, staring at me, wide-eyed. "Who treats someone like that?"

"You're right. It was a bad call on my part." *That's an understatement.*

"You think?"

"At least I provided complimentary doughnuts."

"*Again,* you're an asshole."

"So you keep saying." I scrub a hand over my face. "Are you going to tell your brother?"

She shakes her head. "If I do, he won't go into business with you." She signals between us. "This never happened. You never saw me naked. My brother will never hear a word of it. Got it?"

"What about your little gossip girl club?" I jerk my head toward the door. "From the looks on their faces, they know about us."

"Trust me, they won't say anything." She sucks in a breath before casting me a curious glance. "Who gives people fake names and has business cards with that fake name?"

I shrug, like it's not unusual. "Someone who likes to keep a low profile."

"That's not weird or anything." She scrunches up her nose. "You didn't look shocked when my brother introduced us. Did you know who I was?"

I shake my head. "I don't display my emotions like you. I can handle them maturely without making a scene."

"A scene?" She scowls. "I hardly made a scene. You would've been terrified if I had *made a scene.*"

With that, she walks away, bumping into my shoulder as she leaves.

---

THE COOKOUT WAS A BUST.

Good thing I'm not known for my great entertainment and sparkling personality. I chatted for a while before making up some bullshit excuse about needing to leave for my grandparents' anniversary party.

I'm a lying bastard.

Sue me.

I slump down on my couch, open the Dom Pérignon, and drink it straight from the bottle.

My little brother and father are sitting in a jail cell, and I'm left to pick up the pieces of a family that was already fucking broken.

I do a once-over of my penthouse when I take my next drink. One of the traits I inherited from my family is enjoying the finer things in life, so I'm grateful my shit didn't get seized. The Feds had been watching my family, had fine-combed our finances, but I kept my nose clean. I didn't take a dime of the dirty money, but that didn't mean I wasn't dragged into their mess. At first, the Feds threatened I'd join my father and brother, even when they had nothing on me, and then they switched tactics, begging me to snitch.

My father was embezzling money. It's wrong, yes, but he wasn't fucking murdering people. Even though my loyalty to him isn't as strong as Lincoln's, I stayed silent.

Lucky for me, the bulk of my money is from my inheritance and didn't come from committing crimes and shady shit. The bastards couldn't touch my accounts.

My brother's? They froze all his shit.

Although he was smart enough to sign a chunk of it over to my mother before he got caught up. I'm sure there's money for him in some offshore business account too. My dad is a businessman and was prepared in case this happened.

My head falls back.

*Georgia Fox.*

When I go to bed, flashbacks of our night together keep me awake.

How good she felt and how it killed me to hear her moan out another man's name when it should've been mine.

The reminder that I walked out on her floats through, overshadowing the good, and as I drift asleep, I hate myself.

# CHAPTER NINE

## Georgia

"DO you remember the diner where Mom used to work?" Cohen asks, walking into his living room and plopping down on the other side of the couch.

I toss my phone down next to me. "Mom worked at several diners."

Fast-food joints, factories, cleaning jobs—none of them lasted long. She was more of a fan of getting high than working.

"You know ..." He snaps his fingers, struggling to remember the name. "The one on North Street, close to the park here in Anchor Ridge."

"Dawn's Delicious Café?"

He snaps one more time. "That's it."

"What about it? It shut down forever ago." I grab the bag of Cheetos I brought from home because Cohen doesn't buy junk food—*annoying*—and pop a cheese puff into my mouth.

Dawn, a woman in her late fifties and a recovering addict, owned the café. She took a chance on our mother and gave her a job. The problem was, our mom didn't like being on time or working, nor did she find it wrong to make drug deals in the parking lot.

After she was fired, she moved us a few towns over to

Mayview, Iowa. It's where I grew up, but Cohen moved us back to Anchor Ridge when Noah was born to keep their distance from Noah's mother's family.

"The building is for sale."

"Cool." I pop another Cheetos.

"You think it'd be a good location for a bar?"

I'm quiet while considering my answer.

"The building has great bones," he continues. "Plenty of space, and it's a great location for traffic to maneuver in and out of. It needs work, not going to lie, but I think we can turn it into a kick-ass bar."

I nod in agreement. "I think it'd be cool … but it might drag up old memories."

The excitement on Cohen's face dissolves, and I wish I could take back my words.

"I don't give a shit about memories," he snarls.

Like with our nonexistent father, we don't have a healthy relationship with our mother. I know who she is. I just don't know where she is. She tends to bounce among rehab, jail, and crack houses. When I was seventeen, Cohen forbade her to come around me until she was clean. Unlike him, I don't hate her. I'm more disappointed that she chooses dope over her children. Cohen isn't as forgiving as I am. Once you screw him over, he's done with you. Maybe I'd be different if I were the one picking up all the responsibilities as a result of their neglect.

He shelters me from the struggles he's faced, so at times, I can be naïve. His goal was for me to grow up happy, to feel loved, and it's the same for Noah. Cohen puts up a hard front, but he's all about family. Once you're in his good graces, he's there for you, no matter what.

He stands, nearly a foot taller than I am, from the couch. "I'm meeting with the realtor today. Want to tag along?"

"Sure." I stop myself when a knot forms in my throat. "Will Archer be there?"

He nods, not sensing the change in my mood.

"Is it a good idea for me to come?" I bite into the edge of my lip, already anxious to possibly see the morning-after ditcher. "Maybe it should just be you two. I don't want to intrude."

"Intrude?" He chuckles. "You're my sister. You never have to worry about that ever happening. Archer won't care. He's a laid-back dude."

*Laid-back dude, my ass.*

---

"DAD, THIS PLACE IS SUPER SCARY," Noah whines from the back seat when we pull into the parking lot of the dilapidated building. "It looks dirty and gross. I don't want to go inside. There are probably ninety million bajillion ghosts in there. We'd better call Scooby-Doo so he can get rid of them before we do."

I laugh, unbuckle my seat belt, and turn to look back at him. "Scooby-Doo is on vacation, so you'd better stay close to me if you want to avoid ghosts."

Cohen throws me a *really* look.

"What?" I shrug.

He peeks back at Noah. "Little buddy, don't listen to anything your aunt Georgia tells you. There are no ghosts here. There are no ghosts *anywhere*."

Noah scrunches up his nose, his gaze pinging back and forth between his father and me. "You tell me to listen to her when she babysits me."

"Listen to her then, but when it pertains to ghosts, she's lying," Cohen stresses.

"Aunt Georgia doesn't lie. That's bad."

"Exactly." I hold out my hand for a high five, and he smacks his small palm against it. "I don't do bad things."

My laughter cracks before dying out completely when I twist in my seat and see Archer's car—the same one from the accident.

Meanwhile, I traded my car in for a shiny, *used* VW bug with the money he'd given me.

When his car door opens, my throat clenches, and I give myself a mental pep talk. He steps out, one long leg and then the other, and when his entire body comes into view, my breathing quickens. As soon as we're out of the car, I grab Noah's hand, declaring him my Archer-blocker for the day. I'll keep all my attention on him and act very invested in Scooby and Legos.

He slips his hands into his pockets on his walk toward us.

"Hi, Archer!" Noah calls out, jumping up and down.

My sweet nephew sees the good in everyone, even an asshole like Archer.

"Yo, Noah," Archer replies, failing to glance in my direction. "Hey, Cohen … Georgia."

My name comes out like an afterthought to him, and I narrow my eyes, restraining myself from flipping him off.

As he moves closer, my mouth waters.

*Jesus.*

*Why does he have to look so damn hot?*

I wish I'd had a case of drunk goggles that night—that alcohol had altered my hot-guy meter, and in real life, he was hideous.

But the universe is always against me, and he's just as hot when I'm drunk as he is when I'm sober.

"Hey there!" a woman—her age most likely around my brother's—shouts, walking toward us, her kitten heels crunching against the gravel. "You must be Cohen and Archer." She holds out her hand. "I'm Mariah."

She shakes Cohen's hand and then Archer's. I roll my eyes at the appreciative once-over she gives my brother. When she turns to Archer and does the same, a wave of jealousy hits me that shouldn't exist. Her gaze swoops down his body, taking considerably longer than she did with Cohen, as if she's imagining him naked.

Not that I blame her.

I smile, knowing I've one-upped her.

I *have* seen him naked.

Felt him thrust inside me.

Had his lips on mine.

Archer answers with a head nod, not giving two shits about her presence. Dude does not like conversation. At least it's not just me. He's a dick to almost everyone—with the exception of Noah because the kid is too cute to be a dick to.

If Cohen and Archer go into business together, I'll need to learn how to set aside the hurt he caused and reel in my hatred toward him. I'm not a bitchy person. People refer to me as fun, quirky, a smart-ass with a nosy side.

I'll never be able to fully stomp away the array of emotions I feel for the man. So, as much as I'll hate it, my time at their bar will be limited. Until I get my emotions in check at least. I'll blame it on school, which won't be a complete lie because classes have been kicking my ass lately.

*Scratch that.*

I won't let him win.

It'll be my brother's business too.

Let Archer deal with me *every single day*, like I'm a thorn in his side he can't pluck away.

I give her a slight wave as I introduce myself and Noah.

"As you can tell, the building needs some care," Mariah says, starting her tour of the old restaurant. "A bar would do well here, and you'd hardly have any competition. The owners are moving to Florida and want to sell ASAP, so they're open for negotiation."

The building is large with plenty of space to create a bar front and outdoor seating, and there's room in the back for the kitchen and office space.

It reeks of mold.

Loose floorboards creak with our steps.

The roof slightly sags.

Old kitchen appliances are shoved around the back.

*Needs some care* is an understatement.

Ugly but restorable.

When my brother wants something, he works his ass off for it. I have no doubt he'll do the same with this.

"Daddy, I need to potty," Noah says, grabbing his elbow and glancing up at him.

"Buddy, there's not a restroom in here," Cohen replies. "Can you hold it?"

Noah shakes his head, jumping up and down, and presses his hand against his pants. "I really, really, really need to go."

"My mom owns the alterations shop across the street," Mariah says, pointing toward the entrance of the building. "He can use the restroom there."

"Thank you," Cohen says with a sigh of relief. He grabs Noah's hand before glancing at Archer and me. "Keep looking around and tell me what you think."

The building turns silent as they leave, wood creaking in their wake. I should've faked needing to use the restroom and gone with them.

Archer fishes his phone from the pocket of his jeans and focuses on it without a peek in my direction, as if I were not even here.

"Wow," I say. "I see you're still a rude asshole."

"Still a rude asshole," he answers, his tone flat. "It seems it's your favorite thing to call me, so I won't try to change your mind."

"Why'd you do it then?"

"Do what?"

"Sleep with me. Why would you sleep with someone you can't stand the sight of?"

"Never said I couldn't stand the sight of you. The sight of you is very nice actually."

I snort. "Says the guy who won't even look at me."

He tilts his chin up, and his eyes meet mine with disdain. "Is this better?"

"No," I answer, waving my hand in the air. "Go back to focusing on your phone, or sit in your car, or leave. Any of those would be better."

"You were just mad I wouldn't look at you, and now that I am, you don't want me to?"

"Yes."

He shakes his head, and his attention returns to his phone. "I think this will be a good location for us. Tell your brother that."

"Are you sure? I'm worried if a restaurant didn't survive here, will a bar?"

"From what I researched, the restaurant was run-down, and the food was shit. Our bar won't be any of those things."

"Okay, Sir Know-It-All."

"Why'd you come?" he asks, the question falling from his lips so casually, like it's not rude. "Had you not, we could've avoided speaking to each other."

"My brother asked me to."

"You could've said no."

"Trust me, I tried to. If I'd refused, it would've sounded sketchy." I tap the side of my lips even though he's not looking at me. "Would you rather me tell him you fucked me, so then he'll understand why my new goal in life is to dodge any conversation with you?"

"We decided to keep it to ourselves."

"And that's exactly what I'm doing. That includes not making him wonder why I'm so against being in the same room with you. Cohen and I are close. He knows I'd never miss something like this with him."

"Gotcha. So I should expect to see you around?" He peers up at me.

"You should."

"Noted. Let's try to keep it to a minimum."

His words are a kick through my heart. I hold my head high when I pass him on my way back outside and stand next to

Cohen's car with my arms crossed. As I wait, I'm haunted by flashbacks of the night with Archer—how he said the sweetest things, how he pleasured me like he already knew my body and we were fit for each other. He opened up to me, acting interested in more than a quickie, but it was all a lie.

Maybe Chase is his alter ego.

The pleasant version of him.

It hurt when he acted like he didn't know me at the barbecue, like I meant nothing to him.

Our night together meant nothing to him.

Maybe one-night stands are the norm for him but not for me.

Rich. Cocky. Handsome.

The perfect trinity for an asshole who breaks your heart.

Archer Callahan is a man who screws women and then leaves them notes as a thank-you.

He made a full damn asshole circle.

*Does he not feel bad?*

*Was I just some disposable fuck to him?*

*Fuck him.*

*Fuck one-night stands.*

*Fuck dudes who leave you* don't worry about locking up *notes after they banged the lights out of you all night.*

# CHAPTER TEN

# *Archer*

Six Months Later

"WE DID IT, MAN." Cohen slaps me on the back, a bright-ass grin on his face.

"We fucking did it." I stand tall in pride. No bright-ass grin from me.

After six months of finances, hard work, and Georgia-dodging, we're open. The Twisted Fox is finally open for business and ready to serve drinks. Shockingly, it took only minutes for us to come up with a name. We each chose a word.

Mine was Twisted—since it's how my brain feels.

Cohen's was Fox—after his last name.

We purchased the old restaurant building two days after the showing, then gutted it, remodeled, and created a bar. There were no complaints from me on the location. Anchor Ridge is the small town where Cohen lives and is twenty minutes from my house.

Cohen brought in his friends and Georgia to help, so I sent Kiki, who now has a new job but at least waited until the bar was complete, to do most of my bidding while I handled the behind-the-scenes financial aspects.

The less time around Georgia, the better.

Also, the less I feel guilty about what I did.

When I see her, I'm reminded of how I let her go because I could never have her.

Because it would've been nothing but problems before shattering altogether.

She hates me now, and I fake hate her.

My plan is to make her hate me more.

If she despises me, there will be no temptation.

It's opening night at the bar, and so far, everything is rolling smoothly. Thanks to Silas, there's been talk about the opening. A small radio station is in the parking lot to promote us, and he somehow convinced a few athletes to show up and post their location on social media.

It worked.

It's insane how busy we are.

We created the perfect sports bar with walls of TVs, top-shelf liquor, and an enjoyable atmosphere. I want someone to walk in and feel like they can sit and have a couple of beers with their friends—not caring about a dress code, or bottle service, or a large cover.

The suckiest part is I have no one to celebrate this achievement with. Sure, Cohen and our friends are here but no family. No Lincoln. I would've invited my mother, but she'd have felt out of place. Country clubs and black-tie parties are more her scene.

"I guess congratulations are in order."

I look up to find Georgia slide onto the stool across from me at the bar. It's been a while since I've looked at her—*really looked at her*—since I evade any eye contact, in fear she'd try to start a conversation.

"Yep," I say.

*Be a dick.*

*Make her hate you.*

"How does it feel?"

*Pretty damn good.*

I shrug. "It is what it is."

"All right," she groans. "Having a conversation with you is so much fun." She stands and joins me behind the bar.

"This is an employee-only zone." I narrow my eyes at her.

Shrugging, she snags a bottle of vodka, pours two shots, and hands one to me. "It seems you're only nice when you're drinking, so drink up."

I push the drink away and walk backward. "I'm good."

"I don't get it." She knocks back a shot and sets down the glass. "Shouldn't I be the one pissed at you?"

"Look, Georgia," I sneer, "was I nice to you during our first two run-ins?"

She shakes her head. "Well … no."

"Don't you find it weird that the *only* time I was nice to you was when I was drinking?" I pause to better make my point, to sharpen the knife I'm about to jab through her heart. "And wanted to get laid."

Her eyes widen and then turn cold.

I tap my temple. "Put two and two together."

Her jaw drops. "Are you serious?"

I shrug.

"You listened to me pour my heart out about my father and how hard that day was for me." Her hand holding the shot glass shakes. "You shared your personal demons. All because you wanted to screw me?"

"What can I say? Hennessy goes straight to my dick."

"I regret ever letting you touch me," she hisses.

"You did, though." A sadistic grin passes over my lips. "And if I remember correctly, you liked it."

She gulps down the other shot, drops it, and ignores the glass shattering at my feet. "Wrong. You were the worst sex I've ever had, and your dick is small."

I run my hand over my chin. "Not what you were saying

that night. Something along the lines of, *best sex I've ever had* and *biggest cock ever.*"

"I was faking it. My brother never told you I wanted to be an actress?"

I scoff.

"You know, I came over here to congratulate you, to mend fences, since we'll be around each other a lot."

"That's cool. Say hi. I'll say hi. We don't have to be friends."

"Okay then."

Her face falls, and I inwardly cringe at how I'm treating her.

I reach out to stop her when she turns to leave but immediately come to my senses and drop my hand. Shame washes through me as I clean up the broken glass.

"Dude, it's opening night," Silas calls out from the other end of the bar. "Smile."

I fake a smile before dropping it, and then I drag my finger to my lips and flip him off.

I play it off well, as if this were no big deal, but inside, it's a different story. I'm on top of the world. I own a business—*my own* business. No one can take it away from me or run shady shit through it.

As I take drink orders throughout the night, I can't stop myself from sweeping my gaze over the bar on the hunt for her. A knot forms in my throat when I finally spot her at a table with Grace and Lola. I overfill a beer when a group of guys stops at their table. As I grab a towel to clean my mess, a man has his eyes set on Georgia. Her grin lights the room on fire, and he stops the waitress, gesturing for Georgia to order a drink. She's bubbly as she recites her order, and I wonder what she ordered.

*Cognac?*

I'll be making the drink, so I'll find out soon enough.

I grit my teeth, remembering the high of being the man buying her a drink and holding her attention.

*Don't give it to this guy.*

*Don't give him what you gave me.*

I crack my knuckles. No way can I stomach this night after night. My hope is that she becomes too busy with her job and classes to hang out here frequently.

I can't let this affect me.

I have to pretend not to care.

When she casts a glance in my direction, she runs her hands through her long hair and warily stares at me before mouthing, "*I hate you.*"

I give her a thumbs-up.

The rest of the night flies by in a blur. I make a drink, search the room for Georgia, see what she's doing, and then go back to work. Over and over again.

When the night ends and my work is done, she's gone.

Cohen and I share a celebratory drink after the bar closes.

I don't mutter a word about breaking his sister's heart.

# CHAPTER ELEVEN

## Georgia

One Year Later

"I'M SORRY, but we have to let you go."

*What a shitty way to start the day.*

I wince, taking in my boss's words. "What? Why?"

"Eighty percent of our profit derives from online sales." My boss—*old boss*—Francine shoots me an apologetic smile. "It's just not cost-effective to have a physical store barely dragging in revenue while paying rent and payroll."

I've worked at Boho Doll Boutique, a small shop owned by Francine and her husband, for three years. The pay isn't anything that'll bring me riches, but I get discounts on clothes, and they work with my school schedule.

"Can I help with online orders?" I ask, scrambling for ideas.

She shakes her head.

"Social media? I'm pretty skilled at creating quirky little posts." I poke my finger through the air with the last three words.

"We'll give you two weeks' pay while you look for another job." She reaches out and squeezes my hand. "I'm sorry, Georgia."

I COLLAPSE onto a barstool at Twisted Fox and cover my face in defeat.

"What's wrong, sis?" Cohen asks.

I move my hands, a frown on my face. "I lost my job."

"What happened?" He swoops a towel over his wide shoulder.

"They're going exclusively online."

His eyes soften. "I'm sorry. Any ideas where to go next?"

I inhale a deep breath.

He won't like my answer.

"A couple of clubs in the city are hiring."

Those soft eyes darken in disapproval.

"You banked when you bartended in clubs, and it'll work well with my school schedule."

"You're not working in a club in the city."

"You're not going to tell me what to do. I have bills to pay."

"Work here then."

"Really?"

He nods.

"If I recall, you shot me down last time I asked for a job."

"I'd rather you work at my bar than anyone else's." He points at me, his tone turning authoritative. "As long as it doesn't interfere with your classes."

"It won't. I promise." I've pulled all-nighters before and still aced tests the next morning. I got this.

"Cool. You start Thursday."

I jump up from the stool and clap my hands. "Can't wait!"

That night, the reality that I'll be working with Archer hits me.

I smirk.

*Let him see me all the time.*

*Let him see me make his life hell.*

*Let him see what he's been missing.*

*Let him see what a mistake he made that morning.*

---

"REPORTING HERE for my first day of duty." I salute Cohen when I walk into the bar.

"Reporting for *what*?" Archer asks, stone-faced.

Cohen jerks his head toward me. "I hired her."

"Hired her for *what*?"

"To sell golden chickens on the black market." I roll my eyes. "To work here, idiot."

Cohen gives me a *shut your mouth if you want this to go smoothly* look. "She'll wait tables, bartend, whatever we need her to do."

"Except clean urinals," I say with a shudder. "Sorry, but I'm not cleaning urinals where drunk dudes piss."

"We don't need her to do anything," Archer argues. "We're not hiring."

"Destiny quit last week, so we're short an employee." Tension breaks along Cohen's face. "She'll fill that void."

"Call me the void-filler," I mutter, resulting in another glare from Cohen.

Archer works his strong jaw. "You can't hire people without discussing it with me."

Cohen has hired plenty of employees without Archer because Archer prefers not to deal with it. His tantrum is because he doesn't want *me* working here.

Cohen's voice deepens. "She's my sister. She's working here. End of discussion. Be pissed all you want."

"This is bullshit." He shoots me a death glare before sweeping his hand toward the back of the bar. "My office."

---

THEY SPEND a good twenty minutes discussing if my ass will get canned before returning to the front of the bar. Archer's pissed, and Cohen is annoyed.

"Don't mess up shit," Archer snarls while passing me.

Cohen nods to Trina, a waitress. "You'll train with Trina for a while, familiarize yourself with waitressing duties, and then I'll have you work with Archer and me behind the bar."

"She'll work *with you* behind the bar," Archer corrects.

My next two hours are spent with Trina, and when my time with her is done, I skip over to Cohen. Waitressing isn't bad, but the real fun is behind the bar.

Cohen holds up his hand, stopping me from being loud, and points at his phone. "Sylvia." He walks toward his office at the back of the bar.

I nod, stand in the corner, and watch Archer work. When a woman hits on him, I cringe. Not that I blame her. It's a hot sight. Watching him move around the bar, making drinks, is hypnotic. He gives the woman attention yet doesn't. I'd think he went home alone every night if Cohen hadn't let it slip that he has his fair share of late-night hookups.

Jealousy pricks my veins at the thought of him giving women what he gave to me.

"Sylvia has a family emergency and needs to leave," Cohen says when he returns, referring to Noah's babysitter.

"Uh-oh," I mutter at the same time he calls out Archer's name.

Waving Archer over, he points at me. "Finish training her. Noah's babysitter had to bail."

Archer doesn't spare a glance in my direction, as if I weren't here. "Have Georgia cover for the babysitter, and you stay here."

Cohen shakes his head. "The faster she finishes training, the faster she'll be put to work. It's only for a few hours. No way am I having her train on the weekend. It'll be too chaotic. Let her shadow you."

I perk up. "I'm a quick learner."

"Sure, whatever," Archer mutters, turning away and stalking to the other end of the bar.

"Text me when you get home," Cohen directs me. "Or if you need anything."

I give him a thumbs-up. "I got this. Now, get to Noah."

Cohen leaves at the same time Archer tosses a drink book to me. "Study this."

I play with the book in my hands. "Study this?"

"It's the drink list."

I set it on the bar, flip through the pages, and hold it up. "I'm more of a hands-on learner."

"Whatever," he grumbles. "You don't learn shit from that book anyway."

"Yet you told me to study it."

He's already setting me up for failure.

"Why do you hate me so much, Archer?"

I need the answer. This bickering is a never-ending game with us, and it's getting out of control. Over a year has passed since we hooked up. This rivalry, enemy shit needs to end. All it'll do is ruin company morale and drive a wedge between him and Cohen. If it ever came down to me or Archer, Cohen would choose me.

Archer silently stares at me, working his jaw as though he doesn't owe me an explanation.

"How about a truce?" I thrust out my hand toward him.

"Sure, whatever." He ignores my hand and walks past me. "Now, study your book."

I grab his elbow, stopping him. "You're going to train me, or I'll tell Cohen you wouldn't."

He jerks out of my hold. "Really?"

At his movement, sharp hints of his cologne—a light sandalwood—drift up my nostrils.

It's all man.

Like taking a hike on a crisp autumn day.

"Really." A deviant smirk flashes on my lips. "I was quite the tattletale growing up."

That's a lie. My mother's absence didn't provide much opportunity to have someone to tattle to.

He jerks a glass from a stack and points at me with it. "Have you ever made a margarita?"

I shake my head. "Not professionally, but I've drunk a few." I've also purchased the frozen ones in bags and enjoyed them during our girls' nights. "I tend to drink alcohol in red Solo cups, poured from a keg or cheap vodka." I'm a college student on a budget.

"You were drinking Hennessy at Bailey's," he deadpans.

My breathing slows. *He remembers.*

"You were buying." I grin. "I planned to have the drink and then go home."

"Yet you didn't go home." His eyes turn hooded. "You went home with me."

I nod timidly. "I did."

Something shifts in him, in the mood, and he reaches out. Our gazes meet, his eyes unreadable.

"Georgia." My name is said in a tight whisper.

I close my eyes.

"Bartender!"

My eyes flash open, and Archer pulls back.

"We need to get our drink on!" an obnoxious man shouts. "Which means, we need drinks."

I glare at the jerk.

*How dare he interrupt us.*

For once, since our night together, Archer gave me something other than anger.

His vulnerability screamed his truths.

A moment when he stopped pretending.

Archer clears his throat and swings his arm toward the guy. "He's all yours."

Thankfully, after being here with Cohen so much, I know

my way around the bar and where everything is. I know all the menu items since I helped create it.

After I take the man's drink order, I drift to the group of college-aged guys waving me over. "What can I get you? Forewarning, I'm a newbie, so nothing complicated, please."

A guy with bright blue eyes and blond curls grins. "You know how to make a Can I Have Your Number?"

I chew on my lip.

*Is he asking for a drink or hitting on me?*

Dozens of drinks have sexual innuendos as names. Sex on the Beach or Screaming Orgasm, to name a few.

"I'll be right back," I say.

Archer is pouring a beer when I go to him, but his attention is pinned on the guys I was helping.

"Do you know how to make a Can I Have Your Number?"

He furrows his brow. "A what?"

"A Can I Have Your Number?"

"Who ordered that?"

I jerk my thumb over my shoulder to the curly-haired dude.

Archer slides the beer to the customer and walks around me, and when he reaches the guys, he towers over them. "What's in that drink?"

Curly's face pales. "It's not … a drink."

"What is it then?"

"I was"—Curly's gaze angles to me—"asking for her number."

I smile.

Archer snarls.

# CHAPTER TWELVE

# Archer

GEORGIA WILL BE the death of me this shift.

This job.

Hell, my damn life.

How, out of all people, did I manage to hook up with the sister of my business partner?

Just my luck.

I almost told Cohen I quit for the night if I had to train her. If he wasn't leaving for Noah, I might've gone through with the threat. I hate training, but add in that it's Georgia, and it's a goddamn nightmare.

Guys are hitting on her, not that I blame them.

"We don't serve that here," I bark to the guy who gave her the cheesiest-ass pickup line. "We'll never serve it. Order something else, buddy."

Georgia stares at him intently. "I wouldn't say never, just not tonight. I'm training. Maybe another time?"

The douchebag licks his lips. "I got you. How about a few Coronas for now?"

Georgia smiles sweetly. "I got you."

"Thanks, babe."

When he winks at her, I'm tempted to smash the Corona over his head.

As she turns to grab their beers, I stalk behind her and hiss, "Quit flirting with guys."

"Why?" She tilts her head to the side. "You jealous?"

I shake my head. "I'd say the same to any employee." I snatch the Corona and point at a group of women. "I'll take care of the Justin Biebers. Go serve those women."

As soon as I hand the guys their beers, I turn back to her. She's already a pro at this. Her people skills are on point. She's a smiler, someone who can make conversation with anyone, and she will be a great asset to the bar.

Not a great asset to me, though.

*The death of me.*

*Reminder: tell Cohen I'm making the schedule now.* Georgia and I will be working together as little as possible.

"Well, well, look who it is."

My back stiffens at her voice.

Clear, articulate, and one who once moaned my name.

My past is here to haunt me.

"I heard this is where you started a bar," she says when I shift to face her.

"What are you doing here, Meredith?"

"I wanted to see how you were doing." She sets down her designer bag and climbs onto a stool. "It's been so long."

*Wish we could've made it longer.*

"How are you?" she pushes.

I stare back at the woman who spent years at my side, who was once a part of me. She's just as gorgeous, just as put together, but just no longer for me.

"Good," I clip. "Busy."

"Oh, come on," she says with a sweet laugh. "You can't be too busy for me."

"Go back to the man you're engaged to." That should get her out of here.

We're huddled in the corner, and I hear drink orders being thrown at Georgia left and right. I need to shut this shit down and help her before everyone gets a faulty drink.

"Yeah, that engagement didn't work out."

"Looks like you still haven't bagged a husband your parents approve of."

She flinches at my harsh tone. "I couldn't love him the way I loved you, and he'd never love me the way you loved me before … everything fell apart."

"Our relationship was never perfect."

"True." She sighs, her shoulders drooping. "It was perfect for us, though. You loved me enough to propose, to make me your wife."

"You're the one who wanted out."

"You still don't understand why I left, do you?" She scoffs. "No, you know why. You just don't care."

"Why are you here?" I seethe. "To talk about our past? We're over. Have been over for years."

"I miss you," she whispers. "Back then, I had to walk away."

"You're right. I don't blame you, and there are no hard feelings." *Now, leave.*

"Hello, Mr. Trainer," Georgia sings, sneaking up next to me. "Engaging in secret conversations in the corner isn't productive when I have so much to learn."

Meredith's eyes narrow as her attention pings from Georgia to me.

"Can I get you something to drink?" I ask Meredith, blowing out a strained breath.

She shakes her head. "No, but let's talk tonight. After you close, for old times' sake."

Georgia tenses.

I scrub a hand over my face. "Nah, I'll be exhausted."

Georgia stays, inviting herself into the conversation, and ignores my look of warning. Her employment will not go well here. She's not one to follow rules.

At least she breaks the tension by saying, "If you're staying, how about that drink order?"

"I'll have a Commonwealth," Meredith replies with a phony smile.

Georgia mocks her smile. "Never heard of it, but I'll see what I can do."

"Really?" I glare at Meredith when Georgia leaves.

"What?"

"Commonwealth has seventy-one ingredients."

"She's in training. I'm helping you out." Meredith shrugs. "She likes you," she says matter-of-factly, tapping her manicured nails along the bar. "No surprise. Even with this asshole demeanor, it's hard not to be attracted to you."

I ignore her comment and turn to Georgia. She pokes her cheek while studying the drink book before slamming it shut and grabbing every wrong ingredient.

Without sparing another glance to Meredith, I go to Georgia.

"Did you read the wrong page?"

She shakes her head, pouring random shit into the glass. "Nope, I read it right. My plan is to make her a crappy drink so she'll leave." Throwing a cherry and lemon wedge into the glass, she drops off her concoction to Meredith.

Meredith eyes the drink suspiciously. "That's not what I ordered."

Georgia shrugs. "I followed the book's directions." She forces another fraudulent smile and leaves.

Meredith eyes me, and I throw my arms up.

"What did you expect?" I ask.

The sound of glass shattering stops our conversation, and when I spin around, there's a circle of broken glass at her feet.

"You should leave," I mutter to Meredith, pushing myself off the bar.

"That was totally an accident," Georgia rushes out when I approach her.

She falls to her knees and scrambles for the broken pieces, and I notice a flicker of red before realizing blood is gushing from her finger.

"Shit, Georgia." I bend down and snatch her hand to inspect it.

It's deep but not deep enough to require stitches. I carefully grab her hand and help her to her feet. Tugging a towel from a drawer, I wrap it around her finger. She hisses when I push down on it, giving it pressure.

"Trina!" I yell, snapping my fingers to get her attention as she walks past us.

"Yeah?" she asks.

"Run to the employee room and grab the first-aid kit."

Her attention moves to Georgia before she nods. "On it."

Not caring if blood gets on me, I lead her to the end of the bar and settle her onto a stool. "Hang out here for a sec and keep pressure on this."

"Okay." She peers down in embarrassment. "Sorry, I should've been more careful."

"Shit happens." I pat her thigh before gently squeezing it.

"This is the perfect reason for you to prove to Cohen I shouldn't have this job."

I tilt my head down and wait until her eyes meet mine. "I won't use this against you."

"All right," Trina says, rushing over to us with the kit.

I give every customer who yells out a drink order a *wait for a sec* gesture and bandage her up. I inspect it when I finish. "See, all fixed. Why don't you go home for the night and let that rest?"

"Thank you, but I'm staying," she whispers before sliding off the stool and wincing.

"How about this? I'll explain each drink as I make it. That way, you can give your hand a rest."

She bites into her lip. "Okay."

*I'm only doing this as an employer. I'd do the same with any employee.*

At least that's what I'm fighting to convince myself.

---

"GOOD NIGHT, GUYS!" Georgia calls out, waving a hand through the air. She exchanges a glance with me. "Thanks for training me. You're always such a good time."

"You think you're good to drive?" I ask, stopping her.

She inspects her hand. "Yeah. The ibuprofen I took has helped, and it's only a short distance."

I rub at my face, not wanting her on the road this late. "Let me find Finn and ask him to give you a ride home."

"I'm fine, really. I don't want anyone going out of their way. It's late, and we're all exhausted."

I nod. "Someone needs to walk you out."

It's company policy that one of us guys walks the female employees out or they go out in groups.

Finn, who's been working the door tonight, holds up his non-ringing phone. "Call coming in. You do it, Archer."

He puts the phone to his ear and walks toward the restrooms.

I give him an *I'm going to kick your ass later* look, and he smirks.

Georgia hitches her bag up her shoulder. "If it's that much of a burden for you, I'm fine. I know karate, and Cohen taught me all the pressure points to bring a man to his knees. I might protect myself better than you would. Hell, I might be the one protecting us both."

I shove my hands into my pockets. "I'm not betting my money on a woman who can barely reach the height minimum for the Tilt-A-Whirl to protect me."

She yawns, and I trail behind her as we head out the exit without saying a word.

"Are you leaving?" she asks when we reach her car.

I shake my head. "Nah, I have closing stuff to do."

"Oh, shoot. Is that my job?"

I debate on lying, but in the future, she can't bail on the tasks. "Yes, it is."

"I can go back in—"

"I'll have Cohen show you on your next shift." I stretch out my arms. "I'm exhausted, and I think we both need some rest. I'll do a quick close tonight, and you can learn another day."

She nods. "Good night, Archer."

I nod back without returning the words.

Waiting until she pulls away, I fish my phone from my pocket while walking back inside. After Georgia's finger incident, her attitude scaled down, and we worked together well. Meredith left but was sure to leave a napkin with her number scribbled on it for me. I'm unclear what her intention was by coming here, but I don't want anything to do with her or that life. We had what we had, but it's history now.

I send Cohen a text, letting him know Georgia is on her way home so he can make sure she gets there safely. Finn is wiping down tables when I walk in, and thankfully, he shut off the TVs —an aid to my headache.

"Cohen is going to flip his shit when you fuck his sister," Finn says, no bullshit.

"We're not fucking, so nothing to worry about," I grumble.

"Not yet." He smirks. "It'll happen, though."

"We can't stand each other."

People need to believe this. It's why I put up this entire charade with her.

"You act like you can't stand her because you want to fuck her."

I flip him off.

"You'll fuck her"—he winks—"and then get your ass kicked."

Silas laughs, coming into view.

*Where the fuck did he come from?*

He hasn't been here all night.

"Dude, do you see the size of him?" Silas asks. "No offense to my boy Cohen, but I'd be afraid to fuck with Archer."

"You two keep that thought," I mutter.

*In case you ever find out what has already happened between us.*

# CHAPTER THIRTEEN

# Georgia

WHEN I GET HOME, I head to the bathroom to inspect my finger. It stings when I clean it and change the bandage. Nothing screams, you'll be a bad employee, like breaking stuff and bleeding on your first day.

I've been at the bar plenty of times and helped out randomly, but I've never worked there. It's more intense than what it appears from the outside. Add that chaos with working with Archer, and I'm shocked it was a glass that fell at my feet and not my heart.

It was all a whirlwind. Working with him, his possessiveness sneaking out, and the woman who showed up.

A woman who was no stranger to him.

Ex-girlfriend.

Ex-fling.

There'd been something, and from the way she stared at him, that something was still there for her. She wanted the man I so desperately want myself. Call me stupid—because that's what I am—for still loving his attention and wanting him when he's shown me nothing but hatred.

Even though he shut her down, a pang of jealousy hit me

when they were whispering in the corner like two lovebirds ready to share a strand of spaghetti.

My eyes are heavy as I stroll into my bedroom and collapse face-first onto my bed. The last time I had so much one-on-one time with Archer was when I was in his bed, and our one-on-one time included us all up in each other's genitals.

My problem with hating Archer is that it's fake.

He acts like a dick, but deep down, if you dive into his soul, there's more.

I saw it that night, and throughout his time with my brother, I've caught flashes of it.

*What happened?*

*What pain is he masking with anger?*

I drag myself up, change into my pajamas, and call Cohen while crawling into bed.

"I'm home," I say around a yawn.

"How was training?"

"Super fun."

He chuckles. "I'm sure Archer was the life of the party."

"How can you be friends with him? He's so rude." I fluff my pillow out and relax into it.

"Archer has always been distant, but it got worse when his brother got locked up. He doesn't trust people, so I was shocked when he asked me to partner up with him."

"Why is he distant?"

"Not my story to tell."

"Not your story to tell, or you know nothing?"

"It's his business. If he wants you to know, he'll tell you."

I frown. "Ugh, you're no fun. You're supposed to give me the scoop."

"Be patient. Maybe he'll tell you."

"And maybe I'll grow a horn out of my head."

He chuckles.

I yawn again. "Since you're not up for a gossip time, it's my bedtime."

"Good night. I'll talk to you tomorrow."

When we end the call, I plug my phone into the charger and turn off my lamp, but I don't drift to sleep. Instead, I wonder how my relationship would be if Archer and I had never slept together. He's always a dick, but he doesn't act like Lola's or Grace's existence kills him.

*What gives?*

*Was I sucky lay?*

He had no complaints that night.

Or maybe he didn't care. He did say he went there to get laid.

I could've been a convenient vagina for him that night.

I wish I could see him as a convenient cock for me, but I can't. I'd never had sex with a guy I wasn't dating, and I threw all of that out for him.

Look where it got me.

---

I STROLL into the bar with an iced coffee in one hand and a Cronut in the other.

I'm in my last year of college, and I will soon have a master's in social work. My plan after is to become a school counselor. I want to help children who don't have a Cohen, like I did, and who need someone to talk to or help them.

It's in the middle of the day, and the bar is quiet. Regulars are lingering, eating baskets of fried food and having a drink, but the crowd hasn't made its landing yet.

Choosing a stool at the far end of the bar, I set my coffee and Cronut down before sliding my backpack off and placing it on the stool next to me. My attempt to study at home was a bust. It was too quiet, and I needed background noise. There were no open tables at the coffee shop, so alas, here I am.

I'm collecting my notes and setting my laptop down when

Archer approaches me. I groan, expecting to hear a comment about me hanging out here randomly.

"What are you studying?" he asks.

I freeze, a note drifting to the floor. "Huh?"

He gestures to my notebook. "What are you studying?"

"Oh, law and social work." I bend down to pick up the fallen paper, and when I stand, he's still there.

"I minored in psychology. That shit is hard."

"Really?" I'm shocked he's sharing this with me. "Where'd you go?"

"Stanford." This isn't said with pride or with a cavalier attitude. You would've thought he'd told me he went to Barney's School for Dinosaurs.

"Why are you working in a small-town bar when you have a degree from Stanford?" Hell, I'm staring at him like he said he went to Barney's School.

"It's my father's alma mater. I graduated with a business degree and then started a business with your brother, not just some bar."

"I didn't mean it like that." I chew on my bottom lip. "What I meant was, why aren't you in some ritzy, top-floor office making six, seven figures?"

His face goes slack, a hint of hurt flickering. "That isn't the life for me. I was expected to go to Stanford, no exceptions. Now, I'd rather be here."

I take a seat. "I'm the first person in my family to graduate from college."

He smiles. "That's awesome, Georgia. It's something to be proud of."

My eyes widen in shock at the compliment. "Uh ... thank you."

*Who stuck a nice pill in his coffee this morning?*

A brief silence passes, and I'm thankful Silas is manning the other end of the bar, so no one can steal Archer away from me.

While I have him in this ... *mood*, it'd be stupid of me not to take advantage of it.

I suck in a breath of courage and ask, "Do you not want to be around me because of what we did or because you genuinely don't like me?" Hurt seeps through my blood, outstripping the joy I had from him opening up to me. "When you said I was nothing but a screw to you that night, were you lying?"

He withdraws a step, as if my questions were a blow to the chest. "That was the past, Georgia. Time to move on."

*"Time to move on."*

That can't happen when only one of us is trying.

"Will you stop being a prick for a minute and act like you have a heart?" I question, waiting for him to turn around and walk away. A routine for us whenever I ask something personal.

"Who said I have a heart?" He raises a brow. "And I'm not acting like a prick."

It's my turn to raise a brow.

"This is my shining personality." He chuckles—a rarity. "You didn't know that?"

"You most definitely do not have a shining personality. You have one of the most unchivalrous personalities I've ever encountered."

"Appreciate the compliment." He tips his head down. "Although you might be alone in that opinion."

"Trust me, I'm not alone in that opinion whatsoever."

"Why don't you enlighten me with who my personality haters are?"

"My friends." *And ninety percent of Iowa's population.*

He snorts. "Of course. They know what happened between us and are taking your side."

"Someone would have to be on crack and have no heart if they didn't take my side in our situation." I fight back a smile. "Not to mention, they've seen your *shining* personality aplenty to gain their own opinion of you."

He stares at me, unblinking, before moving closer. "Want to know the truth?"

I nod.

He invades my space and bows his head, his voice sharp and low. "I never saw you as *a piece of ass*. I didn't walk into Bailey's hoping to find a fuck. I planned to get shit-faced and then take an Uber home, but then there you were, sitting at the bar, broken. I couldn't stop myself from going to you, from wanting to talk to you, from wanting to make you whole again." His cheek brushes against mine, the rough scruff like sandpaper against my skin. "It wasn't about me getting my dick wet; it was about how drawn I was to you. Then we talked, and for some damn reason, I shared more with you about my feelings than I had with anyone. You know more about my goddamn life than the woman I was engaged to, than my mother knows—"

As much as I want this moment to last, I wince and pull away from him. "You were *engaged* when we had sex?"

It takes a second for him to register my change in mood. "What? No. I *was* engaged, and it ended years before we had sex."

I nibble on the inside of my cheek and nod, waiting for him to continue. I hate myself for stopping him. His confession has my heart thumping wildly.

I want more.

More of his truths.

Of his conversations.

Of *him*.

"I don't hate you, Georgia," he says. "I just don't trust myself around you." He taps his knuckle against the bar, turns, and walks away.

---

"HEY, BABE," Grace greets when I walk into our apartment. "How was training?"

She's in our kitchen, eating sushi, with a stack of papers on the table in front of her.

We moved into our two-bedroom apartment last year. While I go to school, she teaches at a private elementary school.

Grace became my best friend when I moved to Mayview, and she was my tour guide at our middle school. We instantly clicked. She didn't care about my family's social status, which was in the gutter. The same with her parents, who welcomed me with open arms and helping hands.

Lola joined our circle during our junior year of high school. We were at a party, and after Grace turned a guy down, he called her a bitch. Lola jumped in and told him to get fucked. The three of us have been inseparable ever since.

I grab a plate and steal a sushi roll from her. "Stressful."

She drops the pen in her hand. "Cohen wasn't easy on you?"

"Cohen didn't train me."

"Uh-oh."

I nod.

"On a scale from one to ten, how awful was Archer?"

"A twelve." I grab a bottle of water from the fridge. "Check this out. I went to study at the bar today, and he was nice to me."

Her eyes widen, and she pinches herself. "I'm sorry. Did you say he was *nice to you?*"

"Shocker, right?"

"Huge shocker." She makes strong eye contact with me, her teacher face emerging. "Maybe you and he should sit down and talk. It's one thing to be around each other when we're in a group, but you'll be working directly with each other now."

"I've tried. He always shuts me down."

"I hope working there doesn't break your heart." A shade of sadness passes over her face.

I'm reminded of what Archer said to me earlier today, and chills shoot up my spine. I open my mouth to tell Grace but stop. It's fresh, and I still need to process it. After he dropped that bomb and turned around, I studied. Okay, *tried* to study. Instead of focusing on my homework, I watched him until I eventually left and came home.

"Anyway," I drawl out, "what are you doing tonight?"

"Coming to visit you on your first night at the new J-O-B."

"Second night, thank you very much." Since I'm super classy, I pick up the sushi roll with my hand and take a bite.

She laughs. "Lola and I will be there, ready to order all the drinks from you."

---

"I WAS HOPING you wouldn't show tonight," Archer says when I walk into the bar.

I curl my lips into a smile. "I see Dr. Jekyll has turned back into Mr. Hyde."

He's so hot and cold.

One minute, he's nice.

The next, he's pissed about working with me.

"What if I paid you to get another job?" He makes a show of shoving his hand into his pocket and yanking out his wallet.

I glare at him. "What if I cut off your dick?"

He holds up the wallet. "Five hundred bucks?"

"Five hundred grand will do."

"Funny," he deadpans.

I snatch the pen clipped on his shirt pocket, tap his chest a few times, and walk around him. "Working here or not, you'll see me everywhere, Archer Callahan. There's no getting rid of me."

"Yeah, you're like a bad dream, haunting me."

"A bad dream or a wet dream?"

"Jesus, fuck, Georgia," he hisses.

"What? One of us needs a personality in this rivalry game of ours, and it's not you. You have the personality of a stale piece of bread."

"You have the personality of a hamster who's been on a crack binge for days."

I tie my apron around my waist, and before I move onto the main floor, I glance back at him. "Oh, and, Archer?"

He raises a brow. "Yeah?"

"This little back-and-forth game, you know what it reminds me of?"

"What?"

"Foreplay."

He points toward the incoming crowd. "Get to work."

---

I UNDERSTAND why Cohen didn't want me behind the bar tonight.

It's a madhouse. A boxing match is on pay-per-view, so the place is flooded with people who didn't want to pay for it at home.

I take an order, scurry to Archer, recite it to him, and hop to the next table. Lola and Grace showed up a few hours ago, but I barely had time to take their orders before I was called over by another table. The plus side to the craziness is that I've already made more in tips than I did in a week at the boutique.

While waiting on drinks, I watch Archer. Seeing him work is a lustful sight. He wipes the sweat off his forehead with the back of his arm as he and Silas maneuver around each other behind the bar. At times, I feel him watching me. When I catch him, when our eyes meet, I smile. To which he immediately scowls and quickly glances away.

When the patrons start clearing out at closing, I stroll to Cohen's office, sluggish and exhausted. Waitressing really gave a girl a workout tonight. I barge in without knocking, and he peeks up at me with a smile on his face while sitting behind his desk.

"What'd you think?" he asks, rolling back in his chair and scrubbing his hand over his dark brow.

"It was fun." I yawn. "I think I did a good job."

"You killed it."

We air-five each other.

"Although I think you have to say that since you're my brother."

"I'm also your boss, and as your boss, I'm saying you killed it. You're good with people, so it's no surprise." He jerks his head toward his desk. "Let me finish this paperwork, and then I'll walk you to your car."

"Coolio. I'm going to run to the kitchen and grab a water."

He gives me a thumbs-up, and I leave his office. On my way to the kitchen, I pass Archer's office. His door is open, and I use it as an opportunity to take a peek.

It's similar to Cohen's in size, and the layout is the same, but while Cohen's is warm, Archer's is cold.

My brother's office is decorated with photos of Noah and our family, memorabilia, and cheesy souvenirs from the places we've gone on vacation together.

Archer's is passionless. There isn't a smidgen of anything that shows his character or fires off hints of the life he lives. Not on the walls, on his desk, nothing. I glance in both directions of the hall to make sure the coast is clear before inviting myself in.

A bottle of overpriced water sits next to his iMac, and a jacket hangs off the edge of his computer chair. When I travel to his desk, I pick up the pen resting next to his mouse pad. It's wood and the same one he used to write his information on the day of our accident. It appears handmade, and it's light as I play with it in my sweaty hand. I trace my fingers along the keyboard, somewhat stalker-like, and search for anything to show me who he is.

My heart doubles in speed when I spot a small picture taped to his computer.

It's a boy—my guess, early teens—and an older man on a boat.

The boy's characteristics match Archer's. He's grinning in the picture. It's wide and authentic, and you can tell he's been laughing.

I play with the photo in my hand, moving my finger over the old paper.

"Can I help you?"

I jump, my hand flying to my chest, and find Archer standing in the doorway. His arms are crossed, his stare pinned to me, and his face is red and tight.

I clear my throat and slowly return the photo to its place.

Then I do it again while scrambling for an excuse as to why I'm office-stalking him.

"I wanted to, uh ..." I run my hands down my wrinkled, *smells like vodka and nacho cheese* shirt. "Thank you for training me ... and for making my drinks tonight. You must've done well because I made killer tips."

He nods without saying a word.

*Alrighty then.*

*Convos with him are still a blast.*

I play with my hands in front of me before saying, "Well ... have a good night." I move around his desk, overcome with curiosity, my heart now tripling in speed.

He steps away from the door, giving me plenty of room to brush past him. "Good night, Georgia. Don't visit my office again."

# CHAPTER FOURTEEN

## Archer

STARTING a bar was supposed to bring me peace.

Instead, it brought me Georgia.

My human version of a migraine.

My version of hell.

She's made me question everything.

The kind of man I am, the kind of man I want to be, the life I want to live.

She's puncturing my plan of living lonely.

Night after night, I watch her smile and laugh, and then I go home and think about her. Things have been tense since I found her poking around my office. My pulse sped as I watched her stare at the photo of my grandfather and me. Having the photo in my office is a double-edged sword. I love the memories of hanging out with my grandfather on my father's side growing up but despise the one of his death. I should've never taped it to my computer.

Anger stormed through me, and as soon as she left, I slammed the door shut, plucked the photo off my computer, and slipped it back into my wallet. Had she been anyone else, I would've ripped their head off for snooping through my shit.

She moves around the bar, practically skipping, and all eyes are on her. Her black shirt, branded with the bar's logo, is tied in a knot at the base of her back, right above her ass, and her short-shorts have me remembering what it felt like to be between her legs. She wanders around, throwing smiles at customers and being the sunshine she is.

While I'm standing in the darkness.

*What is it about this woman?*

It could be the connection we shared that night. We bonded over sex, secrets, and our hate of the people who'd hurt us. I'd never opened up to anyone like I did with Georgia.

Not my mother, not Meredith, not Lincoln.

Only her.

*Why can't I stop thinking about her?*

*Solution: find a woman to take my mind off her.*

Not one to date.

One to screw until I forget about her.

"Hi. You're hot. Want to fuck?"

My attention slides from Georgia to the woman in front of me. She plants her elbows on the bar, leaning in closer, and licks her bottom lip while waiting for my answer.

It's as if God had heard my thoughts and sent her to me.

Or possibly the devil since I'm not sure how keen God is on one-night stands.

"My friends dared me to come over and ask you." She grins and winks at me. "I'm newly single, looking for no-strings-attached sex, and there's no ring on your finger." She eyes my hand for a moment as if double-checking. "You game, sexy?"

I hesitate in answering and stare at her. She's gorgeous— plump red lips, dark hair, huge tits. Unfortunately, I'm not sure if my dick would even get hard for her after watching Georgia all night. My new type is apparently a woman who is short, snarky, wears the weirdest damn clothes, and braids her hair too much for someone her age.

I start to decline, but Georgia speaks over me, "I need two

margaritas, stat, bartender! No time for talking while we're this busy."

The woman shoots Georgia a death glare.

I whip around and start on her drinks at the same time Georgia rushes behind the bar. She dodges Silas, who's holding three beers in his hand, and storms in my direction.

"Don't think I didn't hear her little dare with her friends," Georgia seethes as I grab the tequila. "She's lying. She told her friends she could do it, not the other way around. She just wants to bang you and thought that'd be the perfect pickup line."

I continue making the drinks. "Why do you care if it's a dare?"

Her face reddens. "Do you want to bang her back?"

"Bang her back?"

She nods.

"You mean, do I want to fuck her ... like I did you?"

She slides in closer, her waist bumping into mine. "I don't know. Do you?"

I stay quiet, wishing I could tell her I want to fuck *her* again.

Wishing I could tell her I didn't give a shit about that woman.

"Even if you tried, it wouldn't be as good it was with me," she adds with a smirk.

I don't smirk back. "Take your drink orders, Georgia."

"If you sleep with her, I'll be disgusted with you."

"Is that anything new?"

"Yes."

I raise a brow.

"Right now, I just think you're an asshole."

I hand her the margaritas and return to the woman, saying, "I get off at three."

Unable to stop myself because I'm a mean bastard, I glance at Georgia. All playfulness has left her, now replaced with pain ... and disgust, like she said.

The woman grins wildly. "I'll be here."

For the rest of the night, Georgia barks out her orders to me with no emotion and not one extra word muttered in conversation. I even catch her calling out orders to Silas to avoid speaking to me. When her shift ends, she asks Finn to walk her to her car, not sparing me one look.

"So," Dare Girl asks, "your place or mine?"

*"Your place or mine?"*

The same question I asked Georgia.

My stomach churns at the memory. I've had doubts about going home with this woman all night, hoping she'd leave without waiting for me, but as she stares at me in expectation, I shake my head.

"You know what?" I wipe my hands on the towel. "I changed my mind."

---

"THIS IS a collect call from the Oxford Correctional Facility," the recording says after I answer the call.

It pauses, allowing my father to cut in and say his name, before the automation picks back up.

I decline the call and toss my phone to the side.

Twenty minutes later, it rings again. Same number, but this time, after listening to the recording, I accept the call.

"Hey, brother. How are you?" Lincoln asks.

"Same shit, different day." I rub my forehead with the base of my palm, sprawl out on my couch, and tip my head back while leveling the phone against my ear with my shoulder.

He chuckles. "I feel you on that."

"Counting down the days until you're a free man?"

"More along the lines of trying to stay positive. Am I excited? Fuck, yeah. It puts a damper on shit when I think about Dad not coming with me, though."

"He should be in there longer than you." I grind my teeth, hating that he still cares about Dad after what he did.

After the situation he put him in.

After he fucked up his life.

Noticing the tension, Lincoln clears his throat. "*Anyway,* how's everything at the bar? I can't wait to see it."

His subject change is a good one, and our conversation takes a more positive turn as I tell him how well the bar is doing. We talk for twenty minutes before we're kicked off. I toss my phone down and groan—hating that I can only talk to my brother via collect calls with a time limit.

# CHAPTER FIFTEEN

## *Georgia*

I'M FINISHING off a strawberry Pop-Tart when there's a knock on my door.

"Coming!" I scrape the crumbs off the table, pile them in my hand, and drop them into the trash can on my way to answer it.

As soon as I open the door, a wave of dizziness hits me, and I release a sharp breath as we stare at each other.

I'm not sure how long it's been.

Seven, eight years maybe?

Sometimes, when I walk down the street, I ask myself if I'd recognize her if we passed each other. My question is answered, only we're not passing each other. She's on my doorstep.

Seconds pass as neither one of us mutters a word.

"Hi, Georgia," she finally whispers.

Anita Fox.

My mother.

I strengthen my grip on the doorknob, questioning if my next action should be slamming the door in her face.

I can't.

I can't because I'm hit with the reminder of when I showed up at my dad's house, only to be rejected. I'd never hurt someone like that.

It's not in my heart.

Not in my soul.

She moves from one foot to the other.

"Come in," I rush out, waving my hand forward and widening the door to give her room.

Her face registers shock as she digests my words. That clearly wasn't the reaction she expected, and she takes slow steps into my home.

*Did she expect me to be a monster like my father?*

"Can I get you something to drink?" I ask, shutting the door.

*Please don't say alcohol.*

*Or crack-laced water.*

She clears her throat. "I'll take whatever you have."

"Tea? Water? Coffee?"

"Water would be nice." She bows her head. "Thank you."

She follows me into the kitchen, where I pour us two glasses of water. I hand her one before leading us into the living room, and it's quiet when we both sit—me on the couch and her taking a seat on the chair.

I have so many questions.

*Why is she here?*

*Why didn't she come all those years before?*

There's no holding myself back from asking, "Why are you here? How do you know where I live?" My tone isn't angry, yet it's not friendly.

Just because I didn't shut the door in her face doesn't mean I'll get my hopes up or that I'm elated she's here. She's visited Cohen a few times at his house or his job, begging for money. He helps her, and then she disappears in the middle of the night until she needs help again.

One time, I asked Cohen if he thought she was dead. He said no, that he checked on her regularly—whatever that meant —and that I had nothing to worry about. I never knew if he was telling me that to make me feel better or if it was the truth.

Her hand shakes, causing the glass to rattle. "I was in rehab with a woman whose brother is a private investigator. I asked him to look you up because I wanted to see you."

"Why?" I take a small sip of water.

"I'm clean now and getting my life together."

I stare at her skeptically. "How do I know that's true?"

Her shoulders slump. "You don't, and I understand you might not believe me. I'm here because I'd like to prove to you that I am."

I lean back on the couch and take her in, searching for any signs that she's using. She's aged, which is normal, given it's been years since I've seen her. She doesn't look healthy, but she doesn't look strung out either. She was ... or possibly *is still* an addict, and her abuse shows in her every feature.

Briefly, I wonder what she would've looked like had she never become an addict.

*Would she look more like me?*

I see our resemblances—her chestnut-brown hair, her height, even her eccentric style.

I glance down at my phone when it rings, and Cohen's name flashes on the screen. I could answer it, tell him my situation, and ask him what I should do. He'd tell me to ask her to leave, or he'd drive here and do it himself.

I ignore the call and focus my attention on her. "You'd like to prove it to me? How?"

---

"WHAT'S on your mind over there?"

I peek up from my computer. "Huh?"

"You're zoned out," Archer replies. "Everything okay?"

I sigh. "Yes." Another sigh. "No."

The bar has weirdly become my new study sanctuary. Who would've thought I could concentrate better when people were drinking and cheering on sports around me? I move to different sections, different tables, and different ends of the bar to switch it up. Archer doesn't seem to mind, and at times, we make small conversation.

I questioned whether to come in today. We haven't seen each other since the night he went home with Dare Girl. For the first time since I started working at Twisted Fox, I considered quitting. It was one thing to hear about him being with other women or him being an asshole, and another to witness a woman waiting to go home with him. I was lucky enough to be her waitress for the night and had to listen to her brag about him going to her place later.

She couldn't wait to fuck his brains out, wondered how good he was in bed, and made bets with her friends on how big his cock was.

That night, I couldn't leave the bar fast enough. I slipped Trina a twenty to do my closing responsibilities and peaced out.

Archer circles the bar, pulls out the stool next to me—causing me to nearly fall off mine—and sits. Clasping his hands together, he rests them on the bar. "Talk to me, Georgia."

I can't with him today.

For once, I'm not in the mood for nice Archer.

For conversation with him.

It feels tainted now.

All I can think about is him touching her, kissing her, screwing her.

"I don't want to talk about it," I grumble, avoiding eye contact. *It's mommy issues this time.* "Trust me, you don't want to hear about it."

"I wouldn't have asked if I didn't." He chuckles. "You know, I'm not one to stir up conversation mindlessly."

I can't go to Cohen about this.

Not yet at least.

He'd tell me to haul ass away from her, automatically assuming she had shown up to use me.

I downcast my gaze. "My mom … She showed up at my house today."

He stays quiet before saying, "Your mother, she left you too?"

"She didn't leave per se, but she wasn't there either."

He nods in understanding.

"She's an addict. Or was an addict. I'm not exactly sure on what tense I should use at the moment."

*Why am I opening up to him?*

Just like the night at the bar, it comes without thinking, without hesitation.

He can draw the truth out of me by simply sitting down and talking in that deep, smooth voice of his.

How this man can make me hate him and confide in him at the same time is beyond me.

"What'd she say?" He scratches his cheek. "Did she seem clean?"

I shift my weight on the stool. "She said she's in a sober house, and she didn't look strung out or anything."

"Do you believe her?"

I shut my eyes, replaying my conversation with her in my mind. "I do."

"Then follow your gut. If you believe her and think she's changed, give her the opportunity to prove it to you. Put your toes in the water but don't go all in." His voice thickens. "Do not hand all your trust over to her. Don't let her hurt you."

*"Don't let her hurt you."*

*What about the times he's hurt me?*

I struggle to yell at him, to scream that he's just as bad as her and my father.

Making me feel unwanted and unworthy, like the rest of them.

It's become a trend in my life, I guess.

To be unwanted.

"Georgia," he breathes out, "I'll never forget how you looked that night at Bailey's—not just your beauty, but also your heartbreak, the pain of rejection that'd blocked out your light."

He grips the seat of my stool and rotates me to face him. My eyes water at his words, at what today has been, at what this week has been, and I slip him a guarded look. When our eyes meet, a single tear drops down my cheek, and I shiver when he runs the pad of his thumb over my face, brushing it away.

I shut my eyes, savoring his touch, and he drags my stool closer to cup my face in his strong palm. I say nothing, just stare at him, his touch a comfort to my pain.

"Just trust your gut but protect your heart," he whispers, dropping his hand down to curl around my knee. He squeezes it tenderly before resting it there.

*"Protect your heart."*

My eyes flash open.

*"Protect your heart."*

That pertains to him too.

The thought of him sleeping with that woman storms through me.

*Did he touch her with the same hand he's touching me with?*

*Did he use those fingers to pleasure her?*

I shiver, disgust climbing up my throat.

*How dare he.*

*How dare he do this again—play the savior when, behind his walls, he's really the devil.*

I drop my hand down and peel his fingers off me, one by one.

"Don't touch me again, Archer," I snarl, pushing him away and sliding off my stool. "Go call the woman you fucked."

"Georgia."

He attempts to grab my hand, but I swat him away and stick my finger in his face.

"No."

He pulls back but calls my name one last time as I leave.

"HI, SWEETIE."

I peek up from stocking the beer fridge to find a woman plucking a pair of designer sunglasses off her face.

With a gorgeous Chanel handbag hanging from her shoulder and no doubt a monthly Botox budget, she's crawled straight from *The Stepford Wives* movie. The opposite everything of our everyday customer base.

Our regulars don't sport cashmere.

Don't have rocks on their fingers that cost more than it would to feed a small village.

Either she's lost—or from Archer's world.

"I'm looking for Archer," she states, her tone polite.

*Cougar alert.*

*How many more of Archer's women will I have to deal with?*

I can't stop myself from snapping, "Why?" I take a step back with a cringe, wishing I could backtrack my response.

A week has passed since I told Archer about my mother showing up at my apartment.

A week since I told him to keep his hands off me.

A week since I told Grace to punch me in the face to knock some sense into me if I looked at him with googly eyes again.

Archer and I have switched roles.

I'm now the one avoiding any run-ins, conversations, or contact with him.

"Uh-oh." The woman laughs, holding out her hand. "I'm Josephine Callahan, Archer's mother."

*Well, shoot.*

Plot twist.

I pull myself together, embarrassment hitting me, and clasp her hand in mine. "Oh."

*Can I climb into a hole now?*

She grins. "How long have you been dating my son?" She

shakes her head with a tsk. "I swear, he hides everything from me."

A blush creeps up my cheeks as I pull away. "The never day of never."

My response doesn't deflate her smile.

"I see he's being his difficult self," she says. "Difficult, but under that hard exterior is an incredible heart. It's just overgrown from hiding so long." Her smile widens. "It'll be like hitting the jackpot when you make it there, I promise. Don't give up."

My mouth drops open as I scramble for a response. Even with her uppity appearance and barely moving forehead, she's nice. The problem is, she doesn't know my history with Archer. He doesn't want me to find his heart. He doesn't want *any* woman to find his heart. He wants her to find his cock, and then he discards her. I haven't seen Dare Girl since the night he banged her—a clue he most likely played morning-ditcher with her as well.

"We don't exactly get along," I tell her. "That won't be happening."

"My son can be complicated."

"Yes, he can also be a jerk, rude, and inconsiderate—no offense." I slap my hand over my mouth at my outburst, but she doesn't seem fazed.

"None taken." She sighs.

I flash her a genuine smile and point toward a door with an *Employees Only* sign "His office is through there. Down the hall, second door on the left."

"Before I hunt him down, how about a glass of your best wine?"

*Uh-oh.* If she drinks liquor like Lola described her husband did, our *best wine* will taste gross to her.

"Of course." I twist around and eye our wine options. I'm not much of a wine connoisseur, so I pick the one ordered the most. Grabbing a glass, I pour her a glass of pinot blanc.

"He's working through healing," she adds when I hand over her drink. "I promise, he has a big heart."

"That heart seems to shrivel up more and die when we're around each other."

She takes a sip, her face scrunching up as she swallows it down. "Thank you. Don't give up on him, okay?"

# CHAPTER SIXTEEN

# Archer

"KNOCK, KNOCK."

I hear my mother's voice seconds before she barges into my office without knocking.

"Please ask the cute spitfire employee out on a date," she says, shutting the door behind her.

"Hello to you too," I grumble.

She grins. "Hi, sweetie."

*Why is she here?*

My mother doesn't visit the bar frequently. The few times have been when I didn't answer her phone calls and she was worried. It's not her scene, and I understand. Some feel comfortable in sports bars, others in clubs, and galas if you're Josephine Callahan.

She points toward the door. "That spunky little thing behind the bar? I like her, and she likes you."

*Spunky little thing?*

She has to be talking about Georgia.

I toss my pen onto the desk and sink back in my chair. "She doesn't know what's good for her."

She straightens out her knee-length white skirt and sits down in a chair—her posture prim and proper, back brace—

style. "You should pick up dating again. Ask her to dinner."

"She's my partner's sister. Not happening."

Her liking Georgia isn't surprising. They might be from two different worlds, and Georgia doesn't wear designer clothes, but people fall in love with her personality.

Even if Georgia isn't your cup of tea, you can't *not* like her.

I've tried like fucking hell not to.

"What's the plan for your life then, huh?" she asks. "Stay single forever? Work in this bar and sulk while everyone else gets married and has children? You can't hide forever, Archer. Eventually, you'll need to step up and work through your"—she searches for the appropriate word—"grief."

There isn't a right word.

"I have," I seethe. "I face it every damn night."

"No, you *regret* it, not face it. Those are two different things, honey. You can think about those issues all day long. Facing them takes a different type of strength—more work, harder initiative—but the payoff is better. There's a deeper cut, but it's easier to heal without slapping a Band-Aid on it or constantly thinking about it because the scar is what remains."

"I'll work on that," I lie.

She crosses her legs and places her folded hands on her lap. "Your father is shutting down the company."

I wince. "What?"

"He's closing Callahan Holdings and selling all the real estate. He owes restitution, as does Lincoln, and the money will go toward that." Her shoulders sag, shrinking the prim-and-proper posture. "You refuse to work there, and given their felonies, neither Lincoln nor your father can." She squeezes her eyes closed, processing her words.

Her dream life isn't a dream after all. It's a nightmare of fraud and schemes.

"Finally, someone makes a good business decision."

Is my response rude?

Absolutely.

But it's the truth.

I rub the tension on my neck before moving it from side to side.

My ears are ringing, and my chest tightens.

Her tone softens. "It's breaking your father's heart."

*Mine too.*

It's time it happened, though.

Too much damage has been done.

My grandfather's legacy is going to be sold to the highest bidder. The company he built from the ground up will be reduced to ashes from his heirs burning it down.

We're pathetic.

We don't deserve it.

I lean forward to settle my elbows on my desk and throw out my hands. "I hate that it has to end this way."

She flicks away a tear falling down her cheek. "Which brings me to our next conversation."

I shake my head. "One conversation a day is your max. Come back tomorrow."

"Lincoln will be released soon."

"I know this," I reply with a nod.

"Did he talk to you about working here?"

I flinch at her question, my stomach dropping. "No."

"I figured. He's worried you'll say no."

My body tenses. "You have to understand, he's a felon, and this isn't only my business."

If it were only my ass on the line, I'd say yes in a heartbeat.

But it's not.

"Companies won't hire him," she rushes out. "He'll be seen as too much of a liability. Please, Archer. At least until he gets on his feet."

"I'll help with any money he needs."

"It's more than that."

"I'm not the only one who makes business decisions here."

"You know your brother would never bring any harm to your business."

"I trust him. The problem is, I don't want the bullshit, the drama, any of that."

"Think about it. When he's released, he'll need to lean on us. His time away has been an eye-opener for him." Another tear drops down her cheek, and she hastily sweeps it away. Josephine Callahan is also not a public crier. "He's not the same man he was before."

I grind my teeth. "I'm well aware."

Lincoln is smart, a human calculator, and he would be an asset anywhere.

"Everyone makes mistakes," she adds.

"I'll talk to Cohen. The decision isn't only mine."

"Yes, but he's family. And Cohen hired his sister."

"His sister hasn't done time in prison."

# CHAPTER SEVENTEEN

## Archer

### Five Years Ago

"ARCHER, HOW DID THIS HAPPEN?"

I barely make my mother's question out.

My hands shake, my jaw throbs, and I lick my lips to taste the caked-up blood in the corner while staring at my mother.

I open my mouth.

Shut it.

I have no words.

The answer, it will kill them, kill *me,* as it seeps up my throat and out of my mouth.

Fall from my lips, as if I were spitting up poison.

Not that it matters.

It's already assumed that I'm to blame. The accusatory stares and glares of disappointment have been my view for the past hour. It's narrowing down some, thanks to people leaving and one of my eyes now swelling shut.

"Those Callahan boys, wild as can be," I heard someone whisper in the background.

"I can't even look at you," my father snarls, spit flying alongside his fury. "You disgust me."

I welcome the verbal assault, flinch as each word lacerates deeper into my veins, aware the agony will forever be embedded inside me.

I welcome it because I deserve it.

"Dad, stop!" Lincoln yells, pushing forward to separate him from me. He hooks his arms around my father's, saving me from another face blow.

My father stumbles back, and my mother sobs harder.

"Honey," she cries out to him, grabbing his arm before he attempts to deck me again. "Calm down. *Please* calm down!"

Following my mother's lead, Meredith captures my clenched fist. "Come on, baby. You need to sleep."

"Fuck sleep," I grit out, pulling away from her.

Her touch isn't welcome.

Only pain is.

"Listen to your girl and go the fuck to sleep," Lincoln demands, shoving his finger in my face. His eyes are glossy, and his lower lip is trembling.

"I don't need goddamn sleep!" I roar, roughly shoving my palm into my chest.

There'll be no sleeping for me tonight.

My brain can't shut down—can't shut down the adrenaline, the disgust, or the shit I snorted up my nose earlier.

I tip my head up to the sky and scream for a release that'll never come. A single tear—the first I've had in over a decade—slips down my cheek.

"This is all my fucking fault," I whisper into the night, admitting my truth.

# CHAPTER EIGHTEEN

## Georgia

"STOP SUCKING on your Popsicle like that."

"Huh?" I peer up at Archer, and the expression on his face confirms he didn't mean to say that out loud.

He waves to the Popsicle in my mouth.

"What? I was concentrating." I grin and perform a long, dramatic, R-rated suck. "Why? Does it bother you? Are you turned on?"

"It's turning on everyone in here," he hisses.

I do a show of glancing around the bar. "Really? It doesn't seem like anyone *but you* is looking at me."

A few weeks have passed since I told him to keep his hands off me. We've played the *avoiding* game, tiptoeing around each other and only speaking when necessary. He's strictly followed through with my hands-off demand, not even brushing by me when we're working behind the bar, almost as if he's terrified to touch me now.

But as per usual, it's always for awkward reasons that our conversation strikes back up. No regular talks in the soap opera of Georgia and Archer. Nope, it's always super-fun discussions like parent issues, arguments, and debates on me sexualizing my grape Popsicle.

"Just … suck on it like a normal person," he grates out.

I don't.

*He should've never made a comment.*

I suck on it theatrically this time. "How exactly do I suck on it like a normal person?"

I wrap my tongue around the tip, sucking hard before pulling it away. His eyes narrow as they ping from my mouth to my eyes.

I grin, slide my tongue over my bottom lip to capture the juices, and hold it out to him. "Want to show me how normal people suck it?"

"Knock it off, Georgia," he fumes.

The air in the bar grows thicker. It's noon, so it's not busy, and I've been studying while sucking on my Popsicle. Archer is bartending alone tonight, which is typical for a weekday. Weekends are when they tend to double up.

I wave the stick in the air. "You don't have to fake it not turning you on, Archer. There isn't anyone around who can overhear you admit this makes you wonder how it'd feel if I were sucking your cock instead."

"Jesus Christ," he hisses underneath his breath.

I grin.

I'm in a mood.

It started off in a *let's annoy Archer* mood.

Now, it's a *please take me to the back and bang me* mood.

"Quickie in the back?" I raise a brow.

I let out a *humph* when the stick is snatched out of my hand. Archer finishes it off, taking the last bite, and throws it in the trash. I stare at him, wide-eyed and slack-jawed.

"I told you to stop," he clips.

I grin. "But not stopping is more entertaining."

"CAN YOU WORK TOMORROW NIGHT?" Cohen asks, stepping in from the back of the bar.

I'm counting my tips and finishing off a basket of cheese fries after my shift.

Silas and Finn are here, shooting the shit.

Archer is cleaning up behind the bar.

I stack my dollar bills in a pile and shake my head. "I have plans."

"What kind of plans?" Cohen asks.

"A double date with Lola." I shove all my cash together and slip it into my purse.

"That's fucking trouble," Silas says, a smirk on his masculine face.

"At least it's not a double date with Grace," Finn comments with a booming laugh and a gleam in his eyes.

"I'd prefer it to be with Grace," Cohen inputs. "Grace dates respectable guys who wait until marriage to have sex."

"Boring," I sing out, rolling my eyes.

Guys are dumb. They see Grace—strawberry-blonde hair, innocent smile, closet full of denim overalls and summer dresses —and think she's some Virgin Mary. Grace doesn't openly talk about sex, but it doesn't mean she *doesn't* have sex.

Lola, on the other hand, they see as the opposite—straight black hair, deviant smile, closet full of leather jackets and ripped jeans. She openly talks about sex, will give pointers, and creates play-by-plays on the best sex positions, if asked.

Cohen gets a phone call, holds his finger up, and make a beeline toward his office.

"Who's the guy?" Finn asks, stealing one of my fries and shoving it into his mouth, cheese hitting the edge of his lips.

"A friend of the guy she's dating." I shrug.

*Don't know. Don't care.*

I'm not going for the guy.

I'm going for the distraction.

We're going to a club, so it won't be an intimate affair. A group of her friends from work is going, and I'm tagging along because my life is dullsville. I've become a rat on an endless wheel in the dating game. I swear off men, but then I go on these dates even though I'm not interested, nor do I have the time for a new relationship.

Again, the distraction.

The distraction from the brooding dude behind the bar.

"I suggest you ditch the date and work," Archer says. "That's what a responsible adult would do."

I twist in my chair and glare in his direction. "Not everyone is all work, no play, and dull as ditchwater."

"Whoa," Silas says, smirking. "How dare you lie and say Archer isn't fun?"

"We have no one else to work," Archer fires back. "Cohen can't. Silas requested off. You want to go on a date that'll be lame. You lose."

"First, it won't be lame," I argue. "And you have Trina."

He's stopped his cleaning, and I've stopped my eating. We're staring each other down as we throw digs at the other.

"Trina is terrible behind the bar," he points out. "Not to mention, if I stick her behind the bar, we're down a waitress. How does that help?"

"You say *I'm* terrible behind the bar." I twirl a strand of hair around my finger and raise a brow.

"Not as bad as her." He clicks his tongue against the roof of his mouth before pointing at me. "You're working. Cancel your little date," he says, the last sentence turning more mocking with each word.

"That's not fair," I whine and then cringe at how childish I sound.

Archer throws his strong arms up. "Life isn't fair, sweetheart. Consider this a life lesson."

"Too bad you're not my boss." I grin and pop a fry into my mouth.

"Shots fired," Finn calls out in the background, his hands cupped around his mouth.

Archer doesn't oversee me in anything. Everything goes through my brother. Therefore, my brother is my boss and can tell me when I can and can't work.

"I'm not your boss, huh?" His face darkens in frustration. "Who owns this place?"

"You *and* my brother. I consider him my boss. Not you."

"Let me get this straight. You want the bar to be short-staffed so you can do who knows what with some random asshole?"

He taps the side of his cheek, over his stubble, and my legs squeeze together. Even after all this time, I remember what the scruff felt like, rubbing along my inner thighs, marking me.

I cross my arms, hyperaware all attention is glued on us. "Are you mad because I can't work or because I'm going on a date?" I turn to Silas. "I'm sure you're taking off to hit the clubs."

Silas holds up his hands and retreats backward. "It's my brother's bachelor party, babe. We're hitting up Vegas."

I switch my attention to my next victim. "Finn?"

He shakes his head. "Working the door."

"Looks like it's you and me," Archer states flatly. "See you tomorrow—and that's from *your boss.*"

A soulless smile crosses his lips, setting me on fire. When he steps around the bar and stalks toward his office, I'm hot on his heels. He doesn't peer back at me, only makes his strides longer. He opens the door, walks into the room, and sits behind his desk.

"I know why you're doing this," I hiss, slamming the door shut behind us.

He leans back in his chair and spreads his arms out. "Oh, do you?"

"Can you make up your mind on how you feel about me?" I cross my arms. "Anytime you hear about me being with another guy, you act like a dick."

Okay, he *always* acts like a dick.

His mood is on steroids when it involves another man and me.

He pinches the bridge of his nose. "I think you're mistaken."

"Really?" I snort. "When I met a guy for drinks here, you randomly charged over to the table and said I needed to work ASAP because we'd gotten slammed out of the blue, which was a lie."

"This is the place of your employment, not a chance to meet and date guys."

"Like you don't meet women?" I shake my head. "Double standard much?"

"Whatever I do, I do it *privately*. I don't speak about it, don't flaunt it—"

"Whoa," I interrupt, simmering with frustration. "I don't flaunt anything."

"You do." His voice is flat. "You bring guys you're not interested in around to make me jealous. Here, barbecues, when we hang out with friends."

"Don't flatter yourself."

It's true.

For someone who's sworn off men, I do a crappy job of the swearing part.

Swearing off men means swearing off Archer.

I'm fighting to replace him with someone else, but nothing moves past the first date because he takes over my mind.

"This is such bullshit." I advance around his desk to his side. "Admit it."

"Admit what, Georgia?"

"Admit you don't want me with other men because it makes you jealous."

He turns in his chair to face me, and a twinge of exasperation laces his voice. "I don't like you being around other guys. I get jealous." A pained stare clouds his features. "Does that make you happy? Does that make our working relationship any less messed up?"

I dig my nails into the edge of his desk to prevent myself from falling, his words nearly knocking me on my ass.

His words.

His tone.

His anguish.

I hit buttons I never knew existed.

And from the looks of it, he never knew they existed either.

I wasn't prepared for that truth bomb.

His confession is a high before the low.

Excitement but then devastation that he'll never do anything about it.

"Yet"—my throat thickens with heartache—"you don't want to be with me."

He lifts his hands, curling them around my waist, and stares up at me. "We can't be together, Georgia."

The anguish is gone.

Vulnerability in its place.

"Why not?" I choke out.

"It's too complicated." He gives my hips a rough squeeze. "You're my partner's sister. You're too young. You're my employee. I don't do relationships." He shakes his head. "A long list of additional reasons as well."

"You don't do relationships, yet you were engaged?" I shake my head. "That doesn't … it doesn't make sense."

"My failed engagement is what taught me that I don't do relationships." He slides his hands up and down my waist, his touch setting me on fire. "We have enough problems as it is. Us *being together* would create more tension when it fell apart. Our friends would know, and so far, we're finally doing a halfway decent job of being civil toward each other. Think about how that'd go back to hate." His hands shift to my thighs, gripping them. "If something were to happen in this office, if I took you to my bed again, if I fucked you again …" His voice trails off.

I shiver in his arms.

"It'd lead to nothing but problems."

"Do you want to fuck me again?"

"Every time I look at you, I want to touch you. I have to clench my hands to stop myself. I have no right to be jealous, and I'm working on that, trust me."

He drops his head, his forehead against my stomach, and I massage his scalp, running my hand through his hair.

"What if I'm willing to take that risk?"

He expels a long breath when he pulls away. "Georgia, half the time, we can barely stand to be in the same room."

"Because we're running," I say, my voice trembling. "We're failing ourselves in fear. My brother, he'd understand—"

"It's not only about him, Georgia. I'm fucked up in the head. I've done fucked-up shit."

"We all have, Archer." I cup his face in my hands. "We're human."

He repeatedly shakes his head.

I fall to my knees, causing his hands to slide up underneath my armpits, so we're level. "Talk to me."

"You're too pure, too happy to be dragged down with me. You deserve better."

"What if I don't want better than you?" I blink away tears, unable to stop a few.

He drops his hands, smooths his palms over my cheeks, erasing them, and catches my chin between his thumb and forefinger. Silence envelops his office as his gaze explores the features of my face.

"Trust me," he whispers, "you do."

"Archer! Dude, we need you!"

I gasp, jumping, when someone knocks on the door.

Archer kisses my forehead and then the tip of my nose. "If you want the night off, you can have the night off."

There it is.

This conversation has ended us.

"No," I say, my chin trembling. "It's okay."

"Archer!"

We should stand.

Separate.

"Give me a fucking minute!" he barks, rolling back in his chair.

I gasp at the loss of his touch, at the loss of his warmth.

Silas barges into the room, stopping as we come into his view. "I didn't see shit." He slowly backs away, the same way he did earlier. "But seriously, we need you. Wrap this shit up. There's a guy losing his fucking mind in the parking lot demanding to see our camera footage because his wife left the bar with another man."

"Great," I mutter when Silas turns and leaves the room.

Archer stands before holding his hand out. "He won't say anything." He sighs, kisses the top of my head, and walks toward the doorway.

"I'll be here tomorrow," I say before he exits.

He nods. "See you then."

# CHAPTER NINETEEN

# Archer

"I TOLD you something would happen between you two," Silas says in warning. "Your relationship with Cohen is about to get messy as fuck."

"It's not what you think."

"It sure looked like what I think. She was on her knees in front of you—"

"Whoa, she was not about to suck my—"

"Not where I was going with that. The look on her face, the sadness—there's something there. That hate game you play is a bunch of bullshit. I know it. Lola knows it but won't share anything with me because she would never break the girl code. Finn knows it. The only one who's blind is Cohen. Hell, he probably knows it but is trying to convince himself otherwise."

"Just don't say shit."

"I'm keeping my motherfucking mouth shut. When this shit all blows up, don't you dare say I knew."

"It won't blow up."

"It will, and Silas knew nothing."

"ABOUT YESTERDAY," Georgia says when she gets to work.

Her voice sends a chill up my spine. She's all I've thought about since yesterday happened.

Instead of being honest, I lie, "There's nothing about yesterday."

"Archer."

I stop and turn. "You want to know the truth? Let me lay it on you. The day I brought you home and fucked you, I liked you. The day I saw you at the cookout, I knew I was screwed, but once I figured out our only communication was at the bar and a few outings where I could keep my distance, I was relieved. Then you started working here and fucked everything up for me."

"Wow," she says.

"Had this been another time in my life, our situation might be different."

"Had this been another time in your life, you'd probably be married."

"Possible. I don't know." I run my hand through my hair. "But it's not another time in my life. This is now, and now, I'm not the man for you." I gesture between the two of us. "As much as we want this to happen, it can't."

"It's embarrassing, you know, having someone say they like you but not want to be with you. You start to wonder why, you know? Is it because I don't come from money, like you do, that you don't feel like I'm good enough for you, that I'm only your type in bed or physically? You know, it's probably worse that I learned your truth. At least in the past, I thought you hated me. Now, I know you don't hate me; you just don't see me as worthy enough to take a chance with, to be with me, to show me I'm good enough. Yes, my father ran off on my family; yes, we were poor; and yes, my mother was an addict, but that doesn't define who I am."

"This has nothing to do with stature or you and everything

to do with me." I smack my chest. "Me and my fucked-up life, my fucked-up family."

"At least you have a family!"

"Look, whatever you have in your head about us, kill that thought. Fucking slaughter it. We work together. That's it. All I will ever see you as is an employee."

"Jesus, you give me a headache from your whiplash of emotions."

"Georgia, move on. Be with someone else!"

She throws a glass down. "I can't because you don't want me to! You stop me."

I only nod and walk away.

---

SHE ISN'T the same Georgia for the rest of the week.

Somehow, it's like every feeling she had for me is gone … except for the hating part.

I'm an asshole for being sad that she doesn't want me anymore since I'm the one who turned her down.

That night in my office changed everything between us.

It wrote in stone that we're done.

Over.

Nothing.

And never will be.

I grab the most expensive bottle of alcohol from my kitchen and throw it across the room. I wish I were a different man, one who could give her what she wanted, one who wasn't fucked up in the head.

One who wasn't responsible for someone else's death.

# CHAPTER TWENTY

## Georgia

"HOW ARE YOUR CLASSES GOING?"

My mom glances up from her plate at my question. We're at the Moccasin Diner, where she works and the place we meet at once a week. It's not the best diner in Anchor Ridge. The checkered floor tile is dingy, the silverware is always bent, and it's a trucker hot spot. Every time I leave, I cross my fingers I don't get food poisoning.

I don't come for the food. I come for her.

To cheer her on, so she never turns to drugs again.

So far, the ride to developing a relationship has been smooth. It's nice to finally have a mother. Even though it's only halfway, it's still better than nothing.

It should've happened sooner, though.

She should've been there since day one.

I'm working hard not to hold that resentment toward her, but it hasn't been easy. Cohen was the one there for me—when my period started, after my first heartbreak, during my first hangover, preparing me for college.

Not my mother.

Not my father.

Not two people who were meant to be my biggest

supporters.

Cohen.

Every week, I struggle to put it aside, knowing we'll have to talk about it eventually.

People make mistakes.

Drugs make people selfish.

That's why I haven't fully thrown myself into a relationship with her—in fear of her disappearing. Cohen refuses to see or talk to her. He passes off my visits as something that will only break me in the end.

The thing with me is, my heart survives a beating.

It can get fractured in every way possible, nearly destroyed, and I'll still pick up every piece. I'll gather them one by one and then hand them over to someone even more reckless.

Sometimes, my heart is too good for me.

Sometimes, it's too bad for me.

It's also why I am who I am and why I love so hard.

In the end, I can say I tried—tried with my mother, my father, Archer.

I gave every single one of them an opportunity. What they chose to do with it was up to them.

She smiles at me from across our booth, one nestled against a window. "Good. I'm attending them every night I don't work and have been saving up my money to get my own place when I leave the halfway house."

Her cheeks are sunken from the drug's long-term effects. She's gradually gaining weight, and her halfway house drug-tests her every three days. She's missing two bottom teeth, and the others aren't in great condition—another side effect from the addiction. Her plan is to save enough money for dentures.

"That's awesome! Congratulations." I reach out and grab her hand, squeezing it tightly before pulling it away and taking a sip of my strawberry milkshake.

"How are *your* classes going?"

"Good. I'm ready to graduate and forget about midterms and papers and exams."

"I'm so proud of you." She places her palm on her chest over her heart. "My daughter, a college graduate."

I blush.

"All on her own … without a mother."

I open my mouth to tell her it wasn't all on my own. I had Cohen, but she sniffles and keeps talking.

"I'm so sorry, Georgia. For failing you, Cohen, our family." She wipes at her eyes. "My apology will never make up for my absence, and I'm not asking for a pass. You and Cohen will never forget my neglect, but someday, I hope you can forgive me for it."

"I understand," I reply with silent tears.

Her love for the drug was stronger than the one for her family.

I pray that's changed.

That her yearning for forgiveness is stronger than her love for a high.

# CHAPTER TWENTY-ONE

# Archer

WHAT'S HARDER?

Hating someone or acting like you hate someone?

Forcing yourself to push them away?

Georgia stares at me from across the bar.

Every inch of me craves her.

Before she car-blocked her way into my life, I was who I wanted to be.

Who I deserved to be.

Callous. An asshole. Heartless. A loner.

It's who I was.

Enter Georgia Fox.

Coming through with warmth, softening my callousness.

It's unfair to her, us arguing.

Silas calls it foreplay.

I tell him to shut the fuck up.

We haven't touched again.

But that doesn't mean she hasn't touched me in other places. That she hasn't climbed her way into my thoughts and affected me in ways to make me a different man than who I am.

"DON'T FORGET, tomorrow is my birthday, bitches," Silas says, sucking on a lollipop.

Finn slaps his back as he walks by. "I'll be there."

"I'll think about it." Lola smirks, her plump lips bright red.

Silas stops behind her stool, wraps his arms around her shoulders, and nuzzles her neck. "You'll be there. Don't forget my present, my little hellcat."

She tips her head back, staring up at him. "I'll be sure to purchase a value pack of condoms from Costco."

He kisses her forehead. "That's my girl."

"Rule number one," Finn says, sitting down on a stool at the pub table. "No one tells Archer that Georgia is coming."

"I can hear you, dumbass," I grind out, approaching the table. "I promised Silas I wouldn't bail. I'll be there."

I wish *she'd* bail, though.

Georgia perks up in her stool. "I'll be on my best behavior."

Finn snorts and motions to Georgia and then me. "You'll have at least one spat before the night ends."

"Who even says *spat*?" Georgia asks.

Finn shoves his thumbs into his chest. "Fuckers like me."

I want to go to the club like I want to hang out with Lincoln in his prison cell. Silas bribed me into going when I asked him to cover a shift for me. I'm a man of my word, so I'll stop through, have a birthday drink, and then slip out.

Why Silas has his birthdays in clubs is beyond me. Dude is sober and drinks seltzer water at parties. Still a better time than me, though.

Silas has never shared why he doesn't drink. It's been brought up a few times, but he shuts us down—only sharing, "It's not my thing."

As a sober man, he still kills it as a bartender and as our liquor purchaser. Lola has a lot to do with it. She tells him what to buy, and he listens to her every word.

That's why it's no surprise that he invited the girls.

He invites her to everything.

With Lola comes Georgia.

With Georgia comes my aggravation.

With Georgia comes my frustration.

With Georgia comes everything I can never have.

---

## THE CLUB IS PACKED.

Club Soho is the best club in the city.

Once, I lived for this shit.

The loud music, expensive alcohol, drugs.

Now, when I take a seat, I cringe.

"Private tables are the bomb dot com," Georgia says, walking into our VIP section with Grace and Lola. She straightens out her button-up denim skirt and collapses onto the white couch.

*Why did she come looking like that?*

*To torture me?*

Short skirt. Low-cut white top. Black suede boots hitting her knees.

Adorable woven into sexy.

I drink her in as if she were the drink that'd get me through the night.

Instead of the club being my high, it's her.

That blond hair—I've dreamed of it tangled against my pillow.

I had her as a brunette, wild and in my bed.

Now, I need the other.

Tonight, it's our small group—Georgia, Lola, Grace, Silas, Finn, and me.

"It's not hard to get the VIP section when you're the shit," Silas replies, smirking around a blue sucker.

"You mean, it's not hard when *I* set it up," Lola says, elbowing him. "Happy Birthday, asshole."

He points at her with his sucker. "True, *but* it's also easier when you're banging the owner of the club. You got me beat on that one, babe."

Lola flips him off.

"Jealous she's hooking up with him and not you?" Georgia asks—because she's Georgia and she always has to talk some shit.

"Lola knows I'm always jealous of who she's sleeping with." He winks at Lola. "My services are available anytime she wants."

Lola laughs. "Whatever. Everyone knows it's stupid to screw your best friend."

"Love you." He kisses her cheek and drags her onto his lap.

"Hey!" Grace says at the same time Georgia says, "Oh, he's your best friend now?"

"Best *guy* friend," Lola corrects.

"Can I be offended by that?" Finn asks. "I thought we were friends."

"Your best *girl* friend is Grace," Silas answers before squeezing Lola's knee as she squirms in his lap. "Stay away from mine."

"Kinda feeling left out over here," Georgia mutters.

Silas jerks his head toward me. "Then there were two. Looks like it's you and Archer, babe. I know Archer is up for some BFF bracelets."

"Pfft," Finn says. "They hate each other."

"Do they, though?" Silas asks, leveling his eyes on me and stroking his cheek.

Finn is oblivious to his insinuation. Grace and Lola share looks before peering at Georgia.

Georgia raises a brow, her gaze meeting mine. "Do we hate each other, Archer?"

I lick my lips before taking a long draw of my Jack and Coke. "You tell me. I think you've moaned how much you hate me aplenty."

"*Moaned* it?" She cocks her head to the side.

I nod.

"Wrong." Georgia delivers a devious smile. "You know what name I do like to moan?"

I shake my head. "Hard pass."

That devilish smile widens. "Chase."

Grace spits out her drink.

Lola shoves her face into Silas's shoulder to hide her laughter.

"What am I not getting?" Finn asks the crowd before focusing on Georgia. "You have a new boyfriend?"

"Gross." Georgia exaggeratedly shudders. "Chase was some douchebag I had a one-night thing with." She's answering Finn but staring at me. "Totally didn't deliver bedroom-wise, if you know what I mean."

"Keep that from your brother," Finn says, all brotherly like. "He'll lose his shit if he hears about you hooking up with some random dude."

*You have no idea.*

With music blaring around us, I take in the club. Dancers are hanging from the ceiling, doing acrobatic shit. We're on the top floor, a balcony-like layout, overlooking the sea of people dancing to the electric music the DJ is bumping. We talk—I randomly throw in comments—and suck down liquor.

Our waitress returns with a glowing tray of drinks and shooters in her hands and drops them off. Silas slips her a hundred, and she blows him a kiss. Lola and Georgia grab a shooter, and Georgia holds one out to Grace.

She waves it away and yawns.

The girls knock their shots back.

"I'm exhausted." Grace glances at Silas, pouting out her lower lip. "Do you mind if I leave early?"

"You go ahead, Teacher Grace," he replies. "Teach those brats their ABCs."

She rolls her eyes and smacks his arm.

Georgia lifts up, and her ass points in my direction when she slides her phone from her back pocket. "I'll book us an Uber."

My back stiffens, though it shouldn't.

*Don't leave yet.*

Her presence, sipping on her drink and laughing with our friends, has been my entertainment for the night. I'm not ready to end that yet.

Not ready to go home to an empty bed and think about her.

Grace stops Georgia from unlocking her phone. "Nope. Finn is driving me home. He has to leave early, and his house is on the way to my parents'. Stay and have fun."

Silas snorts. "Almost your bedtime, Finn?"

"Hell yeah," Finn says with a nod. "I need my beauty sleep."

"Are you sure?" Georgia asks Grace, chewing on her bottom lip. "I have no problem with going home."

*If she leaves, I'm dipping.*

Grace shakes her head. "I'm going to my parents' for the night anyway."

"Okay. Make sure you text me when you make it there, okay?" Georgia says.

Grace nods, and she and Finn say their good-byes.

"And then there were four," Silas says, relaxing in his seat and throwing his arm over Lola's shoulders.

"Oh my God! Archer?"

My back stiffens as my name is yelled over the music.

*Here we go again.*

I swallow and raise my chin to find Meredith and her two friends walking toward us.

*Keep walking.*

Pretending I don't see them, I lean forward and make myself a drink. As I do, my gaze sweeps to Georgia, who's giving Meredith a death glare.

"Can we join you?" Meredith asks.

"We're pretty full over here," Georgia replies at the same time Silas shrugs and says, "Sure, whatever."

Georgia's icy stare shoots to Silas.

Silas, confused, sends me a curious glance, raising a brow.

We're all looking at each other, not knowing what the fuck is going on.

Meredith chooses Silas's answer and gracefully strolls into our section.

Georgia slides off the couch. "I just remembered, Lola and I have cute guys to meet on the dance floor."

She bumps into my knee while walking toward Lola. Lola stands and grabs her hand, and my eyes are glued to them as the only reason I haven't left disappears through the crowd.

I down my drink, but it doesn't help the dryness in my throat.

So I make another drink.

Meredith sinks down next to me. "Uh-oh," she coos, sliding in too close for comfort. "Looks like Little Miss Jailbait is still crushing on you."

"Jailbait?" I tighten my grip around my glass. "You know she's not jailbait."

Silas signals back and forth between Meredith and me. "How do you two know each other?"

Meredith holds up her bare ring finger. "Archer used to be my fiancé."

"Holy shit," Silas says, pointing at me with his water. "You were engaged to this heartless bastard?"

"He didn't used to be so heartless," Meredith says, brushing her hand along my thigh and resting it there.

I pluck her hand off me as if it were toxic, and Silas arches a brow.

"Wow," Meredith rasps, her mouth slackening.

I bow my head and lower my voice, "Nothing will happen here, Meredith. Give up on that dream. It'll turn into nothing but a nightmare for you."

# CHAPTER TWENTY-TWO

## Georgia

SWEATY AND ANNOYED with men copping feels of my ass, I walk off the dance floor. Heading in the direction of our table, I freeze, remembering Pageant Barbie is there with Archer.

I clamp my eyes shut and release a deep breath.

There are so many reasons I hate the woman.

Archer gave a relationship with her a chance.

Loved her.

Proposed to her.

That's more than he'll ever give me.

And from the way she looks at him, she wants that back.

I dart toward the bar with the urge to drink, to get so inebriated that I have no idea who they are when I look at them. *Become strangers I don't give a damn about.*

As I order my vodka cranberry, a guy slides between me and the person at my side, barely cramming himself in.

"I got this," he tells the bartender. "Add one on there for me too."

The bartender nods and walks away.

Shifting, I smile. "You're in my psych class."

"Georgia." He says my name matter-of-factly, no

questioning himself or throwing out a guess in an attempt to please me.

I nod.

He's attractive with short black hair and bright blue eyes that remind me of the sea, and his blue shirt nearly matches them.

He's the ocean. Happiness.

The opposite of Archer, who's a hurricane over that ocean.

Blowing out a nervous breath, he runs his hand over his head. "Don't judge, but I've been trying to muster up the courage to talk to you for months. Looks like tonight is on my side." He laughs; it's friendly and authentic—something you don't find much from men who ask to buy you a drink at a bar. "Unless you're about to tell me to kick rocks, and in that case, it definitely isn't on my side."

A blush rises up my cheeks. "Nervous to talk to me?"

His shyness is a breath of fresh air, but for some damn reason, Archer comes to mind—the memory of how he was the night he bought me a drink.

No matter what, my thoughts always lead back to him when I should be running like hell away from them.

*Focus on this guy, Georgia.*

*He's not hanging out with his ex. He's talking to you.*

"Hell yeah," the guy says. "You're gorgeous, and you seem chill as hell." He holds out his hand. "Logan."

When I shake it, chills run up my spine as he runs his thumb over the top of my hand.

"You here alone?" His question isn't creepy; it's more concern over me hanging out solo in the club.

I shake my head. "I'm here with friends, but I had to take a break from the dance floor before I kneed a dude in the balls."

"Ah, dudes can get creepy over there."

"Tell me about it," I say. "They know nothing about personal space."

"What about a dance with me?" He presses his hand to his

chest. "I swear not to be creepy, and if I am, I give you full permission to knee me in the balls."

I glance down, biting into my lip as another blush hits me. Maybe Logan is the answer to getting over Archer. We can dance, drink, and exchange numbers at the end of the night.

My thoughts of moving on with him crash and burn when Archer steps behind Logan, his tall body towering over him. My back stiffens, and the bartender drops off our drinks.

"She'll pass," Archer says, his jaw clenching. Pulling out his wallet, he plucks out a few bills and slams them onto the bar in front of the bartender. "I got her drink." He smirks down at Logan, who's curiously staring at him over his shoulder. "Since I'm crashing your little party, I'll pay for yours too."

*I am going to kill him.*

*Murder his ass.*

*Then he won't get a chance to have a relationship with anyone.*

Logan's attention returns to me. "He your boyfriend?"

"Hell no," I rush out. "He's my older brother's friend."

"Ah, so a bit overprotective." Logan slips closer to me and then turns to face Archer.

I'm not sure if it's worry that Archer will rip his head off or so he can get a better look at him.

"Swear to you, man," Logan tells him, "I'll be on my best behavior."

Archer doesn't spare Logan a glance, as if he weren't there, and pins his gaze on me. "*Just* your brother's friend?" He offers a self-satisfied smile. "You're not going to tell him we slept together too?"

My breathing labors, and I gape at him, speechless.

With his piercing eyes not leaving me, he draws out a fifty from his wallet and retreats a step. I wait for him to leave. To run off the guy and then run off himself—the typical Archer and Georgia storyline.

Typical damn Archer.

Wanting no one to have me yet not taking me for himself.

Just as I'm about to grab Logan's hand and lead him to the dance floor, Archer taps a girl on the shoulder.

When she turns in his direction, a giddy smile covers her face.

He shoves the fifty in her hand and motions to Logan. "Dance with this guy."

"What the hell?" I snap, tempted to throw my drink on him.

"Okay," the girl chirps, making eyes at Archer. "*Only if* you save me one for later."

"Yeah, sure, whatever," Archer mutters, not giving her a second glance.

Logan hesitates, his gaze pinging between me and the girl. "No, you really don't have to—"

"Scram," Archer barks. "Or you won't have any legs to dance with." He grabs another bill, as if he were a damn cash cow, and thrusts it into Logan's hand.

Logan smiles apologetically, hands Archer the hundred back, and walks away, deciding I'm not worth the hassle. Not that I blame him. We haven't even danced, and he's already being threatened. I sigh, guilt tripping through me and then annoyance. He didn't take the money. He was a good guy, and Archer ran off him.

Leaving me with Satan himself.

Archer stumbles back, caught off guard, when I push his shoulder.

"You can't just shove your wealth and size around to scare people," I snarl. "I wanted to dance."

He crosses his arms, moving closer into my space, giving me a whiff of his cologne. "I can do whatever the fuck I want actually."

I inhale again, searching for a hint of perfume, of Meredith. *Nothing.*

I cross my arms, mirroring his stance. "News flash, Archer: everything doesn't revolve around you." I invade his space, standing on my tiptoes, struggling to be eye-level with him.

Even with my heels, I'm nowhere close. "What is wrong with you?"

He peers down at me with a mocking grin. "Nothing is wrong with me."

My body is tense. My mind scrambling. Anger firing through me.

I jerk my arm out toward the crowd. "I wanted to dance, and the guy seemed nice, unlike half the creepy guys out there. Of course you had to ruin that like you ruin everything else—fucking me up in the head more and more while you pull shit like this." I shove him again, and his arm hits my drink, spilling it. "Go be with Meredith and leave me alone."

He looks at his arm, grabs some napkins, and wipes up my mess. "Why?"

"Why what? Why do I want to dance?"

He nods, wiping down his arm.

"Uh, it's fun, unlike being at our table and watching you and Pamela Anderson get your flirt on."

He shakes his head, his face unreadable. "Never flirted with her."

I scoff. "She basically sat down on your lap."

"I don't want her, Georgia."

"Do you want *anyone*? Or do you only prefer random women you can screw for a night, and that's it?" It's as if we are alone, the chaos around us fading, and I'm hyper-focused on him.

"I'm selfish, to be honest."

I flinch at his honesty. "So, what? You don't want anything to do with me until a decent guy grabs my attention. Then you stalk over here, all caveman-like, and run him off. I want a boyfriend, and I want someone to fucking dance with!"

This isn't about dancing.

Or a boyfriend.

This is me no longer tolerating his ups and downs.

"And that's what I'm going to do."

I turn to leave, but he reaches out, grabbing my arm, and stops me.

He shoves me into his chest. "Looks like we're fucking dancing then."

I stumble back into him, nearly tripping over his feet. "Wait, what?"

"You want to dance? We'll dance."

His hand captures mine, his grip tight as if he's scared to lose me, and he leads me through the crowd. My heart spirals, pacing as fast as the electronic music playing. Since all Archer and I do is fight, with the exception of orgasm night, I'm clueless on *how* to dance with him.

*Does he know how?*

*Does he think this will be some ballroom shit?*

My dancing is *so not* ballroom dancing.

More Lil Jon & the East Side Boyz.

Lola is dancing with Silas, and she waves me over to them. Her eyes widen, and she smacks Silas, pointing at us when she notices Archer is with me.

"Welp, this is a new development," Lola says, her eyes piercing Archer in warning.

To clear my head, I start dancing, ignoring Archer as he awkwardly stands behind me.

*Why is he even here?*

A pair of masculine hands grip my waist, a strong body behind me, and just as I'm about to swat the person away, I hear, "Relax. It's me."

Archer.

I shut my eyes, relishing the weight of his body pressing against mine, and he drags me in closer. We dance, my ass pushing against his waist, and lose ourselves to the music.

To each other.

I shiver when his lips go to my ear, and his words are a rough whisper. "I shouldn't want you like this."

"But you do," I return.

One of his arms is wrapped around my waist, keeping his hold on me, and the other sweeps over my stomach. "The things I want to do to you …" His voice trails off, as if he's stopping himself from being vulnerable.

"Then do them," I whisper. "Do whatever you want."

"I can't."

"You can."

"You'll hate me more."

I grind into him, his erection growing against my ass.

If he asked me to go home with him, I'd blurt out yes without hesitation.

Be in his bed in a heartbeat.

Archer touching me like this, his honesty slipping from his lips, is the biggest turn-on.

Emotions, honesty, vulnerability are what I'm attracted to.

If a man can screw me well, that's a plus, but he can be taught to do that.

Pouring himself out to me? Revealing his heart?

That can't be faked. That can't be taught. It has to be all him, ready to open up.

I gasp when his fingers feather over the waist of my skirt, gently and barely lifting my top up to allow him better access.

"More," I whisper.

He hesitates.

I squirm against his ass.

He tilts my head to the side, his face falling into the crook of my neck, and his cold breath blows over my skin.

"More." My tone is demanding.

A long sigh bellows from my lungs when he swiftly pushes his fingers underneath my skirt, which allows his large hand hardly any room, and into my panties.

"Look at you, wet as the alcohol you were drinking," he says into my ear, pressing a finger to my clit, adding pressure torturously. If his free hand wasn't gripping my waist, I would've fallen at his feet. "I remember this—how wet you got for me before. I wonder if you taste the same." He flicks my clit, his lips traveling down my neck. "Do you ever think about me inside you?"

I nod.

A gasp.

Another.

A moan.

Until finally, I'm able to say, "Do you think about being inside me?"

He licks up my neck, grinding against me. "All the time. When you scamper around the bar, when I jack off in the shower, when I hear your voice."

I shiver. "Tell me more."

"I remember how good my dick felt inside you, how your pussy was perfect for me in every single way." He sucks on my earlobe and runs his finger through my wetness. "Come home with me tonight." His voice turns pleading. "Please."

"Okay." I tilt my head back, allowing it to fall along his shoulder, and his mouth dips down to mine, our lips touching.

"I will make you feel so good," he says against my lips, slowly gliding his fingers out of my panties.

He turns me around, staring down at me, with heat and need in his eyes.

I nod, a silent go-ahead, and he captures my hand in his.

"Let's go."

"Let's go," I repeat, my throat raw.

"Okay, you cool kids," Silas says, karate-chopping our connection, causing my hand to fall from Archer's. "Time to break it up."

Lola stands behind him, her arm and chin resting on his shoulder, and she stares at me with curiosity and worry.

*Excuse them?*

*What do they think they're doing?*

Archer's face falls, and he steps away from me.

Reality hitting him.

We got lost together—forgetting our hate, how he'd hurt me. All we wanted was the other.

That moment is gone.

Archer's face is pained, and everyone follows him off the dance floor.

"I have to head out." He steps in closer, his mouth lowering so only I can hear him. "I'm sorry, Georgia. That won't happen again."

My hand covers my lips as he walks away. I'm unsure if I'm holding myself back from screaming at him, crying, or vomiting up my humiliation.

"What was that?" I ask, chasing Lola as we return to our section, which is thankfully Meredith free.

"That was me saving you," she says, glancing back at me.

"Saving me? Saving me from what?" My tone is harsh.

*Finally*, Archer and I were going to take that step again.

*Finally*, I was going to get what I'd wanted from him all along.

"You guys were in a moment," she explains, worry in her tone. "Archer doesn't deserve to touch you like that, not until he proves he'll do better than the last time he did."

"What'd he do last time?" Silas asks, raising a brow.

"None of your business," Lola answers, her piercing stare sliding to him. "Whatever you heard and saw stays between the four of us. Got it?"

"Yes, boss woman." He wraps his arms around Lola's waist and kisses her cheek. "Let me hunt down Archer and make sure he gets a ride home before he kicks someone or something."

As soon as he disappears, Lola shoots straight into question mode. "What the hell happened? You were practically screwing on the dance floor. I'm sorry, but Silas and I had to stop it. That rat bastard knows how to play with your head, and I refuse to watch you get hurt. To prevent that from happening, my ass will be lurking around and pulling you away from possible Archer-screwing."

"You're right." I sigh, my stomach twisting as I take in the reality of her words. "You ready to go?"

"Yes." She gives me a hug. "Operation I Will Kill Archer is now in full effect. Let's steer clear from allowing him to have his hand in your panties again. Capisce?"

"Capisce," I mutter, swiping a tear off my face.

# CHAPTER TWENTY-THREE

# Archer

TO CANCEL.

Not to cancel.

Never has a decision had my brain scrambling so hard.

If only I hadn't let my emotions get the best of me.

If only I hadn't touched Georgia when I didn't deserve to.

I'm not worthy of touching her.

I'm unworthy, yet I still stop another man from having her.

Like the selfish bastard I am, I ruined it for her.

And fucking Meredith.

Had she not strutted in and invaded our night, Georgia would've never left. Had she not, I wouldn't have created more problems for myself—for my relationship with Georgia.

There was so much raw tension—sexual and emotional. I was thinking with my dick and not what was good for us.

What was good for her.

Silas played the question game when he met me outside, and I told him to tell the girls I was leaving. Had I not walked away, I wouldn't have cared what Silas or Lola said. I would've begged Georgia to go home with me. I was that desperate for her. Our friends were at least smart enough to stop it.

When I got home, my cock was still hard as a rock. I

showered, punishing myself for my stupid decision and holding myself back from stroking my cock and thinking of her.

Unfortunately, I lack restraint when it comes to thoughts of Georgia.

In my head, she was in the shower with me.

*Wet. Soaked for me.*

I held out my hand, filling it with water, and stroked myself faster. Her name is what slipped through my lips as I came.

Choosing not to be selfish, I pull into the parking lot of the ski resort at the same time as Silas. Ski North is one of the tackiest places I've ever been to, but I'll be here for the next two nights, celebrating Noah's birthday with everyone. It's a small resort, known for its faux snow, where people can ski and snow tube.

I locate my cabin, unload my bag, and meet the gang. Unlike most of them, I rented a place to myself. The girls are sharing a cabin, Finn and Silas are taking another, and the last one will be Jamie, Cohen, and Noah.

Jamie is Heather, Noah's mother's, younger sister. After Noah's birth, Heather ran off to Vegas, and Cohen moved a town over to steer clear of her family. For years, it worked. Until Cohen took a feverish Noah to the hospital, and Jamie was the doctor on duty. After Jamie begged him to allow her to have a relationship with Noah, he finally agreed. Now, they have somewhat of a divorced-couple-visitation like situation. Well, they *did* have that type of relationship. Lately, they're getting closer. I have a feeling their little arrangement is starting to evolve into something more intimate.

Everyone is gathered in the ski shop, where racks of skis and poles fill the room, selecting their rental equipment. They're circled around Jamie and arguing whether she'll die while skiing.

"Whoa," Finn says. "No one expected you to show."

"Why?" I grumble, tucking my skis into my side since I brought my own.

"You bail on half the shit we do."

"It's Noah's birthday. I wouldn't miss it."

The little guy is cool as shit, and his birthday means the world to him. He handmade everyone's invites.

I move farther into the room, and Georgia freezes when I come into her view. We've avoided each other since the club.

"I'm shocked you're here," she warily says when I stop behind her. "You've been avoiding me—no shocker."

"I've been busy."

"Bullshit," she grits out, shaking her head. "Good thing our friends stopped me from doing anything stupid with you."

I flinch.

"Nothing would've changed between us."

She turns away from me and tells Jamie she's not getting out of skiing.

---

*YOU SHOULDN'T WANT to break a ski instructor's neck.*

Yet why do I want to?

Maybe not break his neck but kick him far away from Georgia.

I grind my teeth and tap my foot, watching him flirt with her—clueless that she's my obsession. She smiles, one that's brighter than anything she's ever given me.

I shut my eyes, listening to her laughter.

Watching them is a sucker punch to the throat.

A sucker punch that I deserve.

"Want to share a lift?" he asks her when we walk outside.

I step forward to join their conversation. "Nah, she's riding with me."

Georgia narrows her eyes at me. "I think Finn needs someone to ride with." She jerks her head toward the line waiting at the gondolas. "Ready to go?"

He nods, and his palm rests on the curve of her back as he leads the way.

Lola smacks my stomach as I follow them. "Unless you want to admit your feelings for her, quit cockblocking, asshole."

"I'm not cockblocking shit," I seethe.

"You are, and it isn't fair to her. Georgia deserves someone who wants to be her number one, who wants her to be *their* number one. I don't know what your deal is, but it needs to stop."

Silas laughs, jogging to us, and wraps his arm around Lola's shoulders. "That's my girl. I love her spitfire attitude."

I stay quiet.

"You good to ride with Finn?" Silas asks Lola as they walk alongside me.

"No, I'm riding with you," she answers.

He turns and whispers in her ear.

She rolls her eyes and playfully shoves him. "Fine, whatever. I'll tell Finn he's riding with me. You jerks enjoy each other's company."

She joins Finn in line, and not much time passes before we load into our gondola. When Silas settles next to me, I know he didn't make that decision for shits and giggles. I ignore him and keep my attention on Georgia and Ski Instructor Boy three gondolas up from mine.

"You know, Cohen probably wouldn't care if you and Georgia dated," Silas says. "He knows you're a good dude. We all do. We wouldn't be friends if you weren't. Cohen is being a big brother, but deep down, if he thought any of us would be a threat to her, he'd never allow us around his family."

Every muscle tightens at his comment.

*How much does he know about Georgia and me?*

He and Lola are close, but Lola's loyalty is as strong as Lincoln's. She wouldn't share Georgia's business unless it was cool with Georgia.

I nod in agreement.

I'm not scared of Cohen beating my ass.

It's that him hating me is the best excuse I have.

The reason I give to hide my own truth.

---

*SILAS:* **We're having drinks in the lodge's bar. You game?**

I'm fresh from a shower and drying my hair when I see Silas's text.

Skiing yesterday was a nightmare. Georgia, who seemed like she was a regular at Ski North, didn't need any instructing. Yet the instructor—who I later learned was Calvin—stayed by her side the entire time.

Who did need Calvin's help?

Jamie.

She rolled down the hill, Humpty Dumpty-style, and sprained her ankle.

Today, we had Noah's party, and now, everyone is doing their own thing.

I snatch my phone, ready to ask if Ski Instructor Boy will be there, but then I stop myself. Georgia and I need to talk, to hash out what happened. And what better time than when she might be with another man?

**Me: I'll be there.**

Silas, Lola, Georgia, *and* Calvin are seated at a table in the back of the bar. It's not a dive like Bailey's or a sports bar like Twisted Fox. It's quaint with piano music thrumming in the background and people casually sipping drinks while conversing.

The only open chair at the table is next to Georgia, and Calvin is on her other side. I slip past everyone and drop into the chair. Calvin scoots closer to Georgia, eyeing me suspiciously, knowing damn well there's a chance I'll shove a dagger into his game tonight with Georgia.

*Sure will.*

He won't be sticking his dagger anywhere near her.

Georgia twists in her seat and glares at me, tilting her head to the side. "Can I help you?"

I lean in closer, the same way Calvin did, only looming over her more. "We haven't had a chance to talk since the club."

"You could've solved that problem days ago." She sighs, a twinge of hurt flashing along her face. "Our friends were right to stop us. It would have been a mess had it gone any further."

I nod, hating her honesty. "You're right."

I'm hot and cold.

I don't blame her for finally walking away.

For being done with my ass.

It's what I wanted from day one.

*Isn't it?*

It stings me, but it'll be good for her.

She turns her back to me and starts talking to Calvin.

*This is it.*

*When another man steals her away.*

I order a drink, and when the waitress delivers, I move my cup in circles, studying the liquor as it splashes along the rim of my glass. Everyone talks, and as usual, I'm on the outside, listening.

"You coming, man?" Silas asks me as the night grows later.

All eyes are on me as everyone stands.

I shake my head. "Nah, I think I'll stay back."

As they clear out, I grab my glass and stroll to the bar, taking a seat. The hairs on the back of my neck stand when Georgia approaches me.

"Stay back and do what?" she questions.

I raise my glass and take a swig as my answer.

She chews on her lower lip. "Stay back and wait for another woman to sit down before taking her back to your cabin?"

"To drink." I fasten my attention to her, hoping she sees the sincerity. "I'm not worried about a woman."

"Why not?" She does a sweeping gesture of the bar. "This is a similar scene to what happened before we slept together. Did you forget about that?"

"I'll never forget." My answer is barely audible.

"Should I stay back and drink too?"

"If you stay back, it'll lead to trouble. Your ski boy is waiting for you." I dismissively flick my hand through the air. "Run along."

She gapes at me. "Fingers crossed he doesn't leave me a *see yourself out* note."

"Georgia," I say her name in warning, hating the thought of her with someone else even though it's what I tell myself I want.

Never in my life have I been so fucking confused.

So frustrated.

"Archer," she says, mocking my tone, a hint of a slur in her voice.

"You're wasted."

"Not wasted. Tipsy."

"Same difference." I gesture to the empty stool. "Have a seat if you need proof I'm not leaving with anyone tonight."

"Do you want me to stay?"

"Georgia!" Lola calls us. "Let's go, babe."

Georgia throws me a questioning glance.

*Say yes.*

*Beg her to stay.*

I tip my glass toward her. "Have a good night."

"Don't go home with anyone," she whispers, her voice strangled.

I keep quiet.

"Promise me." Her eyes squeeze shut in pain.

"I'm not promising anything to a woman who's about to leave with another man."

"Georgia!" Lola says again.

Her eyes open, she nods, and then she turns away to be with fucking Calvin.

---

*SITTING at the bar by yourself is a lonely venture.*

I witness it regularly at Twisted Fox.

The brokenhearted who drink away their feelings, positive their lives will never go back to normal.

Tonight, I'm that guy.

My loneliness calls out to me, and I can't stop myself from grabbing my phone. Taking a deep breath, I unlock the screen and hit Georgia's name.

It rings, and as if fate knew what was coming, it goes to voicemail at the same time Cohen slumps down in the seat next to me.

"Damn, dude, you definitely look like you need a drink." I set my phone down next to me. "A motherfucking strong one."

He slides my glass off my napkin and wipes his hand with it. "I need a few of them."

Before answering, he orders us a round of Jack and Cokes. A pained expression is on his face, and his entire body is tense.

"What happened?" I ask. "You and Jamie finally fuck?"

He stays quiet.

"Is that a yes?"

The bartender drops off our drinks, and he mutters a quick thanks. Tonight, I'm seeing a different Cohen, one I've never seen. Cohen is the most grown-up of our group and usually put together. He doesn't make drastic decisions and never allows his emotions to get the best of him.

"How was it?" I push.

*Damn, he's pulling a me with the not opening up.*

*Is this how people feel when they try to get an answer out of me?*

"We didn't fuck," he finally grinds out.

"Something happened, though."

He doesn't deny anything.

"How was it?"

"Fucking wrong. That's what it was."

"Wrong because there was no connection, or wrong because of who she is to you?"

He shoots back his drink, slams the glass onto the bar, and calls over the bartender for another.

"Wrong because of who she is to you, I take it."

"She's my son's aunt." He works his jaw. "Hell, he doesn't even know she's his aunt. She's my ex's sister. Her family attempted to take my son away from me, and now, I'm fucked. If Noah loses her, it'll break his goddamn heart. All because of my stupidity."

I refrain from asking what happened.

From asking for the details.

Sure, I'll give advice, but I won't make you pour your heart out to me to get it.

"What are the reasons it could be right between you two?"

"Nothing."

"Yet you still hooked up."

He glares at me.

I shrug, grab my drink, and take a sip. "You're attracted to her. There's something there. Go for it."

*If only I'd take my own advice.*

*I'm a goddamn hypocrite.*

"Attraction doesn't always mean it's a good idea."

I tip my glass his way. "True." *Hear, fucking, hear.*

My phone rings, and I gulp when Georgia's name flashes across the screen. I quickly silence it but not fast enough.

He side-eyes me. "Why's my sister calling you?"

I shove the phone into my pocket. "Who knows? Probably to yell at me or ask me about work."

*I called her because I can't get her out of my head.*

*I called her because I'm just as confused about my feelings for your sister as you are with Jamie.*

"I didn't know you had each other's numbers."

"We work together." I gulp down my drink. "Look, you're my friend. The situation you're in is weird, and I don't blame you for not crossing a line, but I can't tell you what to do." I poke his shoulder. "Only you know how far you want to take it, how much you want her, how fucking broken you'll be if you lose her. Whatever your choice, just remember, it's on you. Either way, I'll support you, but in the end, I hope whatever you choose makes you happy."

*Practice what you fucking preach.*

My phone rings again, vibrating in my pocket, and I ignore it, hoping my guilt isn't clear on my face.

The bartender returns with another round, and we knock them back together. When Cohen decides to finally head back to the cabin, I tell him good-bye and good luck.

Then I sit there and run the advice I gave him back through my head.

*How can I tell one person to do everything I should be doing myself?*

Time passes until I can no longer take it. I drag my phone from my pocket to text her.

**Me: Can I stop by?**

Three bubbles appear underneath my message.

Then disappear.

Then appear again.

**Georgia: Sure.**

I stand from the stool and walk to her cabin.

# CHAPTER TWENTY-FOUR

## Georgia

"WHAT ARE YOU DOING?" Lola asks when I stand from the couch, grab my shoes, and slip them on.

"I need a breath of fresh air," I lie.

"A breath of fresh air?" she slowly repeats my words. "I call bullshit."

I sigh. "Archer is outside and wants to talk."

"That's trouble," Grace whispers from her chair, snuggled in her blanket.

"Babe, you need to be careful," Lola says. "I love you, and I don't want you to get hurt."

Grace nods. "Agreed."

My heart seemed to freeze when I read Archer's text, asking to come over.

At the bar, when we'd talked, it was hell for me. My stomach dropped as I pleaded, fighting to hold back tears, for him not to bring a woman back to his cabin. Meanwhile, Calvin was standing in the doorway, waiting to come back to ours. The thing was, Calvin coming back to my cabin didn't mean anything. I hadn't wanted him, and twenty minutes after he got here, I told him I was tired, and he left.

I shrug, as if my head isn't spinning. Archer never goes out of his way to be alone with me. It's always been forced, at work, or when we're with friends. Never anything like this, but then again, until the club, he'd never danced with me while his hand was down my skirt. Our relationship is shifting. Whether it's for better or for worse, I have no idea.

"Fucking Archer," Lola grumbles. "I swear, the guy is the coach of mixed signals."

"Yeah, always giving me the red light," I fire back.

"I'd say it's more yellow with you," Grace inputs.

Staring down at my pajamas, I frown, pulling at the bottom of my Nap Queen tee—complete with crown-printed pajama pants. Most definitely not a hot look when meeting the guy you've been lusting over. I peek over at Lola, taking in her black lace romper, and contemplate asking her to do a tradesie. With the way she's staring at me like I have a horn growing out of my head, I doubt she'd be up for it.

"It's one in the morning," Lola continues. "*Are you up* texts are booty-call texts. Remember what he pulled last time. *And,* might I add, this will be harder. Last time, you didn't have feelings for him like you do now."

"Sheesh, Negative Nancy," Grace mutters.

"Not negative, nor am I trying to sound like a bitch." She blows me a kiss. "I just love you, is all."

"Let's just see what he says. Give him the benefit of the doubt," I say.

"No matter what, don't you dare go to his cabin," Lola says. "Even if he confesses his undying love for you, don't. It could be the alcohol talking."

"I got this," I say, expelling breaths before repeating, "I got this."

"And she most definitely doesn't have it," Grace says commentary-style as I head toward the door.

My hand is sweaty when I grip the knob and walk outside onto the porch. There's a bite to the wind, and I cross my arms, scanning the lot. The cabins are set up around a cul-de-sac layout, so you can see all of them from yours. It's quiet outside, everyone in their bed, snug as hell and not waiting for the boy they're obsessed with to come to their porch.

I shiver when Archer comes into view.

Even after everything, I can't stop my face from lighting up. He comes closer and stops at the bottom step of the porch. His heavy-lidded eyes meet mine underneath the dim light.

"Hi," I whisper.

"Hey." He kicks the top of his shoe against the step.

My stomach turns as I take a good look at him.

He smells like a distillery.

There's a hint of desperation in his puffy red eyes.

His stare is pained.

My throat thickens, my heart kicking into my chest, as reality hits me like the bitch that she is.

This is *the talk*.

The conversation that will change everything.

All of our arguments, flirting, sexual tension has led us to tonight.

His drunken lips are about to speak his sober thoughts.

*Am I ready to hear them?*

When I build up the courage to speak, my voice is weak. "Did you need something?"

It takes him a moment before he says, "No."

*That's it.*

I wait for him to continue, but he stays silent.

I swallow down the sick feeling in my throat. "Why are you here, Archer?"

He shrugs, as if he doesn't understand my question. "I don't know."

*For fuck's sake.*

"*I don't know* yourself out of here then." I motion toward the street and point at a random cabin. "Either be honest or go."

"I'm a liar," he states clearly with no bullshit.

"A liar?" I stare at him intensely. "About what?"

"I do need something."

I remain quiet, waiting for him to continue, but in Archer fashion, he only silently stares at me.

"Jesus Christ!" I finally snap, anger rolling through me, causing me to jump down the stairs and step to him until we're inches apart. I swing my arms out, and my voice rises, filling with edge. "Be honest! For once, in this messed-up friendship, relationship, complication-ship we have, please just be honest." The edge in my voice shatters to brokenness. "That's all I'm asking for. It's not that hard."

"You want my honesty?" He runs his shaking hands through his thick hair, tugging at the roots, and his tone is as chilly as the air. "I wanted to see you. I always want to see you." He reaches out, his hands freezing as they cup my face. "You're in my head, in my heart, living inside me, Georgia. No matter how hard I fight, there's no getting rid of you, and it's fucking breaking me. How much I want you and can't have you but other guys can— it tears my goddamn heart out."

Every word of his is a sucker punch to the gut, and I jerk out his hold, my blood on fire. "Is that why you're here? You thought I was with another guy?" I throw out my middle fingers to him. "Screw you! You don't want me, but no one else can have me either?" A strong sigh escapes my lips, and I groan, fighting to restrain my tears.

He winces at my truth, and with hesitation, he comes closer. I shiver as his thumb tenderly brushes my cheek, ridding me of the tears I'm fighting to stop.

"You're beautiful." His voice cracks, the stench of whiskey escaping his mouth. "So damn beautiful and pure, so fucking full of light." He squeezes his eyes together. "I'd kill that inside you, do you hear me? I'd burn you out, be another person in your life who failed you—something you never deserve." He caresses my cheek, moving down to my jaw before tipping his head down and kissing a tear away. "I wish I were a better man for you," he says against my skin.

"Someone who'd help you shine, but all I'd do is put you out."

I wrap my hand around the back of his head, holding him in place, and he rests his forehead against mine.

"Why are you so convinced you'd put me out?" I whisper. "That you wouldn't be good for me?"

"I destroy everything. It's who I am."

I pull back, and this time, it's me cupping his face, his scruff abrasive against my palms. "Whatever it is, I can deal with it. I will deal with anything for you."

"You can't." He shakes his head and releases a heavy breath before pulling away, causing my arms to fall limp at my sides.

As I peer up at him, I read his eyes, and they tell me everything I need to know.

He's not here to be with me.

I take a step back and hold out my hands. "No, this isn't fair to me anymore."

"Georgia," he says around a sigh.

"It's not fair!" I scream. "You can't keep showing up when I'm trying to move on! Stop railroading your way back into my heart, only to crush me over and over again."

"I'm sorry," he whispers.

*"You're sorry?"* I snort, shaking my head. "That's rich. Tell me your truths, tell me what has you so shaken up that you're afraid to open up to me, to give us a chance?"

He stares at me, more defeated.

I scoff, now staring at him in disdain. "Enough. We've played this game for too long. I'm done." A hard sob escapes me. "Just set me free! Let me go!"

"Georgia," he pleads, stepping closer. "Come back to my cabin with me—"

My hand connecting with his face echoes through the empty street.

His eyes are shut as he processes what happened, but he doesn't flinch.

Doesn't feel his face as if it didn't faze him.

"Really?" I shout. "You came here for a booty call? Do you think I'd ever do that again after what you did?"

"I'm sorry," he says, pained.

"You're not," I hiss, pushing him away from me. "You're never sorry, Archer. From the beginning, you've done nothing but play with me. Fuck you." *Shove*. "And your games." *Shove*. "And your bullshit." *Shove*. "And your lies."

"Georgia. *Please*," he begs.

"No." I dash up the stairs and turn to face him. "I'm done."

He's saying my name as I swing open the door and walk in, tears pricking at my eyes as I lock the door behind me.

Grace is waiting and pulls me into her arms as I sob into her shoulder. She leads me into the living room, and I collapse on the couch.

Lola walks in, holding a bottle of vodka. "Time to drink away those feelings for him, babe."

I take a shot, wishing it'd erase him from my brain.

I take another, wishing I'd never parked and blocked him in.

I take another, wishing I'd never asked him to leave the bar with me.

# CHAPTER TWENTY-FIVE

# Archer

*"SET ME FREE."*

*"You're never sorry."*

*"I'm done."*

I shut my eyes.

Georgia's words have been replaying in my mind.

Haunting me.

Rubbing guilt inside the wounds already inside me.

*It's what I wanted all along, right?*

For Georgia to decide she was done with me.

When I'd made the mistake of asking her to come back to my cabin, I'd succeeded in doing what I'd wanted to do when I found out she was Cohen's sister.

Make her never want to see me again.

The problem is, what I wanted then isn't what I want now.

While that moment helped heal her wounds, her scars of us, it only stabbed mine deeper.

I fucked myself over that night—ruined us. My words and actions were a reality smack in her face.

Since then, she's steered clear of me. Our conversations are only work-related or when we're out with our friends. She makes friendly conversation, only if necessary, but that's it.

Hardly any bickering.

And, goddamn it, I miss it.

When we were arguing, at least there was *something*.

Getting nothing from her is worse.

She cut down her hours at work, blaming it on school, and helping with Noah.

That sure went down as a shitshow with his baby momma.

I shudder, thankful I'm not in that mess.

Cohen slaps his hand on the bar. "Don't forget Georgia's graduation party next weekend."

"I'll be there," Finn replies.

"Thanks, guys," Cohen says. "She's ecstatic to graduate."

Silas waits until Cohen is out of earshot before turning to me. "You going?"

I shrug. "Probably best I don't."

"Something has changed between you two."

"She got smart and realized I wasn't worth it."

---

"I CAN'T BELIEVE I'm getting out soon. It seems surreal."

I smile at Lincoln's words.

It does seem surreal.

"You'd better have a party ready for me," he says around a chuckle.

"I'm not throwing you a *congrats on getting out of prison* party."

He groans. "You suck."

I lean back in my office chair and kick my feet onto my desk. "What's your plan when you're released? Staying with Mom?"

"Hard pass." He laughs. "She'll smother me and make sure we brunch like it's our damn jobs. I've been cooped up for a while. Going back to Mom's will drive me insane."

"You want to crash at my place?"

"That's exactly where I'm crashing. It's nice of you to finally offer." He lowers his voice, his words clearer. "Did you talk to Cohen about me working there?"

"If you want a job here, you can have a job here."

Cohen can be pissed, but this is my brother.

I trust Lincoln.

---

I KNOCK on Cohen's office door with my knuckles and wait for him to yell, "Come in," before opening it. Unlike most people around this joint, I wait for people to reply before barging into their offices.

"I need to talk to you about something," I say, walking in.

"What's up?" He tosses his phone to the side to give me his full attention.

"My brother is being released."

He grins. "Sweet! I'm happy for you, man."

I thrum my fingers against my cheek before scratching it. "He needs a job."

His smile drops. "I hope you're not asking me what I think you're asking me."

"I'm asking what you think I'm asking you."

I bite my tongue, stopping myself from saying I'm not *asking* shit. Lincoln needs a job, and I want to hire him. Cohen hired Georgia without consulting me. I can do the same.

"I know he's family, but he's a felon. He was in prison."

"For embezzlement, not murder."

"*Money* embezzlement." He slams his finger onto his desk, his brown eyes widening. "We deal with *money* here."

"Let me correct myself." I hold up a finger, and though I'm not trying to be threatening, there's no stopping my voice from rising. "He went to prison to protect my family. You can't fault him for that shit. You'd have done the same. Give him a shot. If he fucks up, I'll fire him myself."

"No." He stands.

"I'm not backing down on this, Cohen. I don't demand much around here, but my brother needs someone to give him a chance, and he needs a job. And that'll be me and *here*."

"If anything happens, Archer—"

"Nothing will happen," I interrupt. "You have my word."

# CHAPTER TWENTY-SIX

# Georgia

"YOU SEEM DOWN TODAY," my mom comments in her smoke-cured voice.

I stare at her from across our booth and shift in my seat. "Boy problems." I take the last bite of my cherry pie, lick my lips, and drop my fork onto my plate with a *clank*.

*Archer problems.*

Ten thousand times more complicated than just *boy* problems.

Heartless-jerk problem.

Her face falls. "Oh, no."

My relationship with my mother has been getting better and better. She hasn't shown one sign of using again, and next week, she'll be moving into her own studio apartment. I watch as she shoves her last bite of apple pie into her mouth, noticing the changes in her. She's gained weight, and her natural style is showing through. Her clothes scream the '80s—denim vests and pants with bright and over-the-top makeup. I don't have the heart to tell her Smurf-blue eye shadow is definitely out.

Since I've been consumed with midterms and graduation, it's been easier to busy myself and keep my mind off Archer. My game of dodging him has gone well. There have been times he's tried to stop me and attempt to strike up conversation, but I scurry away before giving him the chance.

The night at the cabin was finally my breaking point. When I'd walked outside, in the pit of my stomach, I had known it'd change us.

No longer will I allow Archer Callahan to play with my heart. Every minute we were outside was a kick to the stomach, harder and harder with each word. My brain, finally growing some balls, kicked my heart to the side. It was time I let go.

I tried, begged, for a piece—*anything*—but got zilch.

He slipped up that night. *For once*, he allowed his vulnerability to step out before shoving it back in. He almost showed me his truths and where I stood with him.

He had feelings for me. The pain on his face confirmed it. Someone can be in love with you all you want, but that doesn't mean they know how to love you right.

The worst part, what hurt the most, was him asking me to go to his cabin for a booty call as though that was all I was good for. Never had I been so furious. Never had I slapped, shoved, and screamed at someone so irately. And he gave it to me. He allowed me to give him all my anger. I should apologize, but anytime I start, the memory of his behavior sweeps through me, stopping me.

I cried that night, full of tears, as I remembered his comment from years before.

*"Don't you find it weird that the only time I was nice to you was when I was drinking? And wanted to get laid."*

Nothing said to me has been more hurtful.

"A hot chocolate refill," our waitress says, placing the steaming mug in front of me.

"Thank you," I reply with a smile. A smile that doesn't reach my eyes.

I've decided to be done with Archer, yes, but that doesn't mean all of me is happy about it yet.

My mom wipes her lips with a napkin and sets it next to her

empty plate. "I'm no expert on men—or heck, even life in general, but my advice is to always trust your gut. Throughout my years, my gut has screamed out to me, begging me to listen, but I allowed what I believed was love to blind my rationality. If I'd thought with more than just my heart, it would've saved me from a lot of heartbreak … and making wrong decisions that were destructive to my well-being, to my life, to my children's lives." Her gaze falls to her plate, regret staining her features, and she plays with the pie crumbs between her fingers.

*She has a point.*

I listened to my gut to form a relationship with her, and she hasn't let me down.

She peers back up at me. "What did he do?"

An ache forms in my throat as I squirm in my seat. "It's more along the lines of what he refused to do."

"If he won't fight for you, then it won't work. A relationship can't have only one person fighting for it. Nothing good in life can be one-sided."

I stare at her, unblinking, soaking in her advice.

"That, or show him what he's missing." She winks and waves the waitress over for another slice of pie.

---

MY STEPS ARE slow as I make my way to Cohen's office.

He never calls me into his office. Normally, I just barge in whenever, so I feel like a kid seeing the principal.

I knock and slowly open the door when he yells for me to come in. He peeks up at me from his desk, a thin smile on his face, looking almost keyed up.

I rack my brain for reasons he'd be this tense.

*Does he know about Archer and me?*

*Is Archer dead in his office?*

*Come to think of it, I haven't seen him all day.*

Lately, Archer's mood has been as grumpy as Red Forman's. While Archer and I crumbled on the ski trip, Cohen and Jamie came together. Unfortunately, their happily ever after was happily ever short-term since they've already crashed and burned.

He scratches his neck. "I need to talk to you about something."

"Okay?" I shift from one foot to the other.

"Archer's brother is being released from prison." He frowns. "He's going to work here."

*Phew.*

"Cool." I shrug.

From what I've heard about Lincoln, minus the whole prison vacay, he sounds cool.

"You're not against the idea?" He squints at me harshly as if he's waiting for me to object.

"Nope." I crack a smile.

He blows out a stressed breath. "You should be."

"Oh, big bro." I collapse onto the chair across from him, sitting on it sideways with my feet dangling over the armrest. "Convicts are actually my cup of tea. If he doesn't have a teardrop under his eye, I will be severely disappointed."

"Funny," he grumbles. "For real, if you're not okay with it, tell me."

"I'm cool with it."

"He was *in prison*."

"What's your beef with second chances?"

He massages the space between his brows with two fingers. "It's kind of hard for me to be gung ho on second chances now that I have my son's mother trying to wedge herself into our lives while I'm falling in love with her sister, and it's been a nightmare."

"That sounds complicated." I chew on the inside of my cheek before clicking my tongue against the roof of my mouth. "Have you tried eating a Snickers or something?"

He grabs a piece of paper, crumples it up, and tosses it at me.

I laugh while dodging it, and the sheet falls to the floor.

---

IT'S TIME.

Time to break my Archer-dodging, and what a better way than to give him shit?

"Is your brother hot?"

He peeks up at me before looking at each side of the bar, unsure if I'm speaking to him. "Excuse me?"

"Is your brother hot?" I repeat as if I haven't been avoiding him and we're good ole buddies, ole pals.

"Georgia," Cohen warns, his voice sharp as he walks around me.

I frown. Cohen wasn't supposed to join this game. He was supposed to stay in his office and sulk.

"I'm not asking *you*," I tell Cohen. "I'm asking him." I jerk my head toward Archer.

A confident smile is plastered on my face when I train my attention on Archer. "Well, is he?"

Archer pins his stony stare at me. "I take it Cohen told you about my brother working here?"

I nod, my grin nearly taking over my face. "Yep, and I love myself a bad boy."

"Georgia," Cohen warns again.

"What?" I tilt my head to the side and keep my attention on Archer. "I'm in need of a boy toy."

Archer tightens his jaw, and Cohen is shaking his head when I walk away.

---

CALL ME GEORGIA FOX, M.S.W.

After six years of busting my ass, I finally have my master's in social work.

I stroll through Cohen's backyard with my graduation cap on. Congratulatory gifts for yours truly cover one table, and the other is lined with a taco bar. There's a cake with my face on it—Jamie's idea—alcohol, and food galore. My stomach growls as I snag a plate, ready to eat my weight in tacos.

Even after graduating, I don't have a full-time job yet. What sucks is that jobs want you to have experience before hiring you, but if no jobs will hire people without experience, then how the hell are we supposed to get experience? Luckily, there's a possible job opportunity at the school where Grace teaches. Their guidance counselor is retiring, so until she does and to see if I'll be a good fit, I'm "shadowing" her.

After a heated argument with Cohen, he agreed—with Jamie's persuasion—to let my mother come to his house. She timidly waved to him when she walked in, but he turned around and walked out of the room. We haven't introduced her to Noah yet. I'm still working on convincing him it's a good idea. I bought him a book on forgiveness and left it on his desk last week, only to find it in my book bag later.

Cohen and Jamie finally got their heads' out of their asses' and are in a relationship. Not *only* are they in a relationship, Jamie is also pregnant with his baby. To say they're over the moon is an understatement, and I can't wait for the little one to come.

I open gifts and visit with everyone, and as it grows later, the small crowd clears out. The tacos gave Jamie the gift of heartburn, and Cohen went to check on her, leaving me alone outside for some much-needed quiet time. I toss my cap onto the table next to my green apple Smirnoff wine cooler. Stretching out my legs, I tilt my head back and relax.

"Congratulations."

I slowly raise my head at the same time Archer takes the

chair next to mine. My heart beats like a drum as his gaze locks on me.

He sets a black gift bag with *Congrats, Graduate* scrawled across it in gold glitter.

"Thank you," I whisper, a flush spreading up my neck.

It's easier to talk shit to him when we're at the bar.

Harder during our one-on-one talks.

He stares at me, his masculine face with his strong chin unreadable as the sun sets around us. "How does it feel?"

My gaze falls, and I play with my hands in my lap, fighting a shy smile. "Incredible."

"That's a huge accomplishment, and you worked hard for it. Be proud of that."

I peek up at him, that blush creeping up my cheeks, and repeat, "Thank you."

He signals to the bag. "Open it."

I silently nod, slowly grab it, and shake the bag, like I do with all my gifts, silently guessing what it could be.

It's heavy. Something rattles.

I have no guesses.

With Archer, who knows?

It could be a bomb, and I wouldn't be surprised.

My smile widens as I pull out the gold tissue paper. I peek into the bag before pulling out a liquor bottle.

A bottle of Hennessy.

I play with the bottle in my hands, moving it from one to the other. "Cognac."

"Cognac." He nods, a smile flicking on his lips.

I hold it out toward him. "A reminder that we should never drink this together again?"

"That's not what the gift means." He jerks his head toward the bag. "Keep going, babe."

I bite into my cheek and start withdrawing the rest of the items—a gift card to the coffee shop where I blocked him in, a beginner's guide for driving handbook, and a jewelry box ... a blue Tiffany's jewelry box.

Random.

"What's all this mean?" I ask.

He gestures toward the gifts. "We met at the coffee shop. You forgot how to drive and slammed on your brakes—"

"To prevent a murder," I interrupt.

"To apparently prevent chipmunk murder." He chuckles, waiting for me to open the jewelry box.

"What's this mean?" I ask, holding up the box. "From what I remember, we didn't rob a jewelry store."

He scratches his cheek. "We didn't, but those gifts weren't enough."

*You being here is enough.*

I inhale a deep breath, and we fall silent, the only noise me popping the box open. Gasping, I carefully remove the necklace, holding the chain between my fingers as I take in the gorgeous piece. Two charms with engravings hang from the chain—a long bar with my name and a small circle with *M.S.W.* Next to the charms is a small, sparkling diamond.

"What ... what is this?" I stutter, admiring it.

"A necklace," he states.

"I know that," I say with a laugh. "This ... this is beautiful."

And so thoughtful.

This isn't something he purchased for me at the last minute.

He planned it, had it custom-made—from Tiffany's.

"Thank you, Archer," I say, clasping the necklace in my fist and holding it to my chest, warmth spreading through it.

He subtly nods. "You're welcome." He slides his chair back and stands.

My mouth drops open.

*Is that it? He came to drop off the gift and bail?*

He holds out his palm. "Here."

Relief rushes through me, and I'm hit by a sudden giddiness.

A soft breeze whirls around us, and loose pieces of tissue paper blow across the table. I hand over the necklace, and my palm returns to my chest, hoping to settle my raging heartbeat. He stands behind me and sweeps my hair off my shoulder, bunching it along one side of my neck. His hands are cold, and my breathing turns ragged when he fastens the necklace.

He brushes his fingers along the nape of my neck.

"You're back to your natural hair color," he whispers, grabbing a strand of my hair and curling it around his finger.

"I needed a change."

Rather, I needed to go back to who I was. I've spent hundreds of dollars and made multiple visits, and I am in the ombre stage of returning to my natural hair color.

"It reminds me of our night together." He gives my neck a gentle squeeze and returns to his chair, turning to face me. "You're beaming."

Even if I wanted to hide my smile, I couldn't. "It's been a good day, and your gift, I can't thank you enough. Seriously, this was so thoughtful."

"You're welcome." He thrums his fingers against the table. "I tried to get here earlier, but it was visitation day for Lincoln, and I was running behind. I came as soon as I could because I didn't want to miss the chance to give you that. It looks beautiful on you."

*Who is this Archer, and where can I get him full-time?*

"Want to stay?" I blurt out, shocking both of us. I scramble to grab the Hennessy bottle and hold it up. "Hang out and have a drink, for old times' sake?"

His jaw clenches. "I think we both know that'd be a bad idea."

*We do, but I don't care.*

"So?" I ask, feigning innocence. "Why?"

He licks his lower lip. "From the way you're staring at me and how you look tonight, our night would end the same as our night at Bailey's."

I scan the yard, making sure we're still alone, and lower my voice. "What if that's what I want?"

"It can be what you want, but it's not what you need."

"How do you know what I need?"

"I know what you *don't* need—someone who can never give you what you deserve. I'm that guy."

I sweep my arm over the table, where the gifts are, before running my hand over the necklace chain. "Why show up here with the gifts then?"

"I didn't buy you those gifts so you'd sleep with me. I bought them because you deserve that and more." He briefly slams his eyes shut and bows his head, and his voice is half-whispered. "There are times I wish I could be the guy to make you happy. I might be a heartless bastard, an asshole, but when it comes to you, I stop myself from being the man who crushes your heart."

"Yet you are crushing it," I croak out.

"Babe, trust me." Slowly, he rises to his feet, kisses the top of my head, and says, "Good night, Georgia."

I don't get a chance to say a word before he leaves.

# CHAPTER TWENTY-SEVEN

# Archer

"THANKS FOR LETTING ME CRASH HERE," Lincoln says, tossing his bag on my guest room bed. "Guarantee this shit is more comfortable than what I was sleeping on."

It's the first time my guest room has been used, but since he's been sleeping on a concrete slab for years, I wanted him to be comfortable here. Like the rest of my family, Lincoln grew up with the finer things in life: family trips on yachts, disposable money to blow on whatever we wanted—a lot of times it was blow—and nice-ass bedrooms. I can at least give him the last one of the three.

"I got you," I say behind him, stopping in the doorway and leaning against the door. "How's it feel, being a free man?"

He's four hours free, and damn, it's been a long day. I learned prisons are in no rush to release inmates. My mom and I waited six hours before he stepped out of the building. Our first stop was his favorite restaurant, where he ate his weight in steak and lobster.

I yawn, and my eyes are heavy as he spins and takes in the bedroom. It's almost midnight, and I worked until three this morning. Had I known his release day would be as long as it takes for people to land on the moon, I would've left early and had someone cover for me.

"Damn good," he mutters with a hint of a frown. "Sucks Dad wasn't released with me." He slumps onto the edge of the California king-size bed and hangs his head low, shaking it. "I offered to take a longer sentence to shorten his, but the assholes wouldn't allow it."

*He did what?*

This is the first I'm hearing about his little act of stupidity.

I clench my fists. "Why in the living hell would you do that?" There's no masking the aggravation in my tone.

"He's family," Lincoln points out, peeved, exhaustion overplaying his features. "That—loyalty to our family—might not mean as much to you as it does to me, but Dad's older, and he has heart problems. He doesn't need to be in there."

I unclench a fist and slam my hand against my chest. "Are you saying I have no loyalty?"

"You have loyalty *to me*, sure. To others? Not so much. This stupid game you and Dad have played for years is draining to everyone around you. What happened that night—"

"Don't," I warn, cutting him off. "Don't play that. Whether that happened or not, I still wouldn't be Dad's puppet to his bullshit."

"You threw away your life!" He starts naming off a list on his fingers. "Your job. Your friends. Your family. The woman you were supposed to fucking marry. All because you couldn't get the fuck out of your head and deal with reality." He shakes his head. "I'm not a fucking puppet. I'm living—unlike you."

I didn't plan on us being at each other's throats his first night home. I knew there'd eventually be a conversation about Dad and some back-and-forth shit, talking about loyalty, but nothing this early.

"Oh, piss off," I mutter. "Get off your high horse."

"High horse? I took the job intended for you. You always do

what's best for Archer without giving two shits about anyone else. *You* get off *your* high horse and take a look around. Everyone else is living, not staying in the past, but you won't even try. Hell, I've been in prison for nearly two years, and I still hold no grudges as strong as you."

"What about you?" I seethe. "You sat back while Dad shit all over Grandpa's *legacy*. Where was your loyalty to him? To our name, huh?" I raise my voice. "Where was that goddamn loyalty?"

"What else was I supposed to do, huh?" He rubs the back of his neck. "I took my salary, nothing extra. Did I know what Dad was doing? Yes. I got time because I knew, because I wouldn't turn on my family. Loyalty runs through my blood."

"Your *loyalty* landed you in prison."

*If I hear* loyalty *one more time, I'm going to throw myself out that damn window.*

He stands, plucks his bag from the bed, unzips it, and starts unpacking.

"Look," I say, blowing out deep breaths to calm myself, "it's your first night home. Let's not talk about shit we'll want to kill each other for."

He holds up his arm and flexes his muscles. "Admit you don't want the smoke from these guns."

Lincoln is buff, gym-built buff, unlike me, who'd have a large frame whether I worked out or not. He worked out constantly during his stint in prison and is in the best shape he's ever been. Still doesn't have shit on me size-wise, though. While I got more of my father's size, Lincoln is between my dad's and my mother's.

I tap the door with my knuckles. "Unpack. Get some rest."

"Mom's having a party tomorrow night, and you're coming," he rushes out before I leave.

"No, I'm not."

"Yes, you are."

I shake my head. "You have fun with that."

---

## I CAME FOR LINCOLN.

I'm drinking for my sanity.

There's nothing like celebrating your freedom and being around the fake friends who talked shit when you were arrested, calling you a criminal on the down-low. My mom handled the guest list, and Lincoln, knowing this as well, has steered clear of those people. He insisted my mom have something small, but the seventy-five-plus people in attendance is far from that.

The party is too much for me, and I have to stop myself from bursting out in laughter. There's a harp and piano playing as tonight's entertainment. A fucking harp and piano for a *get out of prison* party. Caviar, Kobe beef, *costs more than my bar makes in a week* champagne.

My mother does not know how to read the room for shit.

I climb up the spiraling staircase at my grandparents' mansion, using the railing as my guide since my tunnel vision isn't doing a great job of leading the way. I walk, weaving from side to side in the hall, until I find the guest room I'm searching for. I slam the door, lock it, and collapse onto the bed as if I hadn't slept in years.

Lincoln decided to crash here after my grandparents offered to have their chef whip up his favorite breakfast in the morning. Considering I told him his ass would be having Lucky Charms at my place, he went with their offer. I might as well do the same.

As soon as my head falls onto the pillow, Georgia comes to mind.

Like my asshole self always does, I shoved myself back into her life. I couldn't show up *without* a gift; that would've been more asshole-like.

At least, that's my excuse.

As I brainstormed gift ideas, I didn't want to give her a generic-ass gift card or a *Congrats!* picture frame. More thought needed to be put into something for her big day.

"Screw it," I groan, reaching across the bed and grabbing my phone from the nightstand. I play with it in my hand while scrambling for the best excuse to call her.

Not that there is one.

*I shouldn't.*

*It's too late.*

*A bad idea.*

*Selfish.*

Selfish or not, I don't stop myself from unlocking my phone and scrolling down my Contacts until I reach her name.

"You selfish bastard," I mutter to myself when I tap it.

Ringing comes alive on the other end, and excitement crawls through my inebriated mind when she answers.

"Hello?" Her voice is cloaked in confusion.

"Hey," I croak out.

"Is, uh … everything okay?"

"Yeah." I'm wasted, in bed, and talking to her. Everything is happy-go-fucking-lucky over here.

The line goes mute for a moment until she finally asks, "If everything is okay, why are you calling?"

*Good question there, woman who's crept her way into my heart. I wish I knew the answer too.*

I tighten my hold on the phone. "I wanted to check on the bar." I tap myself on the arm for my genius answer, too lazy to do the actual *clap on the back* motion.

"Huh?"

"I had the night off, and you worked. I'm calling to confirm everything ran smoothly." Another pat on my arm for me.

"When have you ever called, asking if the bar ran smoothly?" she asks, no bullshit. "Call Cohen if you want to talk *about the bar* while slurring your words."

"Not slurring my words," I reply, slurring my words.

"Where are you?"

I hold the phone between my shoulder and head while dragging my shirt over my head. "A party."

"Archer Callahan, president of the I Hate Parties and Fun Club, is at one? Voluntarily or did someone force you?"

"Hell no, not voluntarily. It's for my brother, and I would've looked like an ass if I hadn't come."

"How is that any different than what you look like on the regular?"

"Funny," I grumble.

She releases a long breath. "Why are you calling me?"

"You're on my mind." The room starts spinning at my confession.

"I'm always on your mind when you're drunk," she deadpans. "You only want to talk to me when alcohol is flowing through your system. But you know what? I refuse to be your tipsy toy."

"Tipsy toy?" I wet my lips. "The fuck is a tipsy toy?"

"Someone you only want to play with when you're drunk."

I swallow hard. "You're not my tipsy toy, and you're wrong. I'm only stupid enough to tell you how much I think about you when I've been drinking."

My drunken brain is the only one that allows me to open up to her.

"I hate this cat-and-mouse game we play," she whispers.

"Me too."

"Then quit playing it."

With that, she hangs up.

———

I SCRUB AT MY EYES, my head taking my over imbibing last night out on me this morning, and yawn.

"Cohen, Lincoln. Lincoln, Cohen," I mutter, signaling between the guys.

Lincoln arrived at the bar fifteen minutes ago. We talked before heading into Cohen's office to introduce him.

"Don't forget about me," Georgia says, strutting into Cohen's office and collapsing into a chair. She presses her hand to her chest. "I'm Georgia, and you're hot."

She peeks over at me for my reaction, and I narrow my eyes at her in warning. It's all a game to her. She's paying me back for all the times I've fucked with her head. My eyes widen as I fight a smile trying to make its way to my lips when I spot the necklace around her neck. She's worn it every day she's been here since I gave it to her.

Lincoln rubs the side of his mouth, no doubt imagining Georgia naked. "Ah, I already like you. Appreciate the compliment, sweetheart."

*Oh, shit.*

Cohen's back stiffens.

"Can I be on training duty for him?" she asks, her voice perky. "I need to practice training, and it'll be the perfect opportunity for me."

"You won't be training anyone," Cohen says with a scowl. "You don't even work tonight."

She cups her chin with both of her hands and dreamily stares at Lincoln—showing off her dramatic acting, apparently. "I'll pick up an extra shift for him."

"How about you pick up yourself and leave my office?" Cohen says, raising a brow and glaring at her as hard as I am.

"All right, all right. Non-training Georgia is out of here." She stands, presses two fingers to her lips, and blows Lincoln a kiss as she passes him before leaving the office.

"Motherfucker," Cohen mutters underneath his breath while I clench my fists.

Cohen points at Lincoln. "My sister is off-limits."

Lincoln's eyes widen. "Oh shit, that's your sister?" He holds up his hand. "My bad, my bad. I really appreciate you giving me a chance, man. I won't let you guys down."

"Archer's family is my family," Cohen answers.

His words are genuine. Sure, he gave me hell when I approached him about hiring my brother, but Cohen knows I wouldn't bring trouble into our bar. He won't mind the extra help since Jamie is close to popping out their baby.

Jamie is good people.

I'm glad Cohen found her.

Found love.

And Noah loves her.

I rub my hands together and jerk my head toward the hallway. "Let's go to my office and get your paperwork started, brother."

He presses his hands together and tips his head toward Cohen. "Thanks again, man."

We walk to my office, and as soon as he shuts the door, he says, "You and the smart-ass sister have something going on, you sly fucker, you."

I stand at my desk, focusing on my computer as I open the folder for the employee documents. "I don't know what you're talking about."

He smirks. "Georgia. Is something going on between you two?"

I drag my finger along the trackpad and hit print. "Hell no."

"That mean she's available?"

"Hell no."

He chuckles, rubbing his hand over his strong jaw. "There's something then."

"There's nothing."

"When she walked into the room, your eyes followed her every move. You were ready to rip my head off my shoulders while she flirted with me. And then you went back to wanting to decapitate me when I just asked if she was available."

"Do you want to get fired before you start?" I level my dark gaze on him.

"I'd prefer not to be."

"Then shut the hell up."

"Cohen seems like he just tries to be intimidating. Ask her out. It'd be good for you. She'd be good for you."

A knot forms in my stomach. "I'd ruin her."

# CHAPTER TWENTY-EIGHT

## Georgia

I'M NEVER HAVING a gender-reveal party.

These things are stressful.

No way could I wait to find out the sex of my baby, but Cohen and Jamie have been patient.

Spoiler alert: I peeked at the cake.

They're having a girl.

After they find out and I get them alone, I'm requesting Georgia at least be thrown in as her first or middle name.

I planned the party with Jamie's best friend, Ashley, but Cohen and I have been planning an additional surprise. He's popping the question to Jamie today, and we set up for the perfect proposal.

A baby-bottle piñata and blue and pink streamers hang from the trees in Cohen's backyard. Games and food are spread along the tables, and the party is half-catered, half-Cohen grilled. He insisted no one but him was grilling his burgers. Friends and family are scattered around the backyard—sitting at tables, playing games, conversing with each other.

Cohen caved again and allowed our mother to tag along with me. After I swore on my life that she'd changed, Jamie and I convinced him that it was time for Noah to meet her. He did, and it only created more sparkle in her eyes. Maybe that's what she needs—a support system, a family—to help her stay sober.

All our friends are here, including Archer and Lincoln. My sleep has been crappy and my stress high since the night of my graduation party. I'd never had anyone gift me something so sentimental. Since then, we've had a few side conversations, but with him training Lincoln and getting Lincoln situated into normal life, we haven't had much time to talk. Not that I'm sure he would talk even if I cornered him.

The man drops bombs and then walks away as if he didn't ignite my feelings for him. I've considered asking Jamie for whiplash medicine because the boy is confusing me with his back and forth.

He's back and forth.

His *I like you, but I'm no good for you.*

His *let me be sweet but make you hate me at the same time.*

When I went home that night, I decided to take my mom's second piece of advice—make him see what he's missing. That's why I've taken on the pastime of flirting with every man Archer can see. Lincoln, guys at the bar, even the man who delivered our beer shipment yesterday.

If you can't beat 'em, might as well create some jealousy.

Strolling through the yard, I spot Lincoln relaxed in a chair, a water bottle in his hand. "Lincoln, Lincoln, Lincoln," I call out, walking over to him before plopping down on his lap and wrapping my arms around his neck. "When are you going to take me out on a date?"

Lincoln wraps his arms around my waist, glancing down at me with a smirk. "Whenever you're available, babe." His lips go to my ear. "Keep making him jealous. It's working."

Lincoln shares some similarities with his brother: chips on their shoulders and not one for small talk, but he's more easygoing than Archer.

These Callahan boys.

Handsome men ready to destroy everything in their paths.

We flirt, but I've never crossed a line with him. Nor will I ever. Even with Archer being a jackass to me, I have more respect for him than that. I have too much respect for Lincoln to use his heart as a pawn. I'm also not so keen on having sex with brothers.

That's my brother's thing ... but with sisters.

*Sorry, Cohen, totally kidding.*

I love Jamie, love how she's fixed my brother, and she's a chill chick.

"You ready, guys?" I hear Ashley yell. "Cohen! Jamie! It's time!"

All eyes are on Jamie and Cohen, and I prepare myself for my fake surprise face—like I didn't cake-peek and I have no idea what's about to happen. Their hands are wrapped around a balloon string, and they have pins in the other.

We count down, and as soon as we say, "One!" they pop the balloon.

Pink confetti rains down on them. The crowd jumps to their feet, cheers, and grabs pieces of the confetti while yelling at them in congratulations.

"Oh my God!" I gasp, my hand on my chest over my heart. "I can't believe this! I so didn't think it'd be a girl."

"You peeked, didn't you?" my mom asks with a smile.

I smirk. "Maybe just a little."

She laughs, shaking her head.

Now comes my other job. I rush into the house, grab a black balloon, and am nearly out of breath when I reach Jamie and Cohen.

*Reminder: get your ass to the gym.*

I hand the balloon to Cohen, my face in a sappy grin, and walk backward to give them their moment but not wanting to miss a second of this.

"Oh my God! Are we having twins?" Jamie asks, eyeing the balloon.

Cohen hands her a pin. "Pop it."

She does, black confetti fluttering to the ground, and everyone else glances at each other in confusion—not noticing what's lying at Jamie's feet.

"Holy shit," she whispers.

"Cuss word!" Noah calls out, making the crowd laugh.

Cohen drops down to one knee and delivers a speech no one can hear.

*Lame.*

She says yes, the celebration continues, and that's my cue to grab the cake.

"I cannot wait to eat, like, ten slices of you," I say to the cake as it sits in the fridge. "Do not let me down with your buttercream frosting, please and thank you."

As I go to take it out, my hand is snatched, the fridge is closed, and I'm being tugged down the hall and led into Noah's bedroom. It happens so fast, and though I don't see who it is, I know it's him.

I feel him.

His presence.

Have memorized his scent, as if it were the perfume I wear daily.

He slams the door shut and turns me to face him. "Stop flirting with my brother."

*And today, we are getting mad-at-the-world Archer, ladies and gents.*

*Well, at least mad-at-Georgia anyway.*

There's no patience in his eyes as he stares at me with disdain.

"What?" I ask, dramatically fluttering my eyes. "I don't know what you're talking about."

"Don't bullshit me," he seethes. "You're flirting with him to fuck with my head."

*I'm fucking with his head?*

*Me?*

*The one who's been straight up, who's begged him not to fuck
with my head.*

My flirting dies and resurrects into anger.

"Screw you, Archer," I snarl, poking him in the chest, my
nail creating a wrinkle. "Maybe I like your brother. Maybe I'll go
on a date with him, and I'll kiss him. And you know what? I
might even fuck him too!"

"Don't say that shit," he grinds out.

"Why? Do you think that because you fucked me, you can
tell me what to do now? You lost that right a long damn time
ago."

When the door swings open, I jump, and Archer flinches.

Cohen is standing in the doorway.

"What the fuck?" he yells.

Silence stretches through the room.

It's like time stands still.

My embarrassment skyrocketing.

Archer's patience dwindling.

Cohen's anger building.

This is mortifying.

I knew there was a chance Cohen would find out what'd
happened between us, but I never wanted it to go down like this.

At his party.

One of my brother's happiest days.

I've ruined it for him.

For Jamie.

Cohen's face is red, and he snarls his upper lip as he stares at
his business partner, his friend, the man he found out had
screwed his sister. "She's my fucking sister!"

Luckily, Jamie saves the situation and stops him from going
Mike Tyson on Archer.

"Nuh-uh," she says, grabbing his arm. "This isn't happening
right now."

"Oh, it's happening," Cohen snaps.

My attention repeatedly pings from Cohen to Archer, back and forth, waiting to see who will make the first move.

*Will it be with punches?*

*With words?*

Archer holds up his hands. "I'm out of here. You can rip me a new asshole tomorrow."

*He's leaving?*

Oh, I'll be ripping him a new asshole for leaving me stranded with these question-askers.

Archer sends me a sympathetic glance, lazily mouthing, "*I'm sorry.*"

I reply with an infuriated stare.

*Do not walk out of here.*

Jamie pulls Cohen back, giving Archer room to exit Noah's bedroom, their eyes locked in anger.

Tears slide down my cheeks—at the hurt, the humiliation, the anguish.

He left, left me to deal with this, and I hate him for it.

Tears are in my eyes when Jamie and Cohen stare at me in question.

"Nope." I sniffle, shaking my head. "Today is about you two. Any dramatic conversations about my life will wait until later."

I leave the room, brushing past them, and rush to the bathroom. After fixing myself, I return to the party, good as new.

One thing my non-relationship with Archer has improved is my pretending skills.

I'm a pro at pretending nothing has built between us, that I'm not stupidly in love with him.

Acting like I'm this happy-go-lucky woman while my heart is cracking with every conversation I have with him.

It's time I stop pretending he isn't crushing my heart and stop allowing him to do it.

# CHAPTER TWENTY-NINE

# Archer

"WE NEED TO TALK," Cohen says, stepping into my office without knocking.

I nod, tossing the pen in my hand down. "We do."

Cohen had the weekend off from the bar, so we had time to cool off before having this conversation. He's my dude, and not saying he's a wimp, but he'd be stupid to fight me.

I should've never gone to the party. Every time I say I'm going to keep my distance from Georgia, I go and do stupid shit like call her while I'm drunk, buy her custom Tiffany's, or show up at a damn party where damn streamers are hanging from the trees.

Watching her flirt with Lincoln was a stab to the throat. They had started flirting on his first day—both of them doing it to fuck with me. At first, I wasn't worried, but the more they did it, the more Lincoln got to know Georgia, the more terrified it made me. Lincoln might think it's a game now, but if he sees the Georgia I do, he'll fall in love with her too.

Jealousy doesn't care who the other man is. All it sees is someone having what you want.

Cohen isn't happy about their flirting either. When I

demanded Lincoln stop, he muttered something along the lines of, "Then make your fucking move on her."

I shouldn't have followed her into the house.

Georgia isn't mine.

After leaving the party, I called and texted her, but no answer. I'd been wrong to walk away, but if I'd stayed longer, the chance of punches being thrown between Cohen and me would have been higher.

Cohen sits, his face unreadable. "Georgia's told me some."

I nod, unsure what *some* is.

"She said you slept together before I introduced you, that it was a one-time thing, hasn't happened since, and you mutually agreed to keep it private between yourselves."

"That's true." I wait for him to tell me what a piece of shit I am for bailing on her the next morning.

He doesn't.

She didn't tell him.

"Is that why you two constantly argue?"

I shake my head and laugh. "Nah, we have conflicting personalities."

"Not conflicting enough to not sleep together."

I stay quiet, worried of saying the wrong thing.

"Archer, you're a good dude. If you like my sister, I'm okay with it. I'm not jumping over the moon, given if you hurt her, it'd fuck up our business relationship. I care about you both. I'll leave you two to handle your business and make your own decisions without worrying if I'll be mad. I know I talk a lot of shit about my friends staying away from my sister, but I'd never allow someone I thought was a terrible guy to be my friend."

I don't tell him I can't date his sister.

I don't tell him that if I try, I'll break her heart more than I already have.

When Lincoln got home that night, we had it out. He was pissed that I'd ditched him and texted him later, telling him to quit flirting with Georgia and to find his own damn way home.

It was a dick move, but I'd had to get out of there. The next argument came when he told me to stop throwing my life away.

Cohen slaps his hands onto his legs and brings himself up. "That's all I needed to say. Whatever you do, that's on you."

When he leaves, I grab my phone and hit Georgia's name, hoping she answers this time.

**Me: *We need to talk.***

I'm surprised when it beeps thirty seconds later.

**Georgia: *I don't think that's necessary.***

**Me: *I do.***

**Georgia: *I don't.***

**Me: *I'm coming over.***

**Georgia: *I'm not letting you in.***

**Me: *I'll stand outside all night then.***

**Georgia: *Bring a sleeping bag then, stalker.***

**Me: *I'll be there in 15.***

**Georgia: *I won't be waiting up.***

I grab my keys, leave my office, and head to Georgia's place.

---

GRACE ANSWERS THE DOOR, wearing the dirtiest look she can manage, which is laughable.

"What do you want, Archer?" she snaps, resting her hand on her waist.

"Is Georgia here?"

"Yep." She taps her foot, her stare cautious.

"Can I come in and talk to her?"

"One moment, please." She slams the door in my face, and I hear her yell Georgia's name before saying, "Asshole Archer is here."

She opens the door again, steps out of my way, and points down the hall.

It's my first time in their townhome. They recently moved into Jamie's place after she moved in with Cohen. It's nice, but

I'm too preoccupied to take a good look around. Making shit right with Georgia is my objective, not admiring the fucking wallpaper.

Georgia is standing in her doorway, her hip nudged against the doorframe, with her arms crossed. "Why are you here? I told you not to come."

"And I told you I was anyway."

I stand a few inches from her, not wanting to creep too much into her space yet. She hesitates, staring so hard at me, as if she's attempting to read my soul. Her hair is down with two messy pigtail-looking buns on the top of her head, and her sweatpants are so large that I'm positive they're Cohen's. At least, that's what I want to tell myself and pretend there's no way they could be another man's.

I'm surprised and grateful when she steps to the side and waves me into her bedroom.

Backing up, she falls onto her bed, grabs a bright purple shag pillow, tugs it against her stomach, and sits cross-legged. "Why are you here?"

I walk deeper into her bedroom. "You're seriously fucking asking me that?"

"I'm seriously fucking asking you that."

"We haven't spoken since the party."

"That's a problem?"

"Jesus, Georgia. Yes, that's a goddamn problem. What we were afraid of happening—Cohen finding out—happened, and you're acting clueless as to why we should talk."

She tightens her hold on the pillow. "I'm well aware of what happened." She taps her chin. "You left me there, by myself, to clean up the mess. I was already worked up after you demanded you have a say in who I can and can't sleep with." She shifts her finger from her chin and points at me. "Then Cohen walked in, and you bailed. I had to force a smile and go back to the party because, unlike you, I don't run away like a scared bitch when problems arise. I put on a brave face and handle it."

Guilt seeps up my throat. If I could go back in time, I'd stay. I'd stay, and poor Noah's room would have some damage to it. In my head, I was thinking about Cohen. He needed time to calm down before we talked. I should've thought more about Georgia and how it would affect her.

"I've been putting on a brave face for years, Georgia." My honesty shocks us both. I sit on the edge of her bed. "I came here to apologize. What I said and how I acted was wrong. Hell, after all these years, all the shit I've done and how I've treated you is wrong."

I fucked us up.

Fucked up everything.

Fucked her up.

At that moment, I realize I've been selfish, doing all this to her.

I should've made it clear in the beginning that there was never a chance for us. Instead, I sent mixed signals.

Fucked with her head and her heart.

"I appreciate the apology," she says gently and genuinely. "This should help with the tension, Cohen knowing."

"Mm-hmm." She nods in agreement. "Does this mean you'll stop acting like I'm the plague you want to steer clear of?"

I wish things were different, wish that I could apologize with more than words. That I could lay her down and ask for forgiveness with my lips, my tongue, my body. I'd slide into her and whisper how much she meant to me.

How my dead heart can't stop pounding against my chest when she's around.

How, even with her arguing, she's kept me going more than she'll ever know.

How she's helped heal me without even knowing about it.

I nod. "I want the bullshit, the games, to stop."

She raises a brow. "Is that you saying you want to be friends?"

"I guess so." This is us settling—something that's necessary but also hurts.

"Friends?" She holds out her hand.

I shake it. "Friends."

One word.

One word I hate when it comes to her.

We'll try, but we'll never be able to go back and start fresh.

CHAPTER THIRTY

# Georgia

*FRIENDS.*

The word hurt when it left my mouth.

I've never been friends with Archer.

We've been one-night lovers and enemies.

But never friends.

We will never be just friends.

Always people who shared an extraordinary night together before one crushed the other.

I've never seen Archer as a friend—only a man who broke my heart and never let me break into an inch of his.

I inhale a deep breath to stop the tears from surfacing. "Friends it is."

There's an uncomfortableness in the room.

Like the air even knows we're lying.

Archer and I have two emotions, two sides to our relationship.

Anger and lust.

Arguing and wanting each other.

No friendship qualities there.

Even though we're calling a truce, I know friends isn't much of an option for us.

I can try.

I can pretend.

It'll be the same as we've been since our morning after, changing my life.

My heart.

Any relationship I have had and will ever have.

"As your new friend, can I ask you one question?" I half-whisper, pulling fuzz off my pillow, unable to meet his gaze.

He slaps my bed. "Shoot."

"Why'd you leave that morning?" I hug the pillow tight. "What did I do to deserve that? To make me feel worthless, like some trash that you were done with?" I hate that a single tear runs down my cheek, and I use my arm to cover it, masking the hurt, as I've done all along.

Masking it with anger.

With sarcasms.

With *I hate you*s.

I tense, preparing to hear that I was a bad fuck, that it was all his drunken dick wanting me, all the reasons he's thrown at me.

"I never planned to leave that morning," he answers, his voice raspy. "If there's anything I wish I had done differently, I wish I'd never taken you to my bed that night."

I wince. "Is that supposed to make me feel better?"

"You deserved better than what I did. You deserve better than me."

"Why'd you leave that morning, Archer?" My tone turns harsh and demanding.

"I was out of coffee, so I went to the coffee shop and picked up some doughnuts. You were sleeping when I got home, and then my mother called in hysterics." He drums his fingers along my comforter. "The reality of my dad being locked up had finally hit her. She'd been holding on to hope that it wouldn't happen—that he and Lincoln would go free because we had expensive lawyers with great records. She'd taken an extra mood stabilizer to help, but it did the opposite—causing her to have a complete meltdown. I had to leave to be with her. I almost—*al-fucking-most*—went to wake you up to tell you I had to go, but when I walked into the room and saw you sleeping, I knew you deserved better than me—a guy who was questioning whether he should ditch you. And even if I had stayed or woken you up, I'd never be the man for you—the kind of man a woman like you deserves."

My voice is hesitant when I ask, "How do you know what I need?"

"Someone who isn't an asshole, who doesn't, for one moment, think about leaving you the next morning."

"Archer, it was for your mom." That doesn't make his excuse acceptable, but I hate that he had to endure that—to see his mother broken.

"The kind of man for you would've woken you up, explained the situation, and given you his number." He scoots forward, toward me, and stretches out his arm, wiping tears from my cheek.

*Here we go with the damn tears again.*

*I need to learn to get control over these damn things.*

"I'm sorry for everything," he croaks out, his hand massaging my cheek. "I have a lot of regrets in this fucked-up life of mine, one of them being what I did to you, how I broke a heart so big —broke a woman who didn't deserve it. For that, along with everything else, I'm sorry."

"Why didn't you just tell me?"

"It's embarrassing. I'd be dragging someone into this life, a depressing fucking ditch, and I never want to do that. You deserve someone to shine light into your life, like you will theirs, and that's not me. I'm not a fucking ray of sunshine like you."

I pull away from him and level my eyes on his handsome yet desolate face. "Are you kidding me? Do you remember how broken I was that night? You provided light for me then, one of the days when my heart was broken more than anything. *You.*

You have no right to tell me what will and won't provide lightness in my darkness."

"I'm glad I was there for you then." He blows out a breath and takes a look around. "I like your room. It screams you."

*Nice change of subject there, ole buddy, ole pal.*

"Thanks." I smile timidly.

I haven't finished decorating my room, but I hung strands of white lights behind my bed and a stardust tapestry on another, and I completed the look with a rattan mirror. My bedding is white and covered in bright-colored shag pillows.

"I'll stop bugging you now." He claps his hands and rubs them together.

*No, wait!*

*Stay!*

*Stay to make up for when you didn't.*

*Stay and tell me that you don't hate me.*

"Good night, Georgia." He kisses the tip of my nose, shocking me, and stands. A short wave is his last move before he leaves my bedroom.

For so long, this man has denied himself, has denied me, of any type of intimacy.

Friendly, romantic, anything.

Just the brush of his lips against the tip of my nose lights me up.

I love this man, and now, I have to be friends with him.

---

"GEORGIA," Lincoln asks when I walk in the bar and head toward the exit after picking up my tip outs. "Have you seen Archer?"

"No?"

*Why's he asking me?*

I'm the last person Archer would report his whereabouts to.

A week has passed since he came into my bedroom and

delivered his truths, and we declared ourselves friends. We've been civil at the bar, tossed a few jokes around, but I don't see us trading friendship bracelets anytime soon.

*Friends.*

*Ha.*

*That was a fake-as-fuck declaration.*

"No one can get in touch with him," Lincoln continues, holding up his phone.

*That's odd.*

Archer never misses a day or calls off.

"Do you have any idea where he could be?" he asks, his tone bordering frantic.

"No idea. He's, uh … not that open with me, if you haven't noticed."

"He wasn't always that way, you know."

"Are you talking when he was, like, six months old, when he couldn't call people names and stomp around because someone had stolen his pacifier?"

"No, it's just … sometimes, shit happens that changes you."

"Like what?"

"Not my story to tell, babe. Not my story to tell."

I nod, accepting the answer I expected. "Maybe he's taking a nap?"

Lincoln slumps in his stool. "Nah, I doubt he'll be sleeping much today. It isn't a good day for him … for our family."

"Why?"

He shakes his head, not answering me.

"If I hear from him, I'll let you know."

He smiles sullenly. "Thank you."

I call Archer when I get into my car.

No answer.

I turn the ignition, and it hits me.

*I know where he is.*

# CHAPTER THIRTY-ONE

# Archer

IF THERE WAS a day I could kick out of the calendar, it'd be today.

Every year, it haunts me.

I've attempted different ways to handle my regret.

Sleep.

Booze.

Sex.

No matter what, there's no escaping my conscience.

Tonight, I've chosen booze.

"Fancy seeing you here."

My heartbeat kicks up a notch at the familiar voice—that sweet, silky voice of hers. The stool next to me is dragged out, and Georgia casually drops onto the seat.

Recollection of the last time we were here zips through my blood—a diversion from my shame.

A recollection of when we attempted to booze through it.

Then sex through it.

I knock back my Hennessy before saying, "What are you doing here?"

Her voice is soothing as she answers, "Thought I could use a drink."

I lick my bottom lip, the taste of warm spice on it. "Lincoln send you?"

She shakes her head. "No, but he is looking for you."

"Does he know I'm here?"

She shakes her head. "I took a guess that you'd be here, but I haven't told anyone."

"Go home, Georgia, and don't tell Lincoln where I am. This has been my perfect hiding spot for years. I don't feel like finding another."

"Your secret hiding place is safe with me." She hums. "Just return the favor if I ever go MIA."

"Go home," I repeat, biting out each word.

In typical Georgia style, instead of listening, she signals to the bartender. "I need a drink." Her attention returns to me after she orders a Coke. "I'll go home when you go home."

I whistle, catching the bartender's attention, and hold up my glass. He nods in understanding.

"Prepare to stay here all night."

"I'd better order some nachos to go with my Coke then, huh?"

This might be what I need.

*She* might be who I need.

Not screwing her but talking to her.

She blows out a breath. "What's going on, Archer?"

"Why does it seem like this is our place?" I ask, in need of a subject change.

"Talk to me."

*And she doesn't take the bait.*

"Even if it's small, talk to me."

"Once upon a time, there was a princess who lived in a castle—"

She shoves my shoulder. "Funny. Why are you here, and what is today to you?"

"Go home." I have a feeling I'll be saying that a lot tonight.

"Not happening." She smiles when the bartender delivers her

Coke, and she orders nachos. "You came to me when I was here. Consider this me returning the favor."

"Does it end the same way?"

"Negative." Her comforting gaze tugs at my heart. "Lincoln said this was a rough day for your family. Why?"

"How did my telling you to leave lead you to believe I'd spill my heart out to you?"

"You're wasting your breath, telling me to go, because you know that won't happen."

I stay quiet.

"Your brother ... all of us ... we're worried about you."

"Tell him ... them ... *you* that I'm fine."

She talks to herself. "Archer said he's fine even though he's most definitely not fine." She pulls out her phone. "I'm at least telling him you're okay."

I eye her suspiciously. "Don't tell him where I am."

"My lips are sealed." She does a zip motion over her mouth. "I don't want anyone knowing about this place either."

"Oh, so is this your place now too?"

"Apparently so." She bumps her shoulder against mine. "I think there's room for the two of us."

She unlocks her phone, her fingers jabbing letters on the screen, and I hear a *swoop* sound when she hits send.

Sliding the phone into her bag, she gives me her undivided attention. "Lincoln knows you're okay, and I told him I'd keep an eye on you."

"I don't need a babysitter."

"Consider me ... less of a babysitter and more as company." When the bartender drops the nacho bowl in front of her, she smiles and thanks him. "I'll sit here silently and devour these nachos." She slides the bowl over to me. "Want some?"

I shake my head as she grabs one, shoving a chip in her mouth before licking the cheese off her fingers.

She eats, offering me nachos every three minutes, and drinks her Coke.

I sulk and drink cognac.

I'm not sure how much time passes before she wraps her hand around my arm.

"Come on. Let's get you home."

I shake my head. "Nah, I'll stay the night here."

"Stay the night here?" Her eyes widen as if I'd lost my mind. "Where are you going to sleep? On the bar?"

"My car."

"Yeah, not happening." She sweeps her hand over the bar. "This isn't the best neighborhood, and you don't do yourself any favors, driving around in that ridiculously expensive car of yours. You'll be a sitting duck, waiting to be robbed." She wiggles her fingers toward me. "Keys."

I tuck my hand into my pocket and slowly drag them out before stopping. "What about your car?"

"Someone would probably pass over a car that resembles a ladybug. I'll drop you off at home and then Uber back."

"I think the fuck not. No way are you taking an Uber that late and coming here. We'll leave my car, and I'll contort myself to get into yours."

"Whatever you say. My goal is to get you out of here. Whether it be in my car, in your car, or on Rollerblades, you need to get home."

I pay our tabs and slide off my stool. I'm not wasted, and I can walk on my own, but watching her help me to her car is comical. I've never been in a car so damn cramped. My head is inches from hitting the top.

She peeks over at me. "Do you want me to go in and grab you a water or something? Please do not puke in my car."

I shake my head before tipping it back on the headrest. "Today is the anniversary of my grandfather's death, and it's my fault he's dead."

# CHAPTER THIRTY-TWO

## Georgia

HIS WORDS SHOCK ME.

My keys fall from my fingers and onto my lap, and I stare at him, mouth dropped open. "What?"

He angles his head to look at me, not lifting it from the headrest. "It's my fault my grandfather died."

I knew Archer was suffering through an emotional agony, and for years, I racked my brain on what it could be. I didn't expect that.

Questions rapidly hurtle through my brain.

"What?" I stutter. "How?"

His head shifts, so he's no longer looking at me, only blankly staring out the windshield. "He died because I was a selfish prick."

"Can you elaborate on that?"

I want to turn on the light, grab his head, and force him to look at me, but I'm scared he'll stop. Maybe in the dark is the only time he'll open up to me. If I have to stay in the darkness for him, I will.

He sucks in a deep breath.

Exhales.

Deep breath.

Exhales.

"My grandfather was my hero, growing up," he says, his voice thick with emotion. "I was closer to him than my father. The summer after I graduated from college, I moved into his pool house. One night, we got into an argument. He thought I wasn't taking life seriously and was partying too much. To be a little dickhead, I threw a big-ass party at the pool house to spite him. I got drunk, coked out, so fucked up that I didn't care what damage was done." He stops, his voice trailing off, and I wait for him to continue.

Another deep breath.

Another exhale.

I situate myself on my knees, moving in closer, and rest one hand on the center console while using the other to run my hand down his arm, praying he takes it as a touch of comfort.

Deep breath.

Exhale.

"He came home during the party and started cleaning the mess." His voice cracks, nearly shattering me. "He tripped, hit his head, fell into the pool, and drowned."

His shoulders slump, his body slouching in my passenger seat, as he breaks down.

We go quiet, and I process his confession.

"Archer," I finally whisper, moving in closer. "I'm so sorry."

He drags his hand through his hair and tugs at the roots. "He probably screamed for help, but the music was blaring. He wasn't found until hours later, and by the time help came, he was already gone. My father blamed his death on me, and he's right. Had I not thrown that party, been a selfish bastard, that wouldn't have happened. After that, I pulled away from everything in my life—the drugs, money, parties, social life. I wanted nothing to do with it. I was disgusted. It was what had killed my grandfather, and he died, knowing I didn't give a shit."

I move his hand and replace it with mine, dragging my

fingers through the strands—an attempt to soothe him. "Archer, it sounds like it was an accident."

"An accident that could've been prevented. He died because of my party."

When he finally looks at me, there's fire in his eyes. I gasp as he grabs my waist, pulls me onto his lap, and smashes his lips into mine.

He grips my face, claiming me, as I wrap my arms around his neck. He kisses me like his life will end if our mouths part. I moan into his mouth when he slides his tongue inside mine, our tongues curling together, and I slowly rock against him.

"Georgia," he moans, his cock hardening underneath me.

I rock faster at the feel of him.

"Georgia," he says, pulling away, and we stare at each other, catching our breaths.

He's breathing heavily while staring up at me. "Georgia, you need to take me home and drop me off, and if I beg you to come in, don't."

My head is still spinning from his kiss. "What?"

"If you come home with me, I will fuck you. I will use you to forget what today is. Don't you dare allow that to happen."

Nothing kills a mood more than the guy saying he'd be using you.

"Well then," I mutter, doing the crawl of shame off his lap. I fetch my keys that fell onto the floorboard and shove one into the ignition, the smell of lust lingering in the small confines of my car. "Can you plug your address into a GPS, so I know where I'm going?"

The last time we left from this bar to go to his place, it was in an Uber. I'd been drinking, and his hand was up my dress, so it was kinda hard to pay attention to when we turned right and left.

He nods, grabs my phone, and punches in his address.

"Thank you," I whisper.

Our ride is silent, our mood somber, while I drive to his penthouse.

*How did we go from dry-humping to hardly muttering a word to each other in minutes?*

I shift my car into park when we reach his place. "I can't leave you alone."

"Lincoln should be here."

I pull out my phone and text Lincoln.

**Lincoln: Hold tight. I'll be right down.**

He turns to look at me, his face inches from mine, before he comes closer and nudges his nose against mine. "I'm sorry, Georgia."

We jump when my passenger door swings open, and Lincoln stares down at us.

"How the hell did you manage to get in this car?"

## CHAPTER THIRTY-THREE

# Archer

"COME ON, MAN," Lincoln says, helping me out of the car before glancing at Georgia, who's next to him. "Thank you."

She smiles, and it lights up my drunken ass before I step out of the car. "Of course."

I stabilize myself and swat Lincoln's hand away. "I can walk."

The last thing I need is my doorman thinking I'm a hot mess and complain about me to the building manager. They're strict about that shit here. I'm straight as I walk in and step into the elevator, and we land in my penthouse.

"You got him?" Georgia asks Lincoln while I grab a water from the fridge.

Lincoln nods. "I'll take good care of him."

I point at Georgia with the water bottle and drag my drunken ass toward the couch. "Pretty sure you'd take better care of me."

Her cheeks turn a bright red, and I can't stop myself from smiling when I see the evidence of my beard rubbing against her face.

We touched. We kissed. I had her in my arms again.

As much as it killed me, I had to stop her.

She deserves better than coming home with me and having drunk sex again.

If I ever get the luxury of touching her again, I need to be clearheaded.

Lincoln turns to Georgia. "Thanks for taking care of him, babe. I appreciate it."

I snarl at him calling her *babe*.

"You're welcome." Georgia's attention slides to me. "Good night, you guys."

"Night," I say, my voice tight.

*Don't go.*

It pisses me off further when Lincoln walks her down to her car and not me.

*I fucked up.*

*I'm fucked up.*

I hang my head low and raise it when Lincoln returns. "Don't flirt with her. Don't call her babe again," I hiss.

Lincoln halts in his steps. "What?"

"Georgia. She's not your *babe*."

He looks at me like I've lost my mind before shaking his head. "Nope. I'm not taking that bait so that you have someone to argue with. My feelings toward Georgia are strictly platonic."

"Good, because she's mine."

"Yours, huh?" He walks farther into the room. "You sure don't seem to claim what's yours. If she's *yours*, why do you keep pushing her away, the only woman who seems capable of putting up with your miserable ass?"

"Fuck you," I snarl.

"Fuck me?" He releases a cold laugh. "I was worried sick about you. I called Mom, the police, even the hospital. You were too selfish to even tell anyone you weren't dead."

"I needed space. I'm tired of people thinking they can fix me every year on this day."

"You sure didn't need space from Georgia," he mutters before catching himself. "Look, I don't even give a shit if it's not me you want to talk to, but a heads-up that you're alive would be nice."

I let out a wicked laugh. "Lincoln, always the martyr of the family."

"Don't start that shit."

"The dude who put his freedom on the line for his family. Who makes sure his brother is alive. Who still attends his mother's parties."

"Don't pity yourself. It's a bad look."

"You doing a stint in the pen isn't a bad look?"

"I'm going to act like you didn't try to throw that shit in my face because you're drunk and hurting. Sue me for being loyal."

"That loyalty put you in prison!" I scream.

He shakes his head and lowers his voice. "It did, and *here we go* with this same bullshit conversation. I went to prison. You blame Dad. I'm out. It's time to move the hell on."

I work my jaw. "Do you regret it?"

"I don't blame anyone but myself. I'm a big boy."

"He played your ass," I release around a snarl. "Straight played your ass."

The more shit I talk, the redder Lincoln's face gets, his patience dwindling.

*Good. Let him sucker punch me like Dad did that night.*

It's what I deserve.

He stands tall, crossing his arms, and anchors his attention to me. "This beef between you and Dad needs to end. No one played me. I wasn't innocent. I knew about the transfers and the offshore accounts. I didn't participate, but I warned him."

I drop my head into my hands, shaking it. "I hate being fucked up in the head."

Lincoln collapses on the opposite end of the sectional. "Everyone is a little fucked up in the head. It's what makes us who we are."

"You're a good brother." I remove my hands, one by one, and stare at him with affection. "A good son."

"So are you."

I shake my head and scoff. "I'm a shit brother, a shit son, a shit person."

"You and Dad need to talk."

"Nothing to talk about. I will never forgive him for blocking me from attending grandfather's funeral, for throwing it in my face day after day that it was my fault he'd died, and drunkenly saying he wished I were the one who had died."

Lincoln shuts his eyes, the memory paining him. That was a tough time for our family, and Lincoln always played referee. "I think it's time you see him."

"You're right."

---

I'VE MADE the drive countless times.

The difference is, I'm visiting someone new.

Someone I swore I never would.

The process is the same—show ID, get searched, walk through a metal detector, wait, and then enter a room filled with inmates until you spot who you're looking for at a table. One advantage of being in a low-security federal prison is, they aren't as strict on you.

My father stares at me from his chair with folded arms and raised eyebrows. Gone is the wealthy and confident man I once knew. His face has aged, his hair peppered with gray sprinkles and thinning, and the suit he's sporting is no longer designer. While Lincoln came out of prison fit, my father isn't in that same boat.

"This is quite the surprise," he comments as I take the chair across from him.

I clear my throat before speaking, "Trust me, even with the long drive to process it, I'm shocked I'm here."

He strokes his chin. "Why'd you come?"

I tap my foot. "It's time we clear the air."

He nods. "Agreed."

I get straight to the point. No use for small talk until we come to terms with our issues and work them out. "Why do you keep asking Mom for me to visit? Why do you keep calling?"

He pinches the skin between his eyebrows with two fingers. "Even before my sentencing, we hadn't held a conversation in years. No matter what, I'm your father, and you're my son."

*His son.*

"The son you blamed for murdering your father." My jaw clenches. "You banned me from his funeral, wouldn't allow me the opportunity to say good-bye to my own grandfather."

"Archer." He releases a long breath. "You have to understand my anger."

"I do. You lost someone you loved, but so did I."

"He died because of your negligence, your selfishness."

"Like father, like son then, huh?" I scoff. "You didn't kill someone, but you put your son in prison."

He winces. "Lincoln and I are working through our issues, and it doesn't concern you. You can't compare prison to death."

"Do you really ..." My voice trails off momentarily. "Do you honestly think *I* killed him?"

He works his strong jaw before replying, "Did you push him into the pool or hold his head underwater? No. But your actions resulted in his death. I'll never go back on that, go back on the truth."

"Wow." I shake my head, planting my palms on the table. "Coming here was a mistake."

He nods in agreement. "You didn't come here to make amends. You came to argue, to vent out your frustrations since his anniversary was a few days ago."

I stand. "Go fuck yourself. Don't call me. Don't speak to me again."

"Archer—"

I turn around and leave.

# CHAPTER THIRTY-FOUR

# Georgia

"I DON'T CARE what anyone says, no one serves margaritas and queso like La Mesa," I say, shoving a chip dripping with queso into my mouth.

"I swear, you'd think I raised you in a barn," Cohen comments from across the table, eyeing me from over his menu and shaking his head.

Noah stares up at him, blinking. "You raised Aunt Georgia in a barn?" He frowns. "Why can't we live in a barn? I love barns because that's where they have horses!" He shakes his chip in the air, shoves it in the queso bowl, and tosses it in his mouth.

Like aunt, like nephew.

Cohen didn't raise no queso haters.

The older Noah gets, the more he reminds me of Cohen. His chestnut-colored hair has grown out and is spiked up with gel, and he's sporting his *Single & Unemployed* shirt—a gift from me. He has the sweetest smile, which cons me out of cupcakes like crazy. Every time I babysit, the kid needs his cupcakes. To which I gladly oblige.

"Oh shit, look who showed up," Finn calls out.

"Language," Grace warns in her teacher voice, jerking her head toward Noah.

"Archer!" Noah shouts, throwing up his arms and swinging them in the air.

At his name, I glance up and train my eyes on Archer and Lincoln approaching us. My mouth waters for more than a margarita. The Callahan men are a sight for sore eyes.

Archer's broad shoulders are covered by a black tee and his hair pulled back into a loose man bun. The man bun isn't a frequent style for him, and I never thought I'd be attracted to them before Archer came along.

Archer has switched up my type.

Shitty attitude.

Allergic to fun.

Plays mind games.

Scruff and man bun.

I scrunch up my face.

He's been a total fuckboy, but after our night at Bailey's, I've grown more understanding of him. It's not an excuse for his behavior, but I know where his pain comes from now.

"How the hell did you convince him to come?" Finn asks, resulting in a playful elbow nudge from Grace. "He's turned us down for Taco Tuesday for years."

Lincoln chuckles, rubbing his hand over his strong jaw. "I told him it was either we come here or I was inviting you over to his place."

"Suckered," Grace says, laughing.

Today is my first time seeing Archer since the night at Bailey's. He texted me an hour after I left, thanking me for taking care of him, and I texted him the next morning to check on him. Neither one of us mentioned the whole *dry-humping in the car* event.

It all finally makes sense.

Why Archer is the way he is and why his family claims he hasn't always been this way. I can't imagine the pain he had when it happened, the guilt he lives with day after day. It makes me want him more, makes me want to help heal him.

That night, when I slid into bed, all I thought about was his mouth on mine. The taste of his tongue. His hands on me. His secrets he'd given to me.

Surprising everyone, Archer takes the chair next to mine. He smiles and doesn't seem fazed that everyone is eyeing him as though he's lost his mind.

"I think motherfucking hell has frozen over but granted me with tacos for some good deeds I did," Finn says.

Grace slaps his shoulder. "Really?"

"Nah," Silas says. "Last I heard, they don't serve tacos in hell."

"Can you guys please stop cussing in front of my kid?" Cohen says in his best dad voice.

"It's okay," Noah says. "I know cuss words, like *shit* and *fu*—"

Jamie cups her hand around his mouth. "Enough of that talk."

"Jamie," Lola gasps. "What are you teaching him?"

Cohen drags his finger down the table, motioning to us. "It's all of you that have no filter."

They start arguing about what words Noah learned where—most of them probably coming from me—and I stare over at Archer.

"How have you been?" I ask, keeping my voice down.

He bows his head, his tone just as low. "Better. Not good, but better."

I offer a small smile. "I'm glad."

"Thank you for being there for me, Georgia." He shuts his eyes and blows out a breath. "My night would've ended a lot worse had you not hunted me down and stayed with me."

"You're finally realizing that no matter what, you can't get rid of me?"

He chuckles. "This is easier, you know. We went about it all wrong."

"What's easier?"

"Us not pretending to hate each other."

"It is, isn't it?"

He gestures to the table. "So this is Taco Tuesday, huh?"

"See what you've been missing?"

He laughs—something I've rarely heard from him. It's deep and husky and manly, and it shoots straight into my soul.

When I glance away from him, I notice everyone's attention is pinned in our direction, even Noah's. Our friends know *something* happened between us, but the only ones who know the full story are Grace and Lola. I doubt Archer is telling people he ditched me that morning. Lola says Silas pressed her for details, but she wouldn't budge. Then Silas brought his interrogation to me, which I ignored. He didn't even bother taking it to Archer.

"Carry on," Archer says, and they return to their different tasks—dipping chips into salsa, studying the menu, grabbing their phones—pretending we're not their chosen entertainment.

As much as I want to ask him a hundred questions about our night at Bailey's, I hold back. This isn't the place for that convo.

"How annoying was Lincoln to get you here?"

"On a scale from one to ten, a good fifteen."

I smile. "I like your brother. He's good for you."

"I'm glad he's home." He opens the menu. "What do you suggest?"

"Uh …" I chew on my bottom lip. "The margaritas are to die for."

"Not much of a margarita man."

My hand dramatically flies to my chest. "Have you ever had a margarita?"

He doesn't answer.

"Shut up." I slap his arm. "You've never had one, have you?"

"Again, do I look like a margarita man?" He gestures to himself.

"You are tonight." I call over our waiter. "Top-shelf margarita for my man over here."

"Nah, I'm good," Archer argues.

"He's good to order one." I smile at the waiter. "Make that two. One for him. One for me."

"Look at Georgia, bossing Archer around like she's his babysitter," Silas says. "I never thought I'd see the day."

"Aunt Georgia is the best babysitter ever!" Noah chimes in. "She buys me extra cupcakes and lets me have sugar in my Cheerios."

Cohen narrows his eyes at me.

I shrug, ignoring Cohen's dirty look. "They don't make it sweet enough."

The waiter drops off our margaritas, and I wait for Archer to take a drink before touching mine. It's almost comical, watching him tip his head down and suck the margarita goodness from the straw.

He swallows it, his face puckering. "Sweet as hell, but not too bad."

I smile. "Don't lie. You love it."

He chuckles.

I laugh.

And I wish we'd had this all along.

***

"YOU KNOW he's in love with you, right?" Lincoln says, stealing Archer's chair after he leaves for a restroom break.

"What?"

*Did he say that, or were the margs stronger than what I thought?*

He jerks his head in the direction Archer headed. "My brother. He's in love with you."

I snort. "Yeah, right."

He leans back in his chair, tents his hands together, and holds them to his mouth. "Archer Callahan is here for Taco Tuesday. You think that's the norm for him?"

"Well, no," I answer softly, chewing on my bottom lip. "You told him it was either come here or there'd be a party at his place. It's no surprise he chose here."

Archer has feelings for me; there's no denying that.

But *love?*

That's on a completely different level.

That's on *my* level.

He chuckles. "Come on. You know Archer would kick each one of you out if he didn't want you there. He's here because he thought I'd flirt and then fall in love with you too. He's pissed I call you babe."

I'm silent, processing Lincoln's claim.

Lincoln squeezes my shoulder. "Give him time, Georgia. He's opening up to you. Hell, he talked to you about our grandfather's death—something he hasn't done with me, my parents, or his ex. You're someone to him, and the closer you two grow, the clearer it gets."

---

I'M IN BED, tossing peanut M&M's in my mouth and catching up on *Schitt's Creek* when my phone vibrates. Setting my snack to the side, I stretch across my bed and snatch my phone off my nightstand.

**Lincoln: Can you do me a favor?**

*Weird.* Lincoln never randomly texts me.

**Me: Depends on what it is. No, I won't have your baby. Yes, I will let you buy me a new car.**

**Lincoln: I know it's late, but can you go to the bar?**

No smart-ass response. Not good.

**Me: Okay …**

**Lincoln: Go see Archer there. It's important. I'll explain later.**

**Me: Give me 15.**

**Lincoln: Thank you.**

I jump out of bed, slip on my shoes, and snatch my M&M's container for the road. Lincoln's text caught me off guard, and my stomach knots harder with every mile I get closer to the bar.

I swerve into the back parking lot, scurry to the door, and let myself in. The bar is silent—no shocker since we're closed—and I stroll down the unlit hall. When I reach Archer's office, the light is on, and the door is cracked open.

I knock.

No answer.

Holding my breath, I peek through the opening. Archer's shoulders are hunched forward in his chair, and his head is in his hands.

"Archer, are you okay?" I ask, hesitating before tiptoeing into his office.

I gasp when he lifts his head.

His face is red.

Tearstained.

"Archer," I repeat, "are you okay?"

I've seen this man resentful—the night his father went to prison.

I've seen him sad—the anniversary of his grandfather's death.

But this is different.

This is broken.

I creep closer.

"My dad is dead," he states with a restrained stare.

I halt. "What?"

"He had a heart attack. He's dead."

I tense, my hand clutching my chest. "Oh my God. I'm so sorry."

His chest rises and falls with rapid breaths. "I visited him for the first time in prison last week. It didn't go well. The entire time he was locked up, I ignored his calls. We hated each other." He slams his hand onto his desk. "He died in prison. We'd argued, and I'd told him to go fuck himself." He bitterly scoffs.

"I argue with someone, and then they die. I'm the goddamn angel of death."

He keeps his vacant stare forward when I stand next to him.

"Archer," I whisper, "that's not true."

"Appreciate you trying to make me feel better, but it is."

"Look at me."

He spins in his chair, and his gaze cuts to me before he rises. I gasp when his lips crash into mine—hard and needy and desperate. He slips an arm around my waist, yanking my body to his, and his tongue slips into my mouth. I taste him while he devours my mouth—the flavor of his booze drawing me in. Picking me up, he steadies me on the edge of the desk, my ass slightly slipping off. He parts my legs and settles his large body between them.

"I need you," he groans into my mouth. "I need to be inside you."

Reaching down, he roughly tugs at the drawstring of my sweats, and just as he's shoving his hand down them, I push him back.

"No. I refuse to be your distraction or how you cope with your loss." I shake my head. "You're not releasing your pain by screwing me."

"Let me eat your pussy then," he pleads. "Let me suck on your clit. *Please.*"

It's tempting.

There's nothing I'd love more than his hands, his tongue, getting me off.

He retreats a step when I slide off the desk and tie my sweats.

"I'll be here for you, but I'm not sleeping with you." I hold out my hand. "I'll drive you home."

"Nah, I'm sleeping here."

"You're not sleeping here." I snap my fingers. "Let's go, or I'll call Lincoln to come get you."

*Speaking of Lincoln ...*

*How's he doing?*

He captures my hand, his grip tight as though I'm his lifeline. Not a word is spoken while I lead him out of the building, lock up, and we walk to my car. I assist him into it, but he moves my hand when I try to buckle the seat belt and clicks it himself.

"Have you talked to Lincoln?" I ask, turning out of the parking lot.

"He's with my mother."

"Do you want me to take you there?"

He shakes his head. "She asked to be alone. I asked to be alone. Lincoln understood my request but was worried about Mom, so he's there with her."

He scrubs at his eyes with his knuckles and tips his head back, not muttering a word during the drive.

When I reach his building, he shifts and settles his gaze on me, torment in his eyes. "Will you stay?"

My eyes widen, and I shake my head.

"Not for sex. To keep me company, so I don't lose my goddamn mind."

"I thought you wanted to be alone?"

"It's different with you. I like to be alone or *with you*. You put me at ease, giving me a peace I've never experienced." He reaches out and strokes my face with the pad of his thumb. "Stay."

"I told you—"

"I'll sleep on the couch; you can have my bed. Just stay with me." Silent tears fall down his cheeks.

"Okay, I'll stay."

His shoulders relax, and after parking, we walk into his building. Swinging his arm back, he snatches my hand and leads me to the penthouse.

I drop his hand when we walk in. "I need to text Lincoln and let him know you're okay."

He nods, kisses my forehead, and heads into the kitchen.

*Me: He's home, safe and sound. I'm so sorry about your dad.*

*Lincoln: Mom popped an Ambien and is sleeping. I can come home.*

I join Archer in the kitchen and read him the text message.

"Tell Lincoln to stay his ass there."

I follow him into the living room, and he collapses on the couch as I'm replying to Lincoln.

*Me: He said to stay your ass there.*

*Lincoln: Not surprising.*

*Me: I told him I'd stay.*

*Lincoln: You're amazing. Thank you, Georgia ... for everything.*

My next text goes to Cohen. I tell him the news and ask him to cover Archer's shift tomorrow night. Archer might not like it, but he needs time to heal.

Sex, working too much, locking up your pain—it will only last so long. Archer has reached his breaking point.

"Can I get you something to drink?" I ask.

"Shit, sit down, Georgia." He shakes his head and rubs at his eyes with the heels of his palms. "Here we are again, you coming to my rescue when it should be the other way around." His voice cracks. "Do you see it now? Why you're too good for me?"

I settle in the space next to him. "Archer, everyone has their issues. Right now, yours are more intense than mine, but I'm sure, somewhere along the road, I'll need you too."

His stares at me vacantly. "Lincoln is crashing in the guest room, so you can have my bed."

"Okay," I whisper, not pushing.

Now isn't the time for relationship talk. He needs time to grieve. Despite his relationship with his father, he's hurting. His wet eyes, broken voice, and desperation are clear.

He stands and jerks his head toward a hall. "I'll show you where it is."

Not that I need the tour.

I've been here before—in this home, in his bedroom, in his bed. The massive bed has a new duvet cover, going from white to black, but everything else is the same.

"Do you need something to sleep in?"

I shake my head. "No, this is fine."

He awkwardly stands in the doorway, his face slack. "Watch a movie with me? Hang out for a minute? Stay with me longer."

I nod and walk out of the bedroom. He rests his hand along my back as we return to the living room. As soon as I sit on the couch, he's dragging me into his arms.

"My last words to him were *fuck off* and *don't speak to me again*," he whispers into my ear, settling my back to his chest.

I reach up, gripping the back of his neck before massaging it. "You didn't know this would happen. You were angry and thought you would have time to make it right, to cool off."

"Did I, though?" He relaxes into my touch. "I told him never to talk to me again, and now, he's gone."

My chest trembles as the man behind me struggles to hold in his hurt, his body shaking behind me—shaking my heart into despair because he's experiencing this pain, this hurt, and just like with this grandfather, he's depositing blame onto his shoulders.

We don't watch TV. I stay with him.

Our breathing is the only noise until he says, "I'm sorry … for everything I've put you through." He squeezes me tight, as if pushing his apology so far into me that he can never take it back. "Now, I know the power of my words, and I'll never do anything to hurt another person I care about."

I drop my hand and rest it over his arm on my stomach. As I stay tucked in his hold, we drift to sleep. I yawn, my eyes sleepy, when he wakes me hours later and carries me to his bed.

---

IT'S ROUND TWO.

Round two of waking up in his bed.

My stomach twists at the reminder of why I'm in his bed, my heart aching for him all over again. I shift when I hear a light snore and find Archer asleep next to me. He's over the covers—as if he wanted to keep distance between us—on his back, and fully dressed.

Our second time in his bed.

Our first morning waking up together.

What he did that morning was inexcusable, but as time passes, my forgiveness for him deepens. It could be the optimist in me, my big heart that seems unwilling to yield to hard resentment.

I shut my eyes, casting my thoughts to his anguish and apologies last night. Kissing two fingers, I press them to his cheek, hoping I don't wake him, and I slide out of bed. Yawning, I stroll to the bathroom, use my finger to brush my teeth, and throw my hair into an even messier bun than I did last night.

As I pass him, it hits me that he'll wake up the same as I did that morning. The only difference is, he'll still be in the house, and I'm too exhausted to go hunting for doughnuts. I pad into the kitchen and realize I'll need to go coffee-hunting since Archer has none. As I grab a water and search the cabinets for breakfast food, the door clicks open.

"Oh, hey, Georgia," Lincoln says, walking in with heavy eyes and a face that screams exhaustion.

I smile gently. "Hi."

He glances around. "He still sleeping?"

I nod. "I think he needs it."

"Agreed." He holds up his phone. "I'm ordering coffee. Want some?"

"I thought you'd never ask."

He walks into the living room. I recite my order to him, keeping my voice as low as I can, and he punches it into his phone.

"How are you doing?" I ask, hugging him, my heart breaking for their family. "How's your mom?"

"Not well." He pulls back. "She lost my father to prison, and now, he's gone for good. My grandparents are with her now, so I could run here for a change of clothes and to check on Archer."

"If there's anything I can do to help, I'm here."

"You're too good to us."

"You're my friends, and friends take care of their friends."

"I'm glad you're in his life. You're one of the best things to happen to him."

"Archer?" I ask even though I already know the answer.

He nods. "When he told everyone to leave him alone last night, I knew he meant everyone *but you*. When our grandfather died and his girlfriend tried to comfort him, he only pushed her away. They had been together for years, and he never let her in like he does you—never let *any of us* in."

I swallow a few times before replying, "People say I'm easy to talk to. It's what I want to do for a living—talk to people and help them through their struggles."

"Georgia, the best psychiatrist in the world couldn't get Archer to do the shit you do. It's not that."

Our conversation is interrupted by Archer coming into view, rubbing at his eyes and looking like he'd been run over, then stomped on, and then run over again.

Lincoln envelops Archer in his arms, giving him a tight hug. Archer squeezes him back, patting his back a few times before pulling away. Their eyes are red, their emotions showing through their usual hard, masculine demeanors.

The doorbell rings, and I answer it, grabbing our coffees.

Lincoln wipes his eyes with the back of his arm before taking his coffee and looking at Archer. "I'm heading back to Mom's."

"How's she doing?" Archer asks.

"Handling. We're trying to keep her mind off it. One good thing that came out of this prison mess is, she's not living in the same house as she did with Dad, where she would have been surrounded by memories of them."

He nods in agreement.

Lincoln packs his bag, tells us good-bye, and leaves.

Archer's attention moves to me.

"Coffee?" I ask, holding mine up. "I can share mine with you, but it's on the sweet side. If you don't mind waiting, I can order you something and have it delivered."

He yawns and shakes his head, now wearing shorts and a tee. "I'm good right now." He yawns again.

We maybe slept for three hours, max.

"You might need to go back to bed," I say when he yawns for the third time.

Another yawn, this one longer.

"You might be right." He tips his head toward his bedroom. "You want to stay? You look like you need sleep as much as I do."

Since yawns are contagious, I do it twice. "Maybe a few more hours would be good for us."

I follow him into his bedroom.

"I know I said I'd sleep on the couch last night," he says, slipping under the blankets. "And forgive me, but when we crashed out on the couch, I knew we'd be more comfortable in here. I never touched you since you told me no last night, so you have nothing to worry about."

"It's fine," I say, joining him but keeping plenty of space between us.

In minutes, his breathing turns heavy, and he's back to sleep.

---

ROUND THREE OF waking up in Archer's bed.

I shut my eyes.

*What'll it be this time?*

I shift from my back to my side, facing him, and my heart

beats wildly when my gaze meets his. There's no shock on his face, no disdain. I blink, my brain playing a guessing game of what's in that unpredictable mind of his.

He's flawed perfection as he returns my stare—his eyes hooded, his face unreadable.

I clear the sleepiness from my throat. "How long have you been staring?"

"Not long." He grimaces, as if struck with a sudden pain. "I fucked up."

I tense, doubt charging through me.

*Round three is about to get messy.*

I slip him a guarded look. "What?"

"I fucked up." His teeth clamps on his lower lip. "This is how we should've woken up that morning, not you in here, alone."

The rejection I expected escapes my thoughts. I'll never forget what he did our first morning, and there will always be a twinge to my heart at the memory, but I'm starting to grasp his reasoning.

"You look perfect here," he says. "Like it's where you belong."

"I feel like this is where I belong," I reply honestly. "It's where I've always wanted to be."

*With you.*

*In your bed.*

*In your heart.*

The bed shifts when he eases closer, and a comfortable warmth fills the air.

"How can you be like this?" he rasps.

"Be like what?"

"So good to me when I've been nothing but a dick to you."

"There's more to you than your anger. You hide behind your pain."

"Not so much with you though, do I?"

Chills spread across my skin when he reaches out to stroke my cheek.

"You're too good to me and too good *for* me."

I tilt my head to the side, into his touch. "That's my decision to make."

His hand drops to my neck, and he captures the necklace he gave me, playing with the charms between two fingers. "I love seeing this on you."

I enfold his hand in mine. "Someone who didn't care, who I was *too good for*, would've never gifted something so meaningful."

He shuts his eyes, and his voice thickens when he drops the necklace. "Georgia, do you still want me?"

My breath catches in my throat, and I repeat his question in my head, as if I misheard him. My heart skitters before battering against my chest.

He stares at me with intent.

Desire radiates between us.

Longing whispers in the air.

His breathing labors as I creep closer, the sheets soft against my skin, until we're inches apart. His breath is chilly against my cheek.

"Always," I answer before brushing my lips against his.

He groans into my mouth.

Our kiss starts slow.

Gentle.

His tongue darts into my mouth.

His heavy hand cups my face as we make out like teenagers, him devouring me.

Everything changes when I grind against him. Long gone is the light kissing, now replaced with an urgency.

"Shit," he hisses into my mouth, wrapping his arm around my waist to tug me close.

Another groan escapes him when I hitch my leg over his waist, and all hell breaks loose. The spark has been lit, and the fire is starting. I'm rolled onto my back, and he climbs over me, our mouths staying connected. I part my legs, giving him access to everything I wish he'd take as his—*make* his. I gasp for breath when he pulls away and stares at me with lust-filled eyes.

"Last night, you said you didn't want to be used to heal my pain, which I understood," he says. "That's not what today is—hell, it wasn't even what last night was. I want you, Georgia—not just intimately—and if you want me to stop, say the word."

"Don't you dare stop." I raise my hips and rub against him.

He groans, throwing his head back, while his hand tugs at the drawstring on my pants. I lift my butt, allowing him to slip them and my panties off me. After he tosses them onto the floor, his eyes flick to me in question, and I nod. Sliding down the bed, he parts my thighs with no hesitation and settles his body between them. His eyes stray, peeking between my legs, and I've never felt so exposed in my life.

Yet I don't feel shy.

My legs are shaking as he sweeps his hands along the inside of my thighs.

"Georgia," he says, staring up at me, "let me make up for the time I should've been doing this, should've been pleasuring you, loving you, showing you how much you mean to me. Let me make up for my stupidity."

I gulp, nodding, and he grips my legs, holding them still. Without wasting a second, he slides the length of his tongue between my folds. My back arches toward the ceiling, and his delivery isn't what I anticipated.

I've had guys go down on me before, but it was nothing like this.

Archer sucks on my clit, shoving two fingers inside me, and I squirm beneath him. He raises my shirt and shoves his hand underneath the cup of my bra, exposing my nipple.

"Please," I beg as he pinches it before squeezing my breast.

I want this to last the rest of my life, but with his fingers and his tongue and *him*, there's no hope for me. When he adds a third finger, I fall apart.

"Yes, come for me, baby," he groans against my core.

I'm still coming down from my high when he lifts himself, his palms slapping on the bed on each side of my body, and claims my mouth.

"See how good you taste?" he hisses between my lips. "I've missed this taste. Have been craving it since our first night together."

Heat rips through my body, begging for another orgasm, and I moan when he peels off my shirt, tossing it across the room. His hand moves to my back, lifting me to unhook my bra. I'm exposed to him, every inch of my body on display.

"Archer," I pant, "I need you inside me."

He stops to shake his head, his eyes meeting mine. "This is for you to feel good. Not me. I don't deserve you yet."

"Your cock inside me will feel good."

He freezes.

I whistle and point at the apex of my thighs. "Your cock, inside me now."

He smirks. "Give me another orgasm, and I'll think about it."

I throw my arms out. "Orgasm me away then."

He chuckles before whispering, "You're beautiful," and runs his hands up and down my thighs. "Perfection," he adds.

And I lose all thoughts as he rains kisses down my body, worshipping every inch of me.

His tongue licks me up and down.

He teases my clit.

I've never been so turned on.

Never wanted someone so desperately in my life.

My need for him is stronger than our first night together.

"Archer," I moan, "please fuck me."

"Say it again," he demands, his voice hoarse.

I tilt my head, all orgasmed/confused out. "Please fuck me?"

"No, my name, say it again."

"Archer."

His name falling from my lips while I'm naked in his bed sets him on fire.

He falls back, shrugs off his tee, and shoves down his shorts, exposing his thick cock. My eyes widen and dart to my parted thighs.

He chuckles. "It'll fit. I promise." Without warning, he shoves two fingers inside me, twisting them. "You're so wet for me, baby. I'll slide right in."

He glides off the bed, kicks off his shorts, opens his nightstand, and grabs a condom. Ripping it open with his teeth, he slides it over his throbbing cock and rejoins me. I gape in anticipation when his heavy body hovers over mine.

He fastens his hands around my wrists, pulls my arms over my head, and tugs them together. "I'm going to take care of you, baby." His lips brush over mine. "Show you that my bullshit will be worth it in the end. Leave these here."

He drops his hands from my wrists and tilts up my waist, and when he slides into me, it's heaven.

Perfection.

Worth the wait.

He wastes no time before pounding into me, and I meet him thrust for thrust, moaning his name. We're sweaty and sticky, and my legs ache.

I'm close to reaching my brink for the third time when he groans, "You feel so damn good. No pussy, no woman, has ever been better, has ever taken my cock better, fucked me better, shown me love better."

His words set me off.

Pleasure shatters through me, and a few pumps later, he shoots his load into the condom.

# CHAPTER THIRTY-FIVE

# Archer

"I HATE that you have to go," I groan.

Now that I have her, I want to keep her.

In my bed. In my arms. In my life.

"Trust me"—she peeks over at me, shyness in her eyes—"I'd love for us to stay in bed and forget everything, but we can't." She turns onto her stomach and rests her chin on my chest. "You need to go see your mom."

"Thank you," I whisper. "For being there for me."

She plants a quick peck to my chest. "Thank you for opening up to me, showing me the real you, letting me in, *and* for all the orgasms."

*That's Georgia.*

Thanking me for showing her the real me—that's all she wants from me.

Oh, and the orgasms.

Coming from my world, that's irregular.

Meredith came with a long list of wants, and her thank-yous came after she received Chanel bags, trips abroad, diamonds.

All it takes for Georgia is a goddamn apology and explanation of why you acted like an idiot.

"It took you long enough to realize this," she adds.

"Yeah, yeah, yeah," I grumble. "We can't all be Georgias."

"The world would be a better place, though." She winks.

"And we'd have more terrible drivers on the street."

I run my hand down her bare back. Waking up next to her this morning was what I'd never known I needed. As I stared at her sleeping, it hit me.

She's changing me.

This spitfire of a woman makes me want to be a better man.

The man my grandfather, my father, wished I were.

It's too late to prove it to them, but I'll prove it to myself.

To Georgia.

To my family.

To my friends.

The first time I slept with Georgia, it was lust.

The anniversary of my grandfather's death, I was falling in love with her.

Now, I'm positive, no doubt in my mind, that I'm in love with this woman more than I've ever loved anyone, more than I love myself.

This broken life led me to her, to a woman who accepts every damn chipped piece of me—imperfections, flaws, despairs. All of them.

I slam my eyes shut and hold in a breath. When I leave this bed, it'll be time to face reality. Earlier, in bed and inside Georgia, my worries faded away, all my thoughts consumed by her.

Us together, making love, owning each other.

She rises, taking our sheet with her, and starts hunting down her clothes, leaving me exposed to all my glory. Good thing she brought the sheet with her because I'm getting hard by the scene in front of me. If she were nude while bending over to grab her panties, we wouldn't be leaving this room for another hour.

She turns around and smirks. "Quit staring. You need to get going."

"Join me in the shower?" I raise a brow.

"Nope." She snaps her fingers and points at the bathroom. "Quick shower and then to your mom's. I know you're not looking forward to it, but she needs you."

I nod. "I know, and I want to be there for her. It's just hard for me … expressing myself."

"No one is asking you to wear your heart on your sleeve. Sometimes, all you need to do is wrap someone in a hug and let them know you care."

I stand as she pulls her sweats on and wrap my arms around her waist. "Will you come back tonight?"

She frowns. "I wish I could, but I told Grace I'd sleep at home tonight, *but* you can stay at my place."

I brush her messy hair away from her face and kiss her. "I might take you up on that offer."

---

BETTI, my mother's housekeeper, gives me a quick hug with tears in her eyes, when I walk into the house. "Your father might've made some mistakes, but deep down, he was a good man."

I stiffen, wondering if she's mistaken me for the wrong brother. Yes, I'm always nice to Betti. She makes the most bomb-ass grilled cheese sandwiches, but I'm not the friendly Callahan brother. Lincoln is the hugger. I'm the avoider.

Lincoln is waiting for me in the foyer, his eyes tired, holding an energy drink in his hand. "You and Georgia, huh? Can we talk about how cute you two look?"

I glare at him. "Swear to God, if you say *how cute you two look* again, I'm smacking you."

He slaps my back, yawns, and chugs the drink. "Don't worry; I'll let you off the hook for now, but I'd bet the fifty dollars the Feds left in my bank account that you'll have a girlfriend soon."

Ignoring him, I glance around the foyer. "Where's Mom?"

"Showering, but she'll be down any minute."

I follow him through the formal dining room, taking in the table blanketed with bouquets, cakes, cookies, pies—all the *sorry for your loss* shit people send. He strolls into the kitchen, opens the fridge for another energy drink, and offers me one. I shake my head and reach around him, grabbing a Coke.

"Does she know I'm coming?" I ask, opening the can.

He nods, and we head back to the foyer.

"How's she doing?"

"Better than I thought she would, but she's Mom. She can smile to our faces and then break down when she gets to her bedroom."

I nod in agreement.

Us Callahans can't stand showing our emotions.

After kissing Georgia good-bye, I showered, dressed, and drove to my mother's, nausea growing in my stomach with every passing mile. My mother is one of the strongest women I know, but she has her slipups. She slipped when my father was sentenced to prison, and that's nothing compared to death.

I hear her heels tapping against the handmade Italian tiles before she comes into view. On the surface, she's not displaying one sign of a grieving widow. Her white pantsuit and heels are all a front.

*I see who I get it from, Mom.*

Like Lincoln said, the world won't see Josephine Callahan break down—only us.

I take long strides in her direction and wrap my arms around her. She stiffens before relaxing into my hold and shoving her face into my shoulder, breaking loose, that emotional wall she put up crumbling.

Georgia's words ring through my mind. *"Sometimes, all you need to do is wrap someone in a hug and let them know you care."*

All along, who would've thought that holding my mother tight was all she needed to let her guard down? Georgia did it for me. I'm doing it for her.

Mascara runs down her face when she pulls away, and she stares up at me in shock, as if I'm a different person, a different son.

"My Archer," is all she says before cupping both hands around one of mine, raising it to her lips, and kissing it. "My Archer is coming back to me."

---

IT'S after midnight when I get into my car to leave my mom's house.

Lincoln and I spent the evening with her, and it was one of the strangest nights of my life.

Growing up, we hadn't spent much time with our parents. They were off doing their black-tie parties and traveling with their country-club friends. Lincoln and I were off blowing their money on partying and drugs. We had been too busy for family time.

We convinced her to eat pizza we'd ordered from the local joint in the city, and from the look on her face, you would've thought we'd asked her to give up her Louboutin collection.

We'd never ordered pizza when we were younger. Ours had been made by our chef with premium, organic, no-bullshit, no-fun, no-greasiness ingredients.

Tonight, she ate three slices before admitting she *sort of* liked it.

Us stubborn Callahans.

After gorging ourselves with pizza, we spent the next four hours in the theater, watching chick flicks she'd selected. They were lame as hell, but as I watched, they reminded me of shit Georgia would like. I sent her a picture of the screen during one movie, and she replied with laughing emojis that it was in her top ten favorites.

We texted throughout the day. Her asking how we were doing, me asking about her day. As I sat there, half-paying attention to the movie, I wondered where we'd go from here.

*Will we start dating?*

*Does she want to date me?*

My eyes are heavy when I drag my phone from my pocket and text her.

**Me: I'm leaving my mom's now. I know it's late, and I don't want to wake you in case you're sleeping.**

I don't want to be a dick and wake her, but I also don't want to be a dick and make her think I've forgotten about her or that I wasn't serious about everything that I said today.

I was serious about every word.

The only times I'd lied to her was when I said I didn't have feelings for her. It was easier to lie than reveal my truth—that I was falling hard for her every single damn second of the day.

The night of my father's death, it hit me. I said cruel words to him, thinking we'd talk again.

The same with my grandfather.

There was a chance that could happen with Georgia. I could lie to her face and make her feel unwanted by me and then possibly never see her again.

It had been a reality check for me.

No more hiding my feelings.

She needs to know every emotion running through my body for her.

My phone rings, and her name flashes across the screen.

I smile.

My lips are probably shocked as fuck since smiling is a rarity for me.

"Hi," I answer.

"Hey," she says around a yawn.

"I woke you up."

"Nope."

"You lying?"

"Yep." She yawns again. "How'd everything go?"

"As good as it could have, I guess." I relax in my seat and massage my forehead, the pain of losing my father hitting me. "We tried distracting her, but the doorbell constantly ringing with sympathy gifts didn't help."

"Poor thing. That has to be hard on her heart."

"She's struggling but working through it well. It helps that Lincoln is here too. Had he still been locked up, it would've been harder on her ... on both of them since he couldn't have been here for her or attended our father's funeral."

"I'm glad he's back for you and your mom. You make a good team."

"Me too." I rub at the tension at the back of my neck. "Is the offer to come over still open?"

I don't want to go back to an empty house, and Lincoln is staying with our mom for the next few days.

"Always," she answers with no hesitation.

———

GEORGIA PRESSES her finger to her soft lips when she answers the door before waving me inside.

I texted her a few minutes ago, letting her know I was here, so I wouldn't wake up Grace by ringing the doorbell. As soon as I walk in, I envelop Georgia in my arms, holding her tight. When we pull apart, she grabs my hand and walks me through the dark hallway to her bedroom. The only light comes from a lamp on her nightstand, and her bed is in disarray.

When she turns to face me, my mouth waters as I eye her up and down, taking in her short-shorts that show off her tanned, sleek legs and an oversize tee that I'd guess was once Cohen's.

At least that's my hope and that it's not some other dude's.

I pull at the bottom of the shirt. "Where'd you get this from?"

She peeks up at me. "Cohen, I think?"

"You think?"

She shrugs. "My brain is too tired to remember."

And I'm too tired to stress the question for answers.

Her eyes fix on me as I strip out of my jeans and tee, leaving on only my boxer briefs. I wait for her to get into bed before sliding in after her.

When I stretch out, half my body is off the bed. "Remind me to buy you a larger bed."

"Hey!" She smacks my arm. "What's wrong with my bed?"

"Baby, have you seen the size of me?"

She bites into her lip. "I have definitely seen the size of you."

I shake my head. "What am I going to do with you?"

"Anything." She yawns loudly, causing me to do the same. "But make that anything in the morning because I can't keep my eyes open."

I kiss her lips, then her nose, and then her cheek before whispering, "Good night."

She curls against me, her back relaxing against my chest, and her legs tangle between mine. Draping my arm over her waist, I make myself comfortable and spoon with someone for the first time in my life.

---

I WAKE UP, half my body dangling off the side of Georgia's bed, and her leg is hitched over my waist.

Her T-shirt rises, exposing the bottom curves of her breast, and my mouth waters.

*She's finally mine.*

Finally, I got my head out of my ass and did the right thing.

I stopped hurting her.

Stopped holding myself back from happiness.

Georgia is the best thing that's ever happened to me.

Through all my sadness, all my bullshit, and my grief, she's been by my side, no matter what.

I sweep my gaze down her body and glare at the tee, remembering no one knows where the hell it came from.

It needs to come off, just in case it didn't come from Cohen.

Thrown in the trash.

Burned.

She stirs when I grip the bottom of the shirt and drag it up.

"You said you don't remember where you got this shirt?"

She stares up at me with tired eyes, taking a moment to process my words.

"Off it goes."

She nudges herself up onto her elbow, assisting me in whipping it over her head, and I throw it across the room.

"This is a better view anyway," I say, rolling her onto her back and hovering over her on all fours.

"That's my favorite nightshirt." She pouts.

I bow my head to nuzzle my nose against hers. "You can raid my closet for a new favorite."

She gasps when I slip my hand between her legs, slide her panties to the side, and plunge two fingers inside her.

"Or just don't wear one at all."

To see all of her, I flip the blanket off us and slide her boy shorts down. I groan, crawling down her body, parting her legs, and lick her clit, swirling my tongue around it before sucking on it hard. She moans as I tease her.

"More," she begs.

"More of what, baby?"

"You. Your tongue. Fingers. Mouth. Cock. Whatever you have for me, I want more of it."

"More of this?"

She gasps when I add a finger inside her without warning.

"Yes, please. Definitely more of that."

Her back arches as I finger her pussy and suck on her clit, loving the sounds of her whimpers.

"Do you want my tongue?"

She spreads her legs wider.

"Answer me," I grind out, pulling my shorts down and releasing my aching cock, slowly stroking it.

"Please, please, please," she gasps.

Her pleas have me parting her folds and diving into her pussy. I love eating her out—tasting her on my tongue, her thighs squeezing against my face, her writhing underneath me.

All the time, at the bar, when she pranced around, I'd remember how she'd let me taste her once and how she was sweeter than any drink I could make.

"Condom," she rasps, pointing at her nightstand. "First drawer."

I ignore the sinking feeling of her having easy access to condoms, snatch one, and cover my cock with it.

"I love your weight over me," she moans as I thrust inside her.

"Yeah?" I ask, edging up onto my knees, changing the direction of my strokes.

"Yes."

"I love being inside you."

I pound into her, resting her thigh along her shoulder, and when I flip her on all fours, I slam into her, causing her headboard to slam into the wall.

---

GEORGIA AND I EAT BREAKFAST, and we kiss good-bye. I go home, shower, and drive to my mom's.

We have an appointment to plan my father's funeral arrangements.

# CHAPTER THIRTY-SIX

## Georgia

I CAN NAME the number of funerals I've attended on one hand.

Lola and Grace are next to me when we walk into the packed cathedral. Finn, Silas, Jamie, and Cohen are behind us. We weave our way around people in the aisle with polished wooden pews on each side of us. Archer is standing at the apse with his mother and Lincoln, surrounded by people making conversation with them. As if he senses my presence, he glimpses in our direction.

It's an Archer I've never seen before. He stands tall in his black suit, tailored to perfection on his body.

His eyes meet mine, and I shyly wave to him. He whispers something into his mother's ear before kissing her cheek and stalking in our direction. We shuffle to the side, allowing people to pass us. As Archer walks through the crowd, a few people attempt to stop him for conversation, but he brushes past them.

His face is blank.

His guard is up.

No shocker.

He won't show these people what he shows me.

"Thanks for coming, guys," he says when he reaches us. "I really appreciate it."

If this were anyone else—Cohen, Finn, Silas—the girls would've already hugged them, but this is Archer.

A man who isn't a hugger.

Who isn't a talker.

Jaws drop, and a gasp falls when he smooths his lips over mine.

"Holy wow," Jamie says as Archer's attention rests on me.

He grabs my hand in his, draping his free one over our connection, and guides me to where his mother is standing. I hear the guys throwing questions at the girls behind us.

"Grandma, Grandpa," Archer says.

An older couple turns to face us. The man's hair is gray, not one strand of color, and he's wearing a pair of thin gold glasses. Archer's grandmother is the opposite—her hair a dark brown and curled out—and there's a Chanel brooch on her black dress.

Archer squeezes my hand. "This is my girlfriend, Georgia." Another squeeze. "These are my grandparents, Evie and Sanders Eubanks, and you've met my mother."

Sanders gives me a head nod while Evie says, "It's nice to meet you, sweetie."

Archer's mother, whose arm is around Lincoln's, steps closer, and I see a timid smile underneath her mourning veil.

"You too," I say, my hand resting on my chest, hoping I don't look bug-eyed and close to passing out—because that's how I feel. "I'm so sorry for your loss."

I stand at Archer's side as his family talks and people approach us—all of who he introduces me to as his girlfriend. When the service starts, he asks me to sit with him. As I take my seat, I notice the photo of his father atop the closed casket. Archer bears a striking resemblance to him. While Lincoln takes more after his mother, Archer looks more like his father.

I peek back at our friends. Cohen stares at me like I'm in a different world, and Jamie's eyes tell me she'll be questioning me about Archer's kiss later. Just wait until they hear him tell people I'm his girlfriend.

That'll really shock them into next week.

Before the service ends, the priest calls for Lincoln to come up to say a few words. Lincoln stands, and as he walks to the podium, I want to smack the bitches behind me as they whisper about his *prison time.*

I squeeze Archer's hand again, dragging my nails into his skin, and hold myself back.

*Who talks shit at a funeral?*

Lincoln is confident as he gives his father his good-bye. He ignores the whispers as he lays himself bare—telling us how he looked up to his father, the kind of man he was, and how much he'll be missed.

It's heartfelt.

Beautiful.

Brings me and those around me to tears.

Including Archer, who's fighting like hell to hold them back.

SINCE THERE WASN'T room for me in the car and I felt his family could use a good bonding moment, I told Archer I'd ride with Lola and meet him at his grandparents' home, where his father's wake is being held.

The back seat door flies open, and Jamie, who rode to the funeral with Cohen, jumps into Lola's car.

"Whoa, what the …?" Grace says next to her.

Jamie pushes her top half forward to ger her head between Lola in the driver's seat and me in the passenger's, her baby belly not making it easy. "How about you tell us how long you've been keeping you and Archer a secret for?" she says, intrigue on her face.

"It's fresh," I reply. "I didn't want to say anything until everything calmed."

"Apparently, Archer didn't share that sentiment," Lola says with a snort. "He strode right through that church and claimed you as his. It was hot. I know I've talked shit about the guy, which he fully deserved, but Jesus, what did you do to him, Georgia?" Lola starts the engine and follows the procession line of cars pulling onto the road.

Jamie falls back to buckle her seat belt. "She gave him time to open his eyes." She cups her hand over her chest, and a tear slips down her cheek. "It was beautiful."

"That's the pregnancy speaking," Lola says.

"It is," Jamie says. "I think it's sweet, but these damn hormones had me crying over a Cheerios commercial this morning."

Fifteen minutes later, we're pulling up to a gated entrance, where a man wearing a suit is waving cars in.

"This house is gorgeous," Jamie says as I stare at it in awe.

Sure, Archer's penthouse is expensive but nothing like this. His is more subtle, and this castle-appearing home is far from subtle.

We drive around the circular driveway before getting out of the car. Lola drops her keys in the young valet driver's hand, and we walk next to manicured hedges to the front door.

The expansive entryway is flowing with people chatting with finger foods and drinks in their hands. I look around and spot Archer sitting next to Lincoln on a sofa.

He stands when I reach them, tugs me into his arms, and kisses my cheek.

"Your girlfriend, huh?" I ask.

He peers down at me, his brow rising. "Is that not who you are?"

*Fine and dandy with me.*

"Does that mean you're my boyfriend?"

"Is there something else you'd rather me be?"

"I mean …" I bite into the edge of my lip.

"Georgia, if you're all in, I'm all in." He kisses my hand before holding it on his chest over his heart. "I'm done being scared, being an idiot, because who knows how long I'll have to be here with you?"

It's been five days since we spent our first night together, and I haven't slept alone since. He's either in my bed or I'm in his. It's been nice in our own little world. Lincoln knew, of course, along with Grace since she heard me moaning Archer's name. At first, she thought I was taking myself to pleasure town until the headboard started banging. She slipped on some headphones and then texted Lola to deliver the tea on my new relationship.

"I'm all in," I whisper.

"Looks like we're boyfriend and girlfriend then, huh?"

"Looks like it."

*Holy hell, Archer Callahan is my boyfriend.*

---

"FOR ONCE, my son listens to me."

I'm sitting in the gazebo with our friends, surrounded by bright-colored flowers and beautiful shrubs, when Archer's mother settles next to me on the bench. He went on a bathroom-slash-refill trip a few minutes ago.

"Huh?" I ask, glancing over at her.

"My son. I told him to ask you out when we met at the bar. It took him forever, but I'm glad he finally came to his senses."

*He didn't exactly ask me out.*

"Me too."

A few times, the worry of not being good enough for his family, of not being *rich enough* for them, caused me some insecurities. Like when I noticed Meredith as Archer led us to the gazebo. She was chatting with his grandparents, and she looked like she belonged in their world.

Josephine clasps her hand over mine. "Thank you for bringing him back into the light, Georgia. You are the only one who could've taken on a task that large. My son loves you, and thank you for loving him."

# CHAPTER THIRTY-SEVEN

# Archer

AT LEAST I was allowed at his funeral.

I stop myself from that thought, working on not holding that grudge.

I owe my father that.

There's nothing like a good support system. When my friends showed up, reality kicked in with a force. These people cared about me—the dick me, the brooding me, the me who hid. Even the girls, who'd never been my biggest fan after what I did to Georgia, came. All along, I'd thought I was this lonely, isolated bastard, but I was wrong. I had family, friends, a business partner, a woman I loved.

I'm headed back to my friends, Georgia's water refill in one hand and mine in the other, when I'm stopped.

"You've changed."

I shift to face Meredith. "I have."

"You love her, don't you?"

"I do."

She cringes before pulling herself together. "As much as I hate that it wasn't me who brought you back, who makes you happy, I'm glad you found yourself."

"You'll find someone." I stare at her, noticing the differences between a woman I thought I loved and the woman I do love.

Who would've ever thought, instead of this woman with her designer dress and David Yurman diamond cuff, the one who saved my heart would sport pigtail buns and sandals that laced up to her knees on the regular?

She swings her arms in the air. "I had a lovely conversation with your mom, and she thanked me for leaving you."

I arch a brow. "What?"

My mother loved Meredith and was devastated when we broke off our engagement.

"She thanked me for leaving you and said had I not, you would've never started to find happiness, where you belong." She tips her head toward Georgia sitting in the garden. "That girl, she's who you need, and your friends over there, they care about you. I'm jealous." She kisses my cheek before squeezing my hand. "I'm happy for you, *but* if it doesn't work out, you know my number."

*Not happening.*

"Thanks for coming," I say before heading back to where I belong.

---

I TOOK a week off from the bar.

Not by choice.

When Cohen heard the news about my father, he had my shifts covered. As much as I hate being away from the bar, it's given me time to grieve and be with my family—something I steered clear of with all my might before.

I stare at Georgia from across the table of the coffee shop. "You have this weekend off, right?"

Now, there's a happy sense of nostalgia whenever I come here. If possible, I park in the spot where we met and she turned my life upside down.

She shakes her head. "I work Saturday night."

"Can you find someone to cover?"

"Sure." She raises a brow. "What's up?"

"We're scattering my father's ashes at my grandparents' vacation home on Jackson Lake. It's a few hours away. Want to come?"

"Will your family be okay with that?" She plays with the straw in her iced coffee. "I don't want to intrude."

"My mom already asked if you were coming."

*So did my grandparents and Lincoln.*

Her face brightens. "Really?"

If it were anyone else, I'd feel weird asking them to attend something so personal for my family, but I want her there. She's the calm to my storm.

My mother has already mentioned an engagement, wedding, and children with Georgia. Even with the few interactions they've had, Georgia has won her over, like she always does with people. I've accepted my mother's comments and recommendations—though I don't follow through with most of them—because it takes her mind off my father's passing.

I nod. "Really."

"I'll be there."

I lean across the table, grip her chin, and kiss her.

———

LINCOLN SLAPS me on the back. "You good to go, brother?"

I nod. "Good to go."

My mother grips the gold urn in her shaking hands, and there's silence as we make our way out of the house, down the stone steps, and to the dock. This was my grandfather's favorite place and then my father's when they needed a breather from the corporate world. When the Feds began seizing my father's assets, my mother's parents purchased the lake home, so our family wouldn't lose something so cherished.

The last time I was here was when we scattered my grandfather's ashes. That day, I refused to stay away, and my father and I went at separate times to avoid contact. He'd already prevented me from saying good-bye to my grandfather at his funeral, and it wasn't happening again.

Lincoln is next to my mother.

Her parents behind them.

Georgia and me following.

My father didn't have much family.

The Callahans are one cursed bunch.

My grandmother passed when my father was young. When my grandfather remarried, she died a decade later. He gave up on marriage after that. The female companions he had later in life were all decades younger and regularly recycled.

Lincoln and I are the only ones to carry the Callahan name.

My mother sobs as she carefully places the urn on the dock and opens it. My stomach turns as a morbid chill hits me.

*That's all you're reduced to when you die.*

*Ashes or a body in the ground.*

*You live your life, only to have your loved ones stare at your urn and weep.*

Georgia stands at the front edge of the dock to give us space while we take our turns with the urn and then scatter his ashes.

We hang out on the dock for an hour, sharing memories, and then my mom and grandparents leave. Last night, Lincoln had asked if I wanted to stay at the cabin overnight, for old times' sake, so we stay behind.

Now, I'm seated upright against the leather headboard of the bed in my old room.

My mouth waters, my cock stirring, when Georgia circles the bed, wearing one of my baggy tees, and my heart races when she climbs into bed with me. As soon as her knees hit the sheets, I bend forward and pull her onto my lap, and she straddles me.

Caressing her cheek with one hand, I use the other to knot

her hair around my wrist, pulling it away from her face. "Thank you for coming, baby."

She smiles down at me as she reaches forward to massage my tight shoulders, easing the constant tension. "Thank you for inviting me to something this special to you."

Jerking her head to the side, I drop kisses along her neck.

"You look so good in this bed." I gently sink my teeth into her skin before sucking hard.

She drops her head back. "You're going to give me a hickey."

"Exactly my goal." I lick up her neck and then suck harder. "I want to mark you everywhere."

She moans. "This used to be your bedroom?"

"Mm-hmm," I mutter into her neck.

I give no shits about talking about this room.

All my focus is on her and how I'm going to spend the rest of the night pleasuring every inch of her body.

"Did you sleep here a lot?"

"Sometimes."

"Did you have other girls in this bed?"

I freeze. *This is where she was going with that.* "Not the time for us to have that convo."

"Why not?"

"I don't want you mad at me, but I'm also not going to lie to you." I raise my hand, slipping it under her shirt, and trail my fingers up and down her spine. "Look at it this way: you'll be the only one here with me from now on."

She frowns, staring down at me, her hands now stationary on my shoulders. "I don't like that answer."

"I don't like that question." I lift my hand and tug on her bra. "Let's get this off."

She gently rocks against me, her thin panties the only barrier between her pussy and me. When she starts pulling up her shirt, I stop her. The sight of her in my clothes is nearly enough to have me busting in my gym shorts.

"Shirt stays on. Lose the bra and panties." Slipping my hand into her panties, I groan. She's soaked, dripping down my fingers. I sink a finger inside her with no warning. "Never mind. I can work with the panties on."

She unsnaps her bra, slightly lifting up to her knees, giving me a better angle to pump my fingers inside her while also pressing my thumb to her swollen clit. As she unshoulders her bra and moves into my touch, her breathing quickens.

"Pull my dick out," I demand. "Fuck what's yours. *Only* yours."

She crawls down the bed, her face at my lap, and she licks her lips before untying my shorts. My back arches when she cups me through my shorts, sliding her hand up and down my hard cock.

"Take it out, baby," I groan.

She tilts her head to the side. "And then what?"

"Jerk it. Suck it. Fuck it. *Anything.*"

"Hmm." She taps the side of her mouth. "Which one should I select?"

"Baby," I rasp. "If you don't take off these goddamn shorts soon, I'm going to *select* it for you by pushing you onto your back and fucking your face."

"Am I not supposed to want that?"

When I rise at the waist, she shoves me back against the headboard. In seconds, she's dragging my shorts down my legs and tossing them off the bed. My knees lock up when she swallows my entire dick into that sweet mouth of hers.

"Fuck, that mouth," I moan.

I used to think all it did was talk shit, but she sucks my dick as if her mouth were made to do it. I've never had to lead Georgia, show her how I like to be sucked; she already knows what sets me off. I wrap her hair around my wrist again, pulling tight, and watch her suck me, her cheeks hollowing out.

"Shit, stop," I grind out when she massages my balls. "Your mouth isn't what's going to take my come tonight."

She smiles. "Then what will?"

She yelps when I haul her back onto my lap, and she wastes no time before grinding against me, her pussy rubbing against my hard cock, which is coated in her saliva.

Her lips go to mine. "We need to be quiet."

I slide my tongue into her mouth.

"Lincoln is in the next room," she says, pulling back.

"Lincoln is the last person I'm worried about hearing us." I jerk my head toward my nightstand. "Condom."

With no hesitation, she stretches across the bed, opens the drawer, and snags one.

"Put it on me."

I hold in a breath when she opens the wrapper and pulls out the condom before slowly sliding it over my erection.

Gripping her waist, I lift her before slamming her onto my cock. Her pussy sinks around my dick perfectly, making us one. She grips my shoulders as she starts riding me, giving my cock the best pussy it's ever had—the only pussy I ever want to have. The more of herself she hands over to me, the more addicted to her I become.

I throw my head back, rotating my waist underneath her. "I could stay inside you forever."

She's biting her lip as she grinds against me, holding back her moans, her groans, the way she gasps my name as my cock fills her.

"Say my name," I moan into her mouth, playing with her clit.

She rides me harder. "Archer."

"Again."

She rides me deeper. "Archer."

"A-fucking-gain."

This time, she moans out my name while falling apart. I keep her still, my fingers pressing into her hips, while I pound inside her until I'm the one groaning her name.

# CHAPTER THIRTY-EIGHT

# Archer

"YOU SURE YOU'RE ready to be back?" Cohen asks, walking into my office. "If you need more time off, I got you."

I shake my head. "Nah, being here is what I need."

Today is Lincoln's first day back too. Like me, he's ready for something to take his mind off losing Dad. It's worse for him, though. Not only was he closer with our father but he also doesn't have much of anyone now. I have Georgia and my friends, but he spends his nights either in the guest room of my penthouse or at Mom's. I need to get my shit together and be a better big brother.

Tonight will be the first night I sleep without Georgia next to me since my father's death. My stomach hollows at the thought. Tomorrow is her first day of working at the school, and I don't want to wake her up after my shift.

Cohen crosses his arms and rests his back against the bare wall. Unlike his office, there are no chairs for visitors in mine—a great preventive measure. If there's nowhere for them to get comfortable, they won't stay longer than necessary.

Cohen kicks his shoes against the floor. "You and my sister, huh?"

I nod, leaning back in my chair, flipping a pen in my hand. "Me and your sister."

Cohen waits for me to elaborate.

I don't.

Dating Georgia won't change everything about me. Yes, I'm coming around more, but I'll always be closed off to everyone but her.

"I forgot about how you talk so much." He shakes his head. "Dude, you need to learn when to shut up."

I shrug. "Mr. Social over here."

He shoves his hands into his pockets. "Is it too soon to ask a favor?"

"Depends on the favor."

"It's a favor for Maliki."

"Yeah?"

Maliki is Cohen's best friend who worked with us before moving home. He owns Down Home Pub, a bar in Blue Beech that's been in his family for decades. Down Home is in the next county, and before Cohen agreed to buy our building, he double-checked to make sure it was okay with Maliki. Cohen didn't want him to see us as competition. Maliki didn't give a shit, of course, and ripped Cohen's ass for thinking he would.

"Sierra's sister needs a job," he says.

I raise a brow. "A job here?"

He nods.

"Sierra is engaged to Maliki, and he owns Down Home Pub. Why doesn't he hire her sister there?"

"Not sure of the full story, but it seems she needs to get out of town for a while."

I shrug. "Fine with me."

"Cool. I'll schedule an interview for her to come in."

"Sounds good."

He turns to walk out, but before he does, he stares at me over his shoulder. "I'm happy for you. You and my sister deserve it, man. Be good to her."

"DUDE, do I even have a roommate anymore?" Lincoln asks, stepping behind me at the bar.

I throw my arms out. "You see me standing here, don't you?"

He flips me off. "Will you be at home tonight or snuggling with your girlfriend?"

I've spent most of my nights at Georgia's—even though I complain about it and offer to buy her a new bed every night I'm there. For some reason, she says Grace doesn't like staying by herself. The nights Georgia has stayed with me is when Grace is at her parents' or siblings' houses. She won't explain why Grace doesn't like shit that goes bump in the night while she's home alone.

"Home tonight," I answer.

"Guess you'll have to watch movies and feed me strawberries instead of Georgia then."

"Funny," I deadpan.

I text Georgia throughout my shift until she tells me good night with a row of kissy-face emojis.

At the end of the night, I close the bar and go home. When I sluggishly walk to my bedroom after work and dive into my bed, I miss the heat of her body next to me. Setting my alarm, I only sleep for a few hours before dragging myself out of bed. Knowing I'll regret it later, I take an energy shot, pick up Georgia's and Grace's favorite coffee, and grab them breakfast sandwiches before heading to her townhouse.

My tired eyes dart open when Georgia answers the door.

"Damn, can I be a student?" I whistle, giving her a once-over and licking my lips at the sight of her in a black pencil skirt and white button-up top. My dick stirs.

She looks sexy and sophisticated. Even with her professional attire, Georgia puts her style into it with her earrings—two hoops with a moon hanging off one and a sun on the other and bright pink heels.

She laughs, slapping my chest, and steps to the side to allow me access into the house. "What are you doing here? You should be in bed."

I drop the coffee and food onto the kitchen table. "Sleep can wait. It's your first day. I came to see you and kiss you good luck." Bowing my head, I give her a quick peck on the lips before wrapping my arms around her waist and dragging her into me. "But now that I've seen you, how about a good-luck orgasm?"

"I wish," she grumbles, resting her chin against my chest as she peeks up at me. "Miss me already, huh?"

My eyes soften as I stare down at her. "You have no idea how lonely I was in my bed. Our sleepovers all week have spoiled me."

She grips my wrist and holds it up to read the time on my watch. "You've only been off work for three hours."

"And those three hours were miserable."

She stands on her tiptoes, her heels still not bringing her to my height, and presses her lips to mine, smiling against them. "I missed you too." She laughs. "Although it did feel nice not to have you hog the bed."

"That's why you should let me buy you a new one." I drop my hands to her ass, grabbing a handful, and pull her closer to me—my cock hard just from the view of her and this conversation. "You're coming over when you get off work, and I'm going to fuck you in this skirt."

She shivers in my arms.

My lips go to her ear, and I know I'm punishing myself by getting us worked up when we can't do anything about it. "When I push it up, do you want me to finger-fuck you or eat your pussy?"

"Oh my God," she groans. "You need to stop before my excuse for being late is that I had to ride my boyfriend's cock."

"Gross, ew," Grace says, walking into the room while

shoving a sparkly pink laptop into her bag. "As if I don't already hear enough of your banging at night."

Georgia turns to face her, and I drag her ass against me, hiding my erection from Grace.

"Hey, he did buy you those noise-canceling headphones."

Grace grabs her curly strawberry-blond locks and pulls them up into a smooth ponytail. "Do you know how hard it is to sleep with bulky headphones on your ears?"

I jerk my head toward the coffee and food on the table. "I at least brought you breakfast and coffee."

Grace, who can't hold a frown for longer than three seconds, grins. "Why couldn't we have had this Archer all along? You are becoming a decent part-time roommate with our coffee and food."

I shrug and kiss Georgia's forehead. "It just took time ... and the right person."

Grace smiles. "I guess so."

We say good-bye to Grace. I walk Georgia to her car, kiss her with a little tongue, and go home to crash for half the day.

"WILL THIS BE WEIRD?" Georgia asks, playing with her hands in her lap.

She's been distant all morning. When I asked her what was wrong, she waved off my question and insisted it was nothing.

Parking in Cohen's driveway, I glance over at her. "Why would it be weird?"

"We've never exactly been nice to each other at one of these."

I shift the car into park. "We were nice on Taco Tuesday. At the funeral."

"Nice to each other while people know that we're"—she pauses, as if searching for the appropriate word—"dating."

I frown. "Do you want us to be mean to each other?" My

voice turns playful, and I hope it perks up her mood. "Role-play?"

She side-eyes me. "You know what I mean."

"It'd make for some hot sex later."

Her frown tips up into a smirk. "How about we ditch the party and go have sex?"

It's my turn to frown. "You want to bail on your brother's birthday?"

This isn't like Georgia. Unless she's had work or class, she's never missed a party or barbecue at Cohen's house—definitely not on his birthday.

"No." She shakes her head as if she's trying to rid it of her thoughts.

"Baby," I say, my chest tightening, "what's wrong?"

She's quiet, chewing on her bottom lip.

"Talk to me."

"I'm scared," she whispers.

"Scared of what?"

She avoids eye contact and plays with her hoop earring. "We've been in our own little world, and with the exception of Grace, we haven't shown our friends how serious we are. If it doesn't work out between us, I'll be humiliated."

"Humiliated? Humiliated over what?" Uneasiness stirs in my stomach.

"The guys, they don't know how deep my feelings for you are. If something happens to us, then it'll be embarrassing. If they think it's casual for us, then it might not be—"

I wince, her words a smack in the face. "Whoa, you think we're *casual*?"

A flush fills her cheeks. "I don't know what we are."

"You shitting me?" Disbelief cracks through me.

"I'm worried I'm a ..." She trails off.

"A what?"

"A distraction," she blurts out. "I'm worried I'm a distraction ... from everything happening in your life."

"A distraction?" I repeat slowly. "You're scared that I'll use you and then discard you after my life isn't shit?"

"A little, yes." She shakes her head and clutches the door handle. "Forget it. It's stupid."

"Whoa, you can't throw that out there and then say *forget it.*" I stop her, my head pounding. "Do you really think that I'm not all in with us?"

"I know how you are when you're in pain," she says softly. "You've used me before."

*"You've used me before."*

I squeeze my eyes shut and force down a sick feeling. "I've introduced you as my girlfriend. I've confided in you in ways I never have with anyone. I brought you to spread my father's ashes with my family. You think that's casual?"

"That's why I said, forget it," she grinds out.

She turns to open the door again, but I speak before she does, "Georgia, look at me."

There's a delay before she does, and my head pounds harder at the uncertainty on her face.

I caress my thumb over her cheek, my stomach twisting at the tears simmering in her eyes, and level my voice. "I'm all in. Every piece of me is in this with you. You're not a distraction. You're the woman I've wanted for years—*years*—and I'm finally done *distracting* myself with other shit to avoid my feelings for you."

She relaxes into my touch, my confession slightly putting her at ease. Three words are at the tip of my tongue. Just as they're about to slip from my lips, Georgia jumps when someone pounds on her door.

"Come on, kids," Finn says as he passes us on his way to Cohen's backyard.

*I'm kicking his ass.*

She wipes her eyes. "What better way for our first *public appearance* than for me to have red eyes?"

"Georgia," I rasp, "I swear on everything, I will never

embarrass you."

She sniffles.

"Come here, baby." I wipe tears off her cheeks and nudge my nose along hers before kissing her. "This is not casual for me. You will never be casual with me. I'm nine thousand percent in this with you."

"Okay." She nods. "I just ..."

"I don't blame you for doubting me."

Our lips brush again, longer this time, and I run my tongue along the seam of her lips. She opens her mouth, curling her tongue into mine, and I pull back.

"I don't know if our first public appearance should involve me dragging you onto my lap and fucking you right before we see everyone."

She traces my lips with her tongue. "That would be a great way to start it out."

I place a kiss on her forehead. "Let's get going."

She turns to grab Cohen's gift bag from the back seat, and I interlace our hands as we walk into the backyard. It's a Monday night—the only day everyone in the gang could get off work. It's hard for us to get together on the weekends since at least one of us needs to be at the bar when it's busy.

To me, it doesn't seem weird. Our friends have been around us together. Hell, Grace has heard us fuck and seen us playing house—eating, watching movies, snuggling on the couch.

Far from goddamn casual.

"Well, well, if it's not the happy couple," Lola says when we come into view. She jumps up from her chair and hugs Georgia. "I feel like I need to move in with you and Grace to see you." Her eyes shoot to me. "*Or* be Archer."

I shrug, holding back a shit-eating grin as Georgia's shoulders relax.

"Girl time," Georgia says.

"You're going to be talking about me, aren't you?"

"Definitely not," she says.

I kiss her cheek while she sits with the girls, and I head over to the guys standing around the grill, drinking beers. We bro-hug each other, and no one acts any differently about Georgia and me. It's as if it's natural, and we've been walking around holding hands for years. I'm sure there's been some talk when we're not around, though.

"Maliki, my man!" Cohen calls out.

I turn around to find Maliki; his fiancée, Sierra; and his daughter, Molly, along with a blonde walking in our direction. As soon as Molly sees Noah and Jamie playing on the swing set, she darts toward them, yelling Noah's name. I'd bet my money those two will date or some shit by the time they hit high school.

"Who's Blondie?" Finn asks.

"Sierra's sister," Silas answers.

"She's cute," Finn comments.

She's young and on the skinny side, and she reminds me of Sierra—pretty, rich, and trouble. Maliki was like me—a loner, not giving two shits or looking for a relationship. Enter Sierra, who kept sneaking into his bar when she was underage. And somehow, they're now engaged. I don't know the full story since I mind my own business.

When he said it took the right one, I snorted.

Now, I get it.

"She's the one we're hiring?" I ask Cohen.

"Hiring where?" Silas asks.

"At the bar," Cohen replies.

"Twisted Fox?" Finn questions.

Cohen nods.

"Why not work at Down Home?" Finn continues.

I have a feeling that will be a frequent question.

"She got into some trouble. Maliki didn't tell me the entire story because he hardly says shit," Cohen replies. "If you want in on any gossip, Sierra is the one you go to."

Georgia, Grace, and Lola trade questioning looks. They're cautious, and they've banned us from bringing random women to the barbecues after one of Finn's flings showed her ass. I didn't give two fucks about the ban since I didn't have random flings I dragged around my friends. When Sierra came with Maliki the first time, they were accepting of her. It could've also been because none of them wanted Maliki.

Since Grace loves Finn.

And Lola and Silas have some weird type of relationship.

Thirty minutes later, we're finishing dinner, and Georgia declares it is cake time before rushing inside. I don't know how she always ends up being the cake-getter.

Deciding we need some alone time, I jog across the yard and wrap my arms around her, dragging her into my side before raining kisses down her cheek and neck.

She laughs, pushing me away, before freezing. "Holy shit, is that my mom?"

# CHAPTER THIRTY-NINE

## Georgia

*WHAT THE HELL IS HAPPENING?*

My jaw drops as my mom slowly walks through Cohen's backyard, gift bag in tow. My attention zips to Cohen, as I'm nervous for his reaction. I didn't invite her since it's his birthday, and when it's your birthday, you get to make the guest list.

*Did Jamie?*

Cohen drops a kiss to Jamie's shoulder, shoves his phone into his pocket, and waves to my mom. His strides are long as he meets her in the middle of the yard. They smile at each other—hers gentle, his inviting.

"Oh, wow," I mutter when he hugs her tightly.

"You want me to grab the cake while you ..." Archer asks, jerking his head toward the scene I'm focused on.

I nod. "Good idea."

"On it."

I wait, keeping my distance, while Cohen and my mom make small talk. I've been begging Cohen to talk to her, and my heart flutters that he finally is, that he's opened up the forgiveness pocket of his heart. The man who doesn't believe in second chances is giving her one.

Taking her hand, he leads her to Jamie and Noah, and when they exchange hugs, my eyes water.

"Got the cake," Archer says, stopping next to me. "Who the hell chose this?"

"Noah." I laugh as I take a look at the Scooby-Doo cake that says, *Happy Birthday, Dad!* "He cons Jamie into letting him make all the decisions."

Archer carries the cake as we approach them.

"Hi, Mom," I say, masking the shock on my face and hugging her.

"Hi, baby." She squeezes me tight.

"Cake is here," Archer says before placing it on the table. He slides his arm around my waist and kisses my cheek.

My mom raises a brow.

"Mom," I say, "this is Archer."

"Hi there," she says skeptically and waves, recognizing his name from the few times I've confided in her.

Her motherly instincts have started kicking in as our relationship grows.

As though he can read her mind, Archer steps forward, and says, "I stopped fucking up."

My mom smiles. "I'm glad to hear that."

Everyone digs into the cake, and when I see Cohen is alone, I pounce.

"You invited Mom?" I ask.

He nods.

"Wow, what am I missing? Are we in an alternate universe?"

"It was time I got my head out of my ass." He runs his hand through his thick brown hair. "Archer's dad's death didn't only help open his eyes; it did mine too. It was time I quit holding a grudge against her. I'm having a little girl, and I'd love for her to have two grandmothers. She's been in the picture with you for a while now, and she hasn't given you any reason to doubt her."

I grin. "I'm happy you and Mom are reconnecting."

He jerks his head toward Archer, who's talking with Maliki.

"After all this time, I kept telling myself that you two just hated each other."

"Were we that good at acting?"

He shakes his head. "I think I was good at turning a blind eye to it because I didn't want it to start drama, but then I sat back and thought, you two dating isn't shit compared to the situation I'm in."

I laugh. "True dat, big brother. Your baby momma's sister is over there, preggo with your next baby."

"Okay, don't make it sound so Jerry Springer-ish."

"Why? It's so much fun."

"Man, you're a pain in my ass," he says, laughing while hugging me.

I take a look around the yard, noticing everyone and everything that's happened.

Everyone around me is taking risks.

And I love it.

---

"I'M SORRY," I say, stretching myself out on Archer's bed, "for what I said about us being casual."

I was nervous.

Scared.

Our relationship had turned serious so fast.

No dating. No foreplay. Just diving straight into each other.

In the car, Archer flinched when I said *distraction*, as if the word was a slap to his face. I was happy with him, on top of the world, but scared. Archer's way of handling stress is by running, drinking, and fucking. I can't be blamed for worrying that he was using me to get through his issues and then would discard me later.

He stands at the foot of his bed—in a pair of gym shorts, shirtless, showing off his buff chest.

His face softens, and he gently smiles. "Baby, don't be sorry for expressing that. My job is to change your mind from feeling that way."

"I mean, I was in a mood—"

"And I'm in the mood to prove to you that this isn't casual."

Leaning over the bed, he grips my ankles in his rough hands, and I shriek when he tugs me down the sheets. My ass is half off the bed, and before I catch another breath, my panties are ripped down my legs. Parting my thighs, he drops to his knees and stares at my bare pussy, his attention riveted.

I gulp, never feeling so on display before.

"Uh … everything okay down there?" I ask before inching my legs closed.

Call me awkward for never having my vagina on display like the *Mona Lisa*.

He stops me. "I'm admiring you."

"Can you, uh … stop admiring and start …"

He peeks up at me, a hungry look on his face. "And what, baby?"

I wave my hands in the air in a *hurry up* gesture.

He chuckles, and anticipation flickers through me when he rains kisses down my thighs and legs and then back up.

My heart pulsates, my body tingling with my need for him.

All of him.

Every damn inch of this guy—mentally, physically, emotionally.

I want him to be my forever.

I want to be his everything.

Without warning, he plunges two fingers inside me.

Laps his tongue around my clit while fingering me.

The attentiveness this man gives my body is like no other.

I've never had a man work to pleasure me like Archer does.

His tongue. His fingers. His mouth. His groans between my legs.

"Come for me, baby," he says.

I arch my back, raising my hips, and he keeps me in place, finishing me off while I ride out my orgasm.

I throw my arms out, catching my breath as my body shakes. He grabs my waist, and I yelp when he tosses me farther up the bed.

He drops his shorts, his cock hard, and slides on a condom. I part my legs, welcoming him, and he kisses me. Darting my tongue in his mouth, I suck on his, and he groans. I wait for him to settle between my legs and thrust into me, but he doesn't.

Instead, he tortures me, cupping my breasts before squeezing them together, sucking and pulling and teasing at my nipples.

Proving this isn't a quick fuck.

That we aren't *casual*.

"I want your cock. So damn much."

He ignores me, sucking on my nipple.

I change direction. "I want you," I croak out. "I want you so damn much. Show me how this isn't casual."

My words set him on fire, and he pulls away, his eyes searching mine. Maintaining eye contact, he situates himself between my legs and eases in and out of me slowly.

Torturously slow.

Unhurried.

Fucking me in a way he's never fucked me before.

His gaze not leaving my face with every stroke until he's close.

He slams his eyes shut, his thrusts rougher and faster, and just as I'm there, he stops and collapses onto his back, rolling me with him to keep our connection so I'm now straddling him.

"Ride this cock you wanted," he demands, his palm cupping my ass before he gently smacks it.

My body tingles with excitement, and I rock my hips, pushing him farther into me.

Heat courses through my veins as I allow him to guide me how he wants it. I ride him hard, and his hips lash forward, meeting mine.

Our sweet fucking has turned into heated fucking.

The sound of my ass slapping into his thighs.

We moan.

We moan each other's names.

My sweat drips down my body and hits his chest.

"Oh my God, Georgia." He throws his head back, slowing his movements. "I love you so fucking much, baby."

I stop.

He gasps, his eyes wide as he stares at me, unblinking.

I'm panting, unsure of where to go from here.

*He said ... he said the L-word.*

He knots his hand in my hair. "Why do you look so shocked?"

"Was that ... it was a heat-of-the moment love devotion, right?" I shake my head. "Totally overthinking that."

I grind against him, but he stops me.

"I mean, yeah, I love when you're riding my cock, but I also love *you*."

I freeze again. "What?"

His eyes search mine, and his voice is rough when he says, "I'm in love with you, Georgia."

My thighs shake, and he grips them under his large palms as a tear slips down my cheek.

"Shit," he hisses. "I'm sorry. I know it's early."

I press a finger to his lips. "I think we both already know that I'm in love with you."

Grabbing my hair, he pulls my mouth to his, and then he flips me over, so he's on top again.

"Mine. So fucking mine," he groans as he thrusts inside me.

I wiggle underneath him. "Yours. All yours."

Archer kisses me. "Never leave me."

"You'd have to kill me first."

# CHAPTER FORTY

# Archer

*"I LOVE YOU."*

Before today, other than my mother, I've only said that to one other woman.

Meredith.

It was part of the natural progression of any relationship.

Date. Fuck. Profess *I love yous*. Get engaged. Marry.

That was the course for all relationships in our circle.

In my case with Meredith, it was fuck and then date—which also seems to somehow be the norm for me. It's easier for me to give someone my cock before giving them my heart.

Sure, I thought I loved Meredith.

I liked her enough to propose to her.

But now that I have Georgia, I know I didn't love her.

Love is when you want to wake up every single day and prove to the other person that you'll work on being a better person than you were the day before—a better lover, a better friend.

Georgia is my girlfriend, the woman I love, but she's also been my best friend and the only person I'm comfortable confiding in.

I glance up at the knock on my office door, and Georgia walks in, closing the door and clicking the lock behind her.

"Our first shift together as a couple," she says.

I nod.

She licks her lips and walks around my desk. "Should we celebrate?"

I turn in my chair to face her, my cock stirring as I take in her short-shorts and V-neck shirt that shows off her cleavage. "What'd you have in mind?"

*God, I want to suck on her tits right now.*

Dropping to her knees, she pulls out my cock, and without warning, she wraps her lips around my length, taking in every damn inch as if she'd been doing it her entire life. She hasn't given me many blow jobs—mostly because I like to come while my dick is inside her pussy, not her mouth.

My knees buckle, my balls draw up, and my hands grip the back of her head.

"Yes, suck me just like that," I groan. "You own my cock."

I stare down at the view of her perfect, plump lips moving up and down my cock.

And as usual, I stop her, wanting to bust my nut inside her pussy.

"Take off your shorts and your panties—and make it quick, so we don't get busted."

She bites into her lip and does what I said.

I bend her over my desk, spread her legs wide, and run my finger through her folds.

"Look how wet you got from sucking my cock," I say into her ear. "You love sucking it, don't you?"

"Yes," she moans when I plunge two fingers inside her.

"Love fucking my cock, don't you?"

"Love it more than anything."

She plants her palms on my desk, knocking shit over, and arches her back as I slide into her.

"Then take it."

I fuck her hard.

One hand gripping her waist, another one over her mouth to mask her screams.

I love this woman, and I pray to God she never leaves me.

---

"I'M a little worried that that's my replacement," Georgia says, signaling to Cassidy when she walks into the bar for her first day of training, wearing cutoff jeans and a crop top.

She's lost her goddamn mind if she thinks she has anything to worry about with another woman. I never wanted anyone to have my heart, but Georgia did the unthinkable. She pushed, she punched, and she shoved her way straight into me, to where she's so deep that I'll never be able to drag her out.

Sure, Cassidy is cute, but she's not Georgia—and that gives every woman a disadvantage when it comes to me.

"Don't even think for a second that I'd be interested in anyone but you," I say, leaning forward to kiss her neck.

We're at a pub table, having a quick bite to eat before our shifts start.

"God, I take back all the times I said Archer needed to get his head out of his ass. You two are gag-worthy," Lola comments, sliding out a stool at the table and sitting.

"I think there's a rule against kissing in the employee handbook," Silas adds, coming into view and stealing the seat next to Lola.

Behind them, I see Grace and Finn, and they join us.

Seconds later, Lincoln is standing behind me.

It's like one big, happy damn family.

"They're cute," Grace says, her voice calm and polite.

"I think it's so cute too," Finn adds, resting his arm over Grace's shoulders. "The bastard has grown a goddamn heart."

I use both of my hands to flip them off as Georgia laughs, finishing off her sandwich.

"Nah. Archer is still the grumpy dick, just not to Georgia," Lincoln argues.

"She's the only one who doesn't deserve it." I stand, brush the mustard off her lips, and kiss her. "Let me know if you need anything."

She returns my kiss with another peck.

"Swear to motherfucking God, I love you two, but this is a working zone," Lincoln says. "Don't be messing up my tips while you guys run around each other with hearts sticking out of your ears."

Georgia laughs, scrunching up her face. "What does that even mean?"

Lincoln shrugs. "I heard the expression on TV once. They don't give you many channels in prison."

I cover my face, shaking my head. "Jesus, you guys are fucking nuts."

This might be the longest conversation I've had with our friends at one time, and damn, does it feel good. I never thought that I could be this way again—sitting and shooting the shit, forgetting about my troubles, being happy and joking around.

This is what I've been missing all this time.

Instead of torturing myself, I could've had this.

A woman who I love.

Friends who are goddamn crazy.

And a great relationship with my brother.

Georgia brought me back to life.

If I didn't have her, especially after my father's death, I don't even know if I'd still be around here.

She's what I needed when I thought I didn't need anyone.

Even when I was shaken, fucked up inside, she took a chance on me.

The woman changed me.

She gave me life again.

Lincoln slaps my back, and we walk to the bar, getting ready for the Saturday night chaos. I'm thankful Cohen didn't give me too much of a hard time about hiring Lincoln. Like with me, I think this bar and these people are also bringing him back to life.

The extravagant parties, the stuck-up and fake friends, the fast chicks—that's not the life for us anymore.

This is.

## CHAPTER FORTY-ONE

# Georgia

I WAVE over Cassidy when she comes into view after she's filled out her paperwork with Cohen. I'm training her tonight.

"Hey, girl," she says with a bright smile—now wearing a black shirt with the bar's logo on it.

Cassidy will do well here. She's gorgeous, outgoing, and smart. A people person, like me.

She sits down at the table with us, and I go through her training packet while my friends make side conversations around us—me having to hush them a few times for being too loud.

When I'm finished, I shut the employee handbook and clap. "You ready?"

"I think so." She holds out a finger to stop me before moving it to the bar. "Who is he? I want him for breakfast, lunch, and dinner."

The table falls quiet as everyone follows the direction of where she's staring with starry eyes ... straight to where Archer is standing.

I inhale a fast breath, ready to storm into Cohen's office and tell him to train this girl himself—or better yet, fire her goddamn ass. She was at Cohen's party. Archer didn't make it a secret that we were together.

Grace drops her fry.

Lola leans back in her chair, crossing her arms, her eyes narrowing in on Cassidy.

Silas laughs—it's one covered in edge and warning. "You might be eating those meals through a straw if you keep talking about Archer like that in front of Georgia."

*At least someone said it for me.*

"Archer?" Cassidy's attention flicks to Silas, shaking her head. "Not him. We met at the barbecue. I'm talking about the guy next to him."

Everyone's gaze returns to the bar, and the tension leaves the table.

My heart settles.

Grace snags a fry.

Lola no longer looks ready to throw her drink on Cassidy.

"Lincoln?" Silas asks. "Archer's brother?"

"If that's the man next to him, then yes," she replies, her eyes following Lincoln as he moves behind the bar. "Is he single? Can I have him? What's his favorite breakfast, so I can make it for him on our morning after?"

*Damn …*

*This girl is confident.*

Silas scratches his cheek. "Be careful, newbie. We have a strict *no relationships between employees* rule around here. Too much drama."

Cassidy glances at me. "Aren't you and Archer dating?"

"They're the exception," Lola inputs.

"Maybe I can be an exception then too," Cassidy says with a smile.

*Oh, she's going to be shaking some stuff up at Twisted Fox; that's for sure.*

Probably why Maliki sent her our way—so he wouldn't have to deal with her.

"All right," I drawl out, taking a quick sip of Lola's drink before standing. "Time to get this training party started."

"Have fun, you cute kids, you," Lola sings out, and I smack her shoulder while passing her.

I train Cassidy—instruct her on our policies, show her around, and introduce her to the other employees.

"You met Archer," I say—even though I doubt Archer said two words to her at Cohen's party. "And this is Lincoln. They're our bartenders for the night."

Cassidy's eyes shine as she licks her lips and stares at Lincoln. "Hi, I'm Cassidy. Your future wife."

I snort, ready for this mini show, and Archer rubs his forehead, as if he doesn't have time for this shit.

Lincoln laughs. "You're working here? Are you even old enough to legally buy a drink?"

"Obviously, or they wouldn't have hired me," Cassidy fires back.

Lincoln whistles and takes a step back. "I stand corrected." He winks. "I'm the fun bartender." He jerks his head toward Archer. "He's not."

Archer's brows furrow, and he looks at Lincoln with a *stay away from her* look.

Lincoln shrugs with a smirk.

Cassidy is eating up Lincoln's flirting.

*Oh well.*

She can flirt with Lincoln all night long, and I'd give no fucks.

Archer slaps my ass with a towel before kissing me on the lips. "You go train away, baby."

I smile, all giddy and flirty, and blow him a kiss as we walk onto the floor.

"So … why aren't you working at Maliki's bar?" I ask Cassidy as she follows me around.

For the first time, Cassidy seems shy, and she rubs her hands up and down her arms. "I got into some trouble, and we decided I needed to get out of town for a while."

"What kind of trouble?"

"Just stupid stuff that got me kicked out of college."

"Oh, I'm going to get that story out of you sometime."

---

TRAINING ON A SATURDAY night has been a catch-22.

Since the bar is slammed, I haven't had much time to train Cassidy, but it's nice having the help. It'll also prepare her for the hectic shifts. I give her the two-top tables to make it easier on her.

"Dayum, sexy," a guy—my guess, early twenties—calls out when I approach his table. His tongue darts out and slides along his lower lip while he eyeballs me.

A little too friendly.

A little too aggressive.

*Great, these tables are always so super-duper fun.*

This asshole is going to ruin the Archer high I've been riding the past few days. I already know it.

Ignoring him, I sweep my gaze around the table, irritated. "What can I get you guys?"

"Your number," one answers with a smirk.

"Dude, back the fuck off," Original Creep—who I'll call OC —says, a sure-of-himself expression on his face. "I called dibs on her."

Feeling a headache coming on, I tap my pen against my notepad. "Seriously, your order, or I'll come back."

"Now, that's some bad customer service," OC says with a tsk. "Don't make us get your boss."

I hold back a snort. I always love when people threaten to tell my *boss*.

These are the times I'm happy that I work for my brother and that he's a good guy. Some bars have that *the customer is always right* mentality. It's a bunch of bullshit because a drunk person isn't always right.

Hell, a drunk person is rarely right.

As a person who works in a bar, I said what I said.

Thank God I didn't give Cassidy this table. My jerk reader must have been alive and well when I saw them sit.

But I did give her instructions on how to deal with customers like him. Tell Finn or one of the other guys and steer clear of the creeps. The problem is, I don't always follow my own instructions. To avoid conflict, I brush off advances, cheesy pick-up lines, and offensive slurs. If I go to Finn and ask him to throw a guy out, he'll tell Cohen—who I don't want to get in trouble for defending me.

I cringe as he scoots closer.

"What do you suggest?" he asks, reeking of booze and weed. From his bloodshot eyes, I'd put my money on more drugs than weed being in his system.

I tense and jump back when his hand scoots up the back of my thigh and up toward my ass.

Swatting it away, I shove his shoulder. "Touch me again, and your ass is out of here."

He smirks deviously. "Speaking of asses, you have a nice one, baby. How about you give me some of that?"

He reaches for me again, but I push him away, my back bumping into his friend, who's just as touchy as him.

"That body is just screaming for me to touch it, lick it, fuck it." He dramatically makes a sucking noise with his mouth.

"That's enough," I say. "Give me your order before I have our bouncer come over and take it for me."

"Oh shit, Chad, she's threatening you," another jerk says.

Chad runs his hands through his curly blond hair. "Nah, she's playing hard to get, but we all know she'll be on her knees with my cock in my mouth by the end of the night."

"All right, you need to leave."

"That's enough."

I peek up at the husky voice to find a guy who's stayed silent until now.

He strokes his chin and smiles at me. "Give her your order and shut the fuck up about her ass."

I release a long breath and send him a smile full of gratitude. He answers with a jerk of his head. As long as he keeps these douchebags in line, I'll grab their orders and ignore their comments the best I can.

"Fine, fine. You're no fun, Brad," Chad grumbles. "We'll have a round of Jäger bombs, and I'll also have a vodka and Red Bull." He smacks his hand on the table. "And keep the bombs coming, baby."

I take their orders and rush away. We don't get too many assholes, but it's a bar, so it's bound to happen.

"You good?" I ask Cassidy as I pass her.

"Yep!" she chirps with a smile while delivering drinks to a table.

My hand is clenching my pen so hard that I break off the clip. I'm scatterbrained as I walk toward the bar and drop my notebook on the way.

"God," I grumble, scrambling to pick it up.

"You okay?" Archer asks, staring at me with concern from behind the bar.

I nod, nearly out of breath. "Just busy."

"Are you getting overwhelmed?" His eyes meet mine in concern. "I'll get someone to help you."

I wave off his offer. "No, it's fine."

"You look like you're on the verge of tears," he snaps. "What the hell?"

"Nothing," I rush out. "Drunk people. They just suck sometimes."

His nostrils flare. "Is someone fucking with you?"

"No, it's just …" I shake my head and start rattling off my drink order.

He makes them, and before handing them over, he says, "If something happens, you run your ass over here. You hear me?"

"I hear you," I croak out.

My heart is racing when I deliver their drinks, nearly spilling one, and then I rush away from their table. As I run around, helping other customers, I feel their eyes on me.

––––––––

"HEY, bitch, you're taking too long on our drinks. I shouldn't have to hunt you down," Chad hisses in my ear, fastening his hand around my elbow and jerking me toward him before I could walk away from the bar, toward another table. "I said to keep 'em coming."

I pull away from him. "Go to your table, and I'll grab them for you."

He blinks rapidly while staring at me. "You afraid to get in trouble, baby?"

When he grabs my arm again, a drink topples off my tray, shattering to the floor.

"You bitch!" Chad snarls, holding out his shirt to examine the bright red blotches—courtesy of the vodka cranberry that was on its way to table fifteen. "You ruined my shirt."

I guess that's my thing with assholes.

I spill drinks and mess up their shirts.

Serves them right.

I don't pick up the glass. No way am I bending down in front of his waist. I can only imagine what the creep would try.

"You okay, Georgia?" Cassidy yells over at me.

I nod, giving her a thumbs-up, and force a smile at Chad. "I'm really sorry. Your drinks will be on me tonight."

Chad smirks. "How about *you* be on me tonight to make up for it?"

Cassidy's question must've caught Archer's attention because I hear him calling my name from behind me.

"Look," I breathe out, "go to your table. I'll get your drinks, okay? I'm really sorry about your shirt."

He laughs manically. "Sorry won't cut it, sweetheart. Sucking my dick will, though."

I swallow down the nausea seeping up my belly. "Go back to your table before I tell my boss you're harassing me, and he kicks you out of here."

"Harassing you?" He snorts, his voice slurred. "Baby, this is harassing you."

When he grabs my ass, I drop my tray, every glass breaking, and push him with all my power. He stumbles back, hitting a few people and knocking down a chair.

I smile, proud of my badass self.

"What the fuck?" I hear Archer roar.

When I peek back at him, he's jumping over the bar and storming toward us, venom in his eyes, as the crowd parts, providing a straight line to Chad.

"You motherfucker!"

Knowing this won't end well, I turn and scurry in front of Chad just in time. "Archer, no!"

"Fuck that shit," Archer snarls, emphasizing each word. "Move, Georgia." His hands tighten into fists as he levels his gaze on Chad.

Everyone's awareness is on us now. Since it's a small-town bar, they know that Archer is an employee here. The main bartender. A few know he's also the owner. The last thing the bar needs is talk that an owner beat the shit out of a drunk guy. I've already spotted three people recording us.

I hold up my hand. "He's drunk. Let Finn kick him out."

"Nah, I'll take the trash out myself."

My breathing hitches as I straighten my back.

*Relax.*

When Lincoln appears at Archer's side, there's a hint of that relaxation. I exhale another breath when Finn stops next to me, his eyes shooting back and forth between Archer and Chad.

"I got this," he says.

Then Chad stupidly decides to make things worse. "Oh, look, the assholes are coming to her rescue."

"Georgia, goddamn it, move." Every muscle in Archer's body goes rigid.

We're in a standoff, and I can't believe I'm standing between my boyfriend and a man who grabbed my ass, asking my boyfriend to let it be.

There isn't one person in the bar who isn't looking at us, and panic charges through me when Cohen joins us, his gaze bouncing between me, Archer, and Chad.

Archer doesn't look at Cohen or Finn for backup.

His glare is fixed on Chad, waiting for me to step aside so he can unleash his rage.

"No," I say, my voice shaking. "He's drunk, and I don't want you doing anything stupid."

"He fucking touched you!" Archer screams. "Don't fucking defend him!"

"What do you mean, he touched her?" Cohen yells, tapping in and ready to play sidekick to Archer's ass-kicking.

"Cassidy," I call out, my voice pleading, "tell his friends they need to take him home." They've been watching the scene, but so far, none of them have come to his rescue.

Cassidy nods and scrambles toward his friends. With groans and looks of annoyance, they get up.

Chad tilts his shoulder in a half-shrug, and now that he knows his friends are coming, he grows braver. "She's been asking for it all night. You should've seen the way she was looking at me, practically drooling for my cock."

My hands are shaking in anger as I attempt to tune out Chad's words. I whisper Archer's name, struggling to grasp his attention.

*Look at me.*

*Only me.*

Chad pounds his fist against his chest and stares at Archer

mockingly. "You want a piece of her pussy too? I'll share after I've had my fill."

His words light a match underneath the fire that is Archer, and there's no stopping him. Archer swings around me to reach Chad.

I fall, and everything goes black.

# CHAPTER FORTY-TWO

## Archer

I SHOULD WALK AROUND with a D on my chest.

A scarlet letter kind of way.

A signal that says, *If you love me, prepare for death.*

Guilt spreads through my chest, as if an infection, controlling my every thought.

This is all my fault.

I was on too much of a high—a high where I thought my life could be different.

That I could be happy.

That'll never be me.

I'm a curse.

Poison to the heart.

Unlike my grandfather, everything I touch doesn't turn to gold.

It turns to black.

Into flames.

Obliterated.

If only I'd walked away from that fight.

If only I'd listened to her.

After Georgia fell, everything became a fog.

The man who'd groped her became the least of my worries. I should've been paying more attention, but the fury I had toward the guy consumed me. He needed to get his ass kicked.

For hurting her.

For touching her.

For the vile shit he was spitting from his lips.

She took a hard blow to the head and was bleeding. Her eyes were shut, and she wasn't speaking, like she was in a deep sleep. She was breathing but not lucid. I desperately yelled her name, gently shook her shoulders, snapped my fingers in front of her face until Cohen pushed me to the side and did the same.

Someone called 911, and she was rushed to the hospital. Chad and his friends ran out of the bar, and since our attention was on Georgia, no one tried stopping them.

I hate myself.

I veer into the first open spot I find in the hospital's parking lot and slam my fists against the steering wheel. Cohen rode with Georgia in the ambulance, and I followed them. Lincoln and Finn stayed behind to work the bar until someone could cover for them.

My head is bowed in shame when I step out of my car and rush into the emergency room.

I ignore other patients, ignore the workers at the front desk, and say, "I need to see Dr. Jamie Gentry."

Name-dropping Jamie is the fastest way to get to where I need to be. She's the doctor on shift at the hospital tonight, and Finn called, giving her a heads-up to expect Georgia. The woman behind the counter surprisingly nods, and the double doors electronically open. The scent of antiseptic invades my nostrils, and I rush over to Jamie, who's talking to a nurse.

"She wasn't waking up," I say, my voice quivering. "She wasn't waking up."

Never have I felt so vulnerable around someone other than Georgia.

Jamie's face is professional, her look both serious and packed with concern. "She's awake. Well, she's conscious but sleeping. She's going to be okay." Her voice is soothing. "We're thinking it's only a mild concussion."

I shake my head and repeat, "She wasn't waking up."

Just like the memory of dragging my grandfather out of the pool, begging him to wake up, Georgia lying on that dirty bar floor, unconscious, will forever haunt me.

Visit me in my dreams.

Reminding me of my fuckups.

Jamie steps closer and wraps her arms around me.

"Where's she?" I ask, my voice nearly a plea. "Can I see her?"

"Room four." She tips her head toward a room and takes my hand. "Just … if Cohen tries to argue, don't engage."

I nod, holding back the urge to barge into Georgia's room, sit by her side, and apologize.

When the door clicks open, Cohen's eyes narrow, looking at me to blame.

I slip my hands into my pockets and walk farther into the room. I have to see her. He can punch me, beat my ass, do all the shit he should've done the day of his gender-reveal party so that this would've never happened.

He exchanges a look with Jamie, and she stops behind him, wrapping her arms around her fiancé from the back. He runs his hand over his face, shielding his silent tears.

"I'm sorry," I tell him, taking the few long strides to Georgia.

Cohen massages his temples. "It's not your fault. It's that asshole's fault."

"Archer, it was an accident," Jamie says.

*Thanks for trying to make me feel better, but you're wrong.*

Cohen stands. "Can you sit with her while I use the restroom?"

"Yes."

"They'll be coming and getting her for a CT scan," Jamie

says. "We want to check for internal bleeding on the brain. She's on pain medicine, so she'll be groggy."

I scrub my hand over my forehead and nod.

Cohen tips his head down and leaves the room with Jamie, giving me the alone time I so desperately need.

"Baby," I say, stepping to her side, wiping my watery eyes and my face with the back of my arm.

A white bandage is wrapped around her head, covering the wound she wouldn't have if I was able to control myself.

Her eyes slowly open, brimmed with confusion, and she fights for them not to close again. I reach out, running my hand along her sweaty forehead, and my chest aches.

"I'm sorry," I cry out in a whisper.

This is why I didn't want to get close.

Her voice is hoarse, and my name comes out in a long breath. "Archer." She looks down, noticing the IV in her arm, and winces when she touches her head. "What am I doing here?" She scans her body, as if it were foreign, inspecting her hands and arms.

"You fell." I clasp my hand over her clammy one. "You hit your head, but you'll be okay."

She struggles to keep her eyes open, and I tip my head forward, drawing closer.

"Get some rest." I caress her face, as if it'll never happen again, my goal to lodge it into my memory, never forgetting the perfection I had but ruined.

She relaxes into my touch, her head resting against my palm. "Will you be here when I wake up?"

"Always," I say, squeezing my eyes shut, my pain clutching my throat. "I'll always be here." I brush my lips against hers, lingering for a moment, and then I pull away and press one to her forehead. "I love you."

There's a gentle knock on the door, and a nurse walks in. "Hi there, I'm here to take her to her CT scan."

Georgia's eyes are heavy as she whispers, "I love you."

My shoulders hunch forward as I take one last look at her, aware I'm losing everything again.

Walking away is what I should've done.

Not invite her into my bed, into my heart, only to fall in love.

This time, I need to stop being selfish and do what's right for her.

# CHAPTER FORTY-THREE

## Georgia

"I'LL ALWAYS BE HERE. I love you," are the words I remember when I wake up.

As the woman wheeled me away, I noticed there was a deep pain on Archer's face.

My eyes are heavy as I open them, and Jamie is standing over me.

"Hi, Georgia."

"Hi," I say in hesitation around a scratchy throat.

My gaze darts around the room as questions ram through my aching skull, so fast that I can't keep up.

"Do you know why you're here?"

I hear her voice, but it's as if she were speaking to me from across the room. I shut my eyes, thinking back to earlier.

"A little. I hit my head?"

It's obvious *something* happened to my head. I've never felt a headache so throbbing, so powerful, and if I had a choice at the moment, I'd rip the damn thing off my shoulders and throw it across the room.

"Headache?"

"Like no other," I grumble.

"Sleepy?"

"I could sleep for the next month."

I shut my eyes and listen to people talk around me.

"No internal bleeding on the brain. No vomiting, slurred speech, or seizures," Jamie says. "It's a concussion—a hard hit to the head—and we want to keep an eye on her, but she'll be okay."

"Thank God for that," Cohen inputs.

"Can someone help me sit up?" I ask, feeling like I have no control over my body.

"Of course," Jamie answers, but it's Cohen who's at my side to help.

His face is red and puffy. There have been few instances when my brother has cried. He's always the strong one—the shoulder you cry on, the one who assures you everything will be okay.

I hiss a few times in pain as he helps me, and I take deep breaths as I scan the crowded room. Lola, Grace, my mother, Silas, and Finn are scattered around the room, standing or sitting in chairs.

My mother's face is splotchy.

Lola's and Grace's faces are red.

Worry creases Silas's forehead.

Finn's muscles are strained, as if he wants to kick someone's ass.

I'm thankful they're here.

I'm just missing one person.

My stomach churns, as I'm expecting the worst, when I ask, "Where's Archer?"

*He should be here, right?*

*Maybe he went for a restroom break?*

*Grabbed a coffee?*

Nervous glances are shared around the room.

No one says a word.

Cohen, noticing the panic, says, "We think he went home."

Untruth is plastered on his face.

I know my brother too well.

"You think? Can't you ask Lincoln if he's home?"

"Sweetie, he might be napping," Jamie says, coming to my brother's rescue.

"Jesus, be honest with her," Lola snaps, standing and walking to my side. "Head injury or not, she deserves for us to be up front with her."

Lola, always the one to give no bullshit.

The one who will give you the ugly truth to save you from harder heartbreak later.

"Babe," she says, taking my hand in hers, a doleful expression on her face, "Archer is MIA."

"Lola," Silas snaps.

Lola holds her palm toward him, not looking in his direction, her face falling as she delivers the blow. "I know it's not what you want to hear, but from your face, I know you wouldn't have stopped asking questions until someone told you anyway."

"What ..." My hands tremble. "What do you mean, *MIA*?"

She shakes her head in disappointment. "No one can find him, and he's not answering his phone."

"He was here earlier. Maybe he's sleeping or something." I gesture to Cohen as nausea consumes my stomach. "Can I have your phone, please?"

"Georgia—" he starts.

"Your phone!" I shriek frantically. "Someone give me a phone, *please*." My voice breaks; my heart breaks.

Cohen shoves his hand into his pocket, fishing out his phone. He unlocks it and hands it to me. I go to his contacts, hit Archer's name, and listen to it ring.

And ring.

And ring.

No answer.

I call Lincoln next.

"Do you know where Archer is?" I ask without offering a greeting.

"No clue," he replies. "Sorry, Georgia."

"Don't lie to me."

"I wouldn't. No one knows."

I ignore the IV in my hand, the sound of beeping machines next to me, the fact that I don't even know the full story of why the hell I'm sitting in the hospital as I break down and sob.

"I hate him," I cry out, my gut already telling me he's gone.

"You don't hate him," Silas says. I've never heard his voice so gentle. "Maybe he's taking a breather."

"He's gone," I say, no doubt in my voice.

No hesitation.

No being an optimist.

I fall back asleep, and when I wake up again, he's not there.

He walked away as if I was nothing, as if I meant nothing, as if our relationship meant nothing.

Just like the first time we'd slept together.

# CHAPTER FORTY-FOUR

# Archer

I CAME HERE to clear my head.

I tried my penthouse, but I knew that was the first place they'd look.

Every single friend has called me, even the girls.

After the hundredth call, I shut off my phone.

"How'd I know you'd be here?"

I peek back to find Lincoln walking down the long dock as I sit at the edge, my legs hanging over, the water splashing against my feet.

He groans while sitting down next to me. "Everyone is looking for you."

No one, other than Lincoln, would think to look here.

Like my grandfather and my father, I've chosen to take solace here.

I stare ahead. "You didn't tell them—"

He cuts me off, "No. As much as I like them, you're my brother."

"You and your loyalty."

"Maybe you should try the shit for a change. Quit being a selfish dick."

His honesty is a nasty bitch slap.

"Fuck off," I growl.

"Georgia is in the hospital, man."

My voice is flat. "I'm well aware."

"That's where you should be."

"I saw her. Made sure she was okay. Told her good-bye." The last part is a half-lie. I did my good-byes, but I lied to her. While I knew it'd be my last time, she thought I'd be there, waiting for her. My stomach clenches. I hate myself.

"The fuck you mean, you *told her good-bye*?"

I shrug.

He scoffs. "You know that's a punk-ass move, right?"

I finally shift to look at him, my upper lip snarling. "You know I'm fucked up in the head. Why are you here, starting this shit with me?"

"You're not fucked up in the head. You have guilt."

I stab my skull with my finger. "Guilt makes you fucked up in the head."

"Don't walk away from her."

I don't say anything.

"She's asking for you. She's *crying* for you."

His words are a blow to the chest, delivering the truth I already knew. "She might be hurting now, but in the end, she'll be happy I did this."

"Happy you broke her heart? That's the dumbest bullshit I've ever heard."

"In the end, when she finds the right man for her, she will."

"In the end, where will you be? Alone, in your self-pity hell? You'll regret turning your back on a woman who'd fight any battle for you, who dealt with your demons as if they were her own, who was willing to walk down the darkest roads to be with you ... all while you were still playing games with her head. If you don't get your dumbass up and go to the hospital, it'll be the biggest mistake of your life."

I do what I do best—stay quiet.

He stands. "You coming?"

"Nah."

He blows out a stressed breath and nods. "Whatever, but keep in touch with me. Even if it's a simple emoji or *I'm still alive* text, I want it."

# CHAPTER FORTY-FIVE

## Georgia

One Week Later

"GEORGIA," Lincoln says when he walks into the bar.

I stare at him with the dirtiest look I can muster. "Unless you're here to tell me where the hell your bastard of a brother is, I'm not speaking to you."

He knows where Archer is but won't tell anyone.

There's been no word from him.

The first few days, I called and texted.

No response.

So, I stopped.

What I want to say to him needs to be said in person.

Lincoln has covered his shifts.

I told Cohen to fire his ass—even though I knew Cohen wouldn't go through it.

It's not Lincoln's fault his brother is a spineless jerk, but all I need is an address. An address to march my butt over to, so I can deliver the hardest kick in the balls my little body can muster.

Provide him temporary pain to ease my eternal hurt.

"Archer asked me to give you this." He holds out an envelope to me.

I stare at the envelope as if it's filled with anthrax. "What Archer needs to do is grow some balls, face me, and tell me why he left me."

Lincoln thrusts the envelope closer. "Archer doesn't always do what he needs to do. You know this."

"What's his plan then?" Cassidy asks, sitting back in her chair and crossing her arms. "He's just never coming back?"

"I think that's his plan," Lincoln mutters.

Cassidy's eyes widen. "What about you? Are you leaving too?"

Lincoln shrugs. "I have no idea. Now, take the envelope."

"What's in it?" I glare at it.

"He didn't say. Only asked me to give it to you." He holds up his hands. "Don't shoot the messenger."

I snatch it from his hand, and their eyes are on me as I rip it open. Papers are folded inside. I jerk them out as if they'd stolen today's coffee and unfold them, and then my mouth turns dry as I read his bullshit letter.

*Georgia,*

*I'm sorry.*

*Fifty percent of the bar is yours.*

*Do what you want with it. Sell it to Cohen or be a partner but make yourself happy.*

*Archer*

"You've got to be kidding me," I hiss, glaring at Lincoln. "Tell me where he is."

Lincoln shakes his head. "No can do, babe."

"Goddamn it, Lincoln!" I shriek, tossing the letter onto the table. "Forget your stupid loyalty for one damn minute and tell me where he is." I flick the letter away. "He's trying to sign over the bar to me."

"What?" he sputters out.

I jerk my head toward the letter. "Read it."

He does, slamming it down when he's finished, and exhales a frustrated breath. "He's at our grandparents' lake house."

*Okay, I know where that is.*

*Kinda.*

*Not really.*

I could pick it out of a line of houses, but no way can I just drive there.

I played passenger when I went with Archer and was too busy introducing him to every TLC song to pay attention to where exactly we were going.

"Address, please," I say.

He gives me a *good one* look.

"Directions."

"Fine, fine, but don't say I'm the one who gave it to you."

Cassidy chuckles. "There's no way you're getting out of this one." She slaps his arm. "Think of it as your good deed of the day."

He peers over at Cassidy, fighting back a smile. "Listen, youngster, don't you have some frat boy's heart to break or Barbies to play with?"

She flips him off. "Don't you need to go find your vitamins to keep your bones strong and pick up your Viagra from the pharmacy?"

Lincoln stares at me. "Georgia, since you might be the new part owner, fire her ass."

Cassidy throws her head back. "Lincoln, dear, the chances of you being fired are much higher than mine since you're related to the devilish heartbreaker."

Cassidy has made it her mission to get under Lincoln's skin, and as much as he tries to fight it, he always caves in, engaging with her.

Lincoln rubs his forehead. "He's going to kick my ass for this, so be happy that I like you."

"Just tell him I went through Lincoln's phone and gave it to you," Cassidy says with a shrug. The girl is a brave one, not even flinching at the possible wrath of Archer.

Lincoln shakes his head. "I'll text you the address."

Cassidy peers up at me. "You okay to drive? I can take you if you want?"

"She wants a front seat to the shitshow," Lincoln comments.

She whips around to glare at him. "Rude. I *also* want to make sure she's cool to drive."

"I'm fine. They told me to wait forty-eight hours before driving, and it's been a week. I haven't felt dizzy at all. All I need from you is for you to cover my shift tonight."

She points at me and clicks her tongue. "I got you."

# CHAPTER FORTY-SIX

## Archer

AS SOON AS I answer the door, papers are shoved into my chest.

"Fuck these papers," Georgia shouts, storming into the lake house. "Fuck your games. Fuck your excuses. *Fuck you, Archer!*"

The papers plummet to my feet, and stepping to the side, I slam the door shut. "Georgia, calm your ass down."

Her thick hair is wet, dripping at the ends, and her shirt is soaked to her skin from the downpour outside.

*Why the hell was she driving?*

*Why the hell did my dumbass brother tell her where to find me, give her directions, and not give me a heads-up?*

Georgia stares at me, shivering. "No, I won't calm my ass down." Her voice cracks as she continues, "You left me, Archer! You left me in the hospital."

I shake my head before laying out my bullshit excuse. "I went to the hospital and made sure you were okay."

"Then you left!"

"What did you expect me to do?" I pound my finger against my chest. "My actions were what landed you in that hospital bed. It's time you find a man who isn't a toxic son of a bitch like me."

"What did I expect you to do? I don't know … uh, stay! I've been there for you over and over, but when it came time *for you* to be there *for me*, you ran." Tears fill her eyes, mascara running down her cheeks—pain and the rain the culprits.

My stomach knots, blistering with torment. "I'm sorry. It was the wrong way to end things, but by now, you should know that it was best for me to walk away."

"You're right." A cold smile creeps up her lips, sending chills down my spine. "I don't want to try to make it work with you anymore. You're selfish."

I stumble back a step, her words a blow to my chest.

*Isn't that what I wanted?*

*For her to be done with my ass?*

"What? You have nothing to say?" she rasps. "Of course you don't. I'm out of here."

My head spins, and I thank God I put down the bottle of Jack I'd been sipping on earlier, finally realizing it was time I quit relying on alcohol to mask my torment. Being alone in this lake house with hours upon hours to think has opened my eyes. Lincoln, Georgia, everyone was right. It's time for me to sit down, pull through my shit, and be the man Georgia deserves.

That means I have to let her go.

*Who knows how long it'll take me to sort out my shit?*

I teeter back when her shoulder smacks into mine on her way to the door.

Whipping around, I circle my arm around her waist to stop her. "No way are you driving in this weather."

She jerks away from me, venom in her tone. "In what?"

*She shitting me?*

I gesture outside. "It's dark, like a fucking monsoon out there. You're upset, and it's a long drive. You're not getting behind the wheel."

Her face burns with anger. "I'm sure as shit not staying here and hanging out with you."

"Too damn bad. You're the one who drove here, stomping and ready to kick my ass—"

"Which is fully deserved."

"I'll take that."

She crosses her arms. "Take me home then."

"*Neither* one of us is driving in this weather." I'll confiscate her keys, hide them, flush them down the damn toilet if I have to.

"This is entrapment."

"I'll let you go tomorrow."

She slips a glance at the papers on the floor, and I follow her gaze, recoiling as I stare at my handwriting, at the bullshit letter I wrote. Sure, it was a stupid move on my part, but it was what I felt was best.

Tapping her foot, she goes quiet, as if weighing her options. "Fine. Entrap me away."

My shoulders relax. "Let me grab you some dry clothes."

I wait for her argument, for her to tell me she isn't wearing any of my shit, but she doesn't. I hold in a breath while rushing into my bedroom, grabbing the first shirt and gym shorts I see, in hopes that she won't bail on my ass. Chasing her through the rain sounds like a bad time. When I return, she's on the couch, shivering and running her hands up and down her arms.

I hand them over. "Here."

With hesitation, she takes them, rises, and walks to the bathroom. I search for a blanket, raid the pantry, and pull out the instant hot-chocolate mix. She's tugging at the ends of her hair, the black blotches cleaned from her cheeks, and her bare feet slap against the floor as I stir hot-chocolate powder into a mug filled with warm water.

"Sit," I say, wrapping her up in the blanket and settling her down before handing over the mug.

She shifts, making herself comfortable. "How did we go from screaming at each other to you snuggling me in a blanket and providing hot chocolate?" She shakes her head. "Swear to God, our *whatever this is* between us is super dysfunctional."

I run my hand over my jaw and sit in a chair across from her, my legs wide. "Don't you see, that's what I've been trying to tell you?"

She raises the mug to her lips but doesn't drink. "Is dysfunctional a bad thing, though?"

I raise a brow, a *really* expression crossing my face.

"I don't mean *Sammi Sweetheart and Ronnie* dysfunctional. Let me reword it. Would you rather be boring? The few problems we have are nothing compared to others. When you're not running away, we get along perfectly. You're a great boyfriend and thoughtful. Well, you *were* a great boyfriend."

I grind my teeth at the word *were*.

"Archer, why do you feel like you can't love?"

"It's not that. Trust me, I *feel* love. I love you with every inch of my being. That's why I'm letting you go. I don't deserve you."

She pats the couch, and because I don't think and I long to be near her, I go to her.

My hand caressing her hair, I kiss her forehead. "I can never be perfect for you."

"I don't want perfect. I want *you*. When you're not acting like a jerk, we're good. Growing up, I saw bad relationships. I witnessed men treating my mother terribly. That's not you. It's not us."

"If you're okay with disappointment—"

"Jesus, you're not a disappointment." She yawns, exhaustion on her face, and takes a gulp of hot chocolate, like it'll give her a rush of energy. "I don't want the perfect man. That sounds scary, very Stepford Husband-ish."

I chuckle.

"Like you, I have issues. Daddy issues, an attitude problem, I've been called a sarcastic bitch more times than I can count, I get hangry like no other, I kill my bank account with my iced-coffee addiction, and I am stupid in love with you."

I gulp at the *stupid in love with you* comment. "All I care about is your happiness."

She squeezes her eyes shut and shrinks into the blanket. "What if my happiness is with you?" Another yawn escapes her. "I love you, Archer."

My back straightens. Hearing her say *I love you* is a knife through my heart.

She nibbles on the bottom of her lip. "It's really over for us, isn't it?"

My mouth opens to tell her yes, but I can't do it. I can't look at the woman I love and say I'm done with her, with us. I can't. As much as I tell myself I can walk away from her, I'm too weak. Selfishly, I can't let her go.

Her eyes are wet when she sets her mug on the coffee table and flips the blanket off her lap. "While I appreciate the warm drink, staring at the man who's breaking my heart isn't a good time."

"Stop."

She freezes.

"I can't." I shake my head, my voice breaking. "I can't let you go, Georgia. I thought I could, but ..." I hang my head low. "Stay tonight, please. Get some rest, and we can talk about this tomorrow."

I need to find the right words, the right way to fix us, to show her I can be a changed man. In doing that, she needs her space, needs time to process everything. And like so many other times, I don't want to use her body as I attempt to cope and deal with my issues.

"I'm not sleeping with you, only for you to tell me to kick rocks tomorrow."

"Take the guest room."

She's quiet.

"I promise, it's way more comfortable than your bed."

"Always hating on my bed." She stands. "Show me the way to my room, heartbreaker."

I lead her up the stairs and down the hallway. I open the door, and when I turn, she's wiping away silent tears from her blotchy face. I clench my fist, fighting back the restraint to hold her, to drag her to my bed so she never has sadness again.

I kiss her forehead. "Get some rest."

# CHAPTER FORTY-SEVEN

## Georgia

THUNDER ROARS OUTSIDE, knocking me out of my sleep, and I peek around the dark room. I left the bedside lamp on, but when I lean forward to turn it back on, it clicks, and nothing happens. The power must've gone out.

With no hesitation, I jump out of bed and creep down the hallway. His bedroom door is cracked. It squeaks as I open it all the way. I tiptoe into the room, and the sheets are soft when I crawl into bed with him.

"Don't say anything," I whisper when he stirs.

He nods, wraps his arm around me, and pulls me into him.

No words are spoken, and I fall into a restful sleep.

---

*I MISSED THIS.*

Missed waking up next to him, his strong body warming mine, his grip on me tight. I missed the happiness of opening my eyes and having him with me first thing in the morning—this man who I've gone through so many highs and lows with.

When I stormed out of the bar and drove to his grandparents' lake house last night, I had no plan. My lack of plan also included my lack of checking the weather. I didn't expect all hell to break loose on my drive here. Even though I fought it, I was glad he'd told me to stay.

I'm in his arms, the broad expanse of his chest against my back, and I feel his light breathing.

We need to talk.

No more arguing.

Running.

Back and forth.

Whatever is happening between us needs to be sorted out.

He stirs behind me, a yawn leaving him, and I roll away from him to settle on my back. His face is unreadable, and my sleepy eyes meet him in question.

"Morning," I whisper with a nervous smile.

"Morning."

"Last night was interesting."

My heart rages against my chest while I wait for his response.

*Will he want me out of his bed?*

*Ask me to leave?*

*Beg me to stay?*

*Push me down and do every dirty thing he did to me the last time we were in here?*

He yawns again, stretching out his arms. "A gorgeous woman crawling into my bed is indeed interesting."

My stomach settles.

"Really?" I playfully shove his shoulder. "It was pouring outside, I was in a random room, and there were weird-ass noises."

"You scared of the dark now?"

"No, I actually thought you needed consoling. You were talking in your sleep, whining about monsters. So, like the nice person I am, I came in to keep you safe from them."

He chuckles. "Appreciate that, babe."

*Babe.*

My head is dizzy.

"We need to talk." He pulls himself up, resting his back against the headboard.

I raise myself, shoving my elbow onto the bed, and peer up at him. "Agreed."

He blows out a breath, and his voice is level when he speaks, "I was wrong. I should've never run. I should've been by your side every minute you were in the hospital."

And I only grow dizzier.

I rub at my face, telling my head to straighten the hell up so I can process this conversation. "Why'd you do it? Why'd you leave?"

He doesn't lower his gaze or try to hide the guilt on his face. The firmness in his tone confirms our talk will be filled with truths and decisions. "I was scared." No bullshit, no excuses, the words coming out strong.

"Of what?" I whisper.

"Losing you?"

"Are you kidding me?" I shriek. "You chose to lose me."

"I fucked up. I thought I was doing what was best for you."

"I'm confused as to why *you* think you know what's best for *me*."

He groans. "Do you not realize why I'm scared? My grandfather and I argued, and he died. My father and I argued, and he died. You and I argue over me kicking a guy's ass, and you end up in the hospital with a concussion."

I raise a brow. "How'd you know it was a concussion?"

"Lincoln kept me updated."

"Snitch bitch," I grumble. "He had no problem giving out my business, but it was like pulling teeth to get him to give me anything on you."

"Lincoln likes you, likes us together."

"He's the brother with the brains."

He chuckles. "You're probably right."

I slide in closer to him. "Archer, what happened was an accident. You didn't mean to hurt me, and I don't blame you."

"I know." His face drops. "As I lay here last night when you were in the other room, I questioned everything I was doing wrong in my life. Then at the time I was mustering up the courage to let you go, you climbed into my bed. I realized, at that moment, I always want you in my arms. I don't want to lose that—to lose you and being the man who makes you happy. I love you, and I need to quit telling myself that I don't deserve our relationship."

"What are you saying then?"

"I'm saying, I love you, and though I don't deserve it, I'm asking for another chance."

My heart swells in my chest. I don't want it to seem like I'm letting him off the hook too easily, but I've never doubted Archer having feelings for me. It's whether Archer is willing to take the steps to be with me. There's no way I can look at this man that I love and turn my back on him.

Archer isn't a bad man. He's just gone through some bad shit.

"I lost my way," he continues. "Thinking people only wanted who I'd been before—the guy full of life, who didn't hold guilt on his shoulders like it was a part of him he'd die without. I'll never be that guy again, and I'm realizing that's not who you want. You didn't fall in love with that guy. You fell in love with who I am now, the man I've turned into, and for that, I realize that maybe I've found who I was supposed to be all along."

"Archer," I breathe out his name, making it longer as I search for the right words. "If I let you back in, if I put my heart on the line, then you need to promise me that you won't pull this shit again."

His shoulders curl forward. "I'm not perfect. I can't promise I won't fuck up, but I give you my word. There will be no running."

"Your word doesn't mean much right now. You gave me your word at the hospital."

"I fucked up."

"I can take flaws and haunted pasts, but I won't take disappearing. If we do this, it's all in. Period. If you can't commit to that, then walk away now. You can still work in the bar, and we'll be friends."

My stomach churns.

Friends.

I hate that word when it comes to Archer.

"I'm all in. I'm so damn sorry, baby. I was fighting to convince myself you'd end up being happier with someone else."

"Never going to happen."

"I love you, Georgia, more than you'll ever know." He grabs my arm and pulls me onto his lap. "You've changed me into a better man. You're inside me. You ripped yourself into my veins, shaking every bone in my body, until my heart finally broke free."

Tears are in my eyes.

He's fighting back his own.

I circle my arms around his neck, my stomach fluttering. "You know you have some making up to do, right?"

"Oh, baby, I know."

I giggle when he rolls me over onto my back. We're undressed in minutes, he slides a condom on, and when he positions himself at my opening, he stops.

His hand spreads on my chest over my heart. "This right here, I've never seen someone have such a big heart after going through the pain you have." He moves his hand to kiss the spot and then sucks on my nipple. "Not only is this body mine, but this heart is too." He grabs my hand and presses it to his chest. "And this, this belongs to you—the woman who saved me, who gave me a life again."

# CHAPTER FORTY-EIGHT

# Archer

"ARCHER." Cohen is standing in the doorway of my office with a scowl on his face and his hands shoved in his pockets.

I scrub a hand over my forehead. "Why do I feel like I'm about to get grounded?"

Cohen's face is blank as he walks in. "Maybe because what you did was fucked up."

I nod, understanding his anger. "I was in a bad place."

"You still in that bad place?"

"I can't say I'm not, but I'm also working through it."

His brows furrow. "Don't disappear on me again. You left me with a brokenhearted sister in the hospital, a son, a baby on the way, and a fiancée who craves Skittles one minute and a goddamn cheeseburger the next. I don't have time for your bullshit."

*Damn.*

Cohen isn't fucking around today. I feel bad. I'd assured him that there wouldn't be any issues with me wanting to pull out, but then I tried to give away my half of the bar. Cohen should have looked at the plus side. He'd have owned the bar with his family.

"I got your back, man. I'm clearing out my head."

"We all get one fuckup." He holds out his knuckles.

*I think I've had more than one.*

I bump my knuckles against his. "It won't happen again."

He gestures toward the door. "Now, come on. We have some drinks to make."

I stand, and he claps me on the back on our way to the floor. "It's good to be back."

---

"MMM, BACK THAT ASS UP," I groan, my hard cock rubbing against Georgia's ass crack.

We're in my bed, and damn, it's missed her.

She laughs, peering back at me with a smile. "What little ass I have."

I cup her backside before giving it a firm smack. "I love your ass, baby."

"You have to say that. You're my boyfriend."

"I don't have to say shit." I run my hand over one cheek and then the other. She shivers, pressing her ass into me, moving her hips in circles. "Ah, you kill me."

Hitching her leg over my waist, I find her clit, using my thumb to play with it, and she writhes against me. She shifts, and I groan at the loss of her. When she situates herself on all fours, my dick aches.

Crawling behind her, settling myself on my knees, I eye her adorable ass. "How bad do you want it, baby?" I slide my cock between her cheeks, my free hand massaging one.

She arches her back, her ass more in my face, and her grin is devious as she looks back at me. "How bad do *you* want it?"

I chuckle and lift forward to kiss her. She slides her tongue into my mouth and moans my name, knowing that's my weakness. Tilting her hips up, her ass in the air, I give it a quick slap before sliding inside her, inside heaven.

Her pussy tightens around my cock, gripping it hard, owning it.

My hands cup each cheek of her ass while I set a slow pace, waiting for what she wants.

There are times we fuck hard.

There are times we make love.

It isn't until she says, "Harder," that I slam into her with no restraint.

My bed thumps against the wall with each thrust.

My eyes are transfixed as I watch my cock slide in and out of her.

Our moans are loud.

The sound of my thighs smacking into her ass is music to my ears.

"I could stay inside you forever," I moan. "Touch yourself, baby. Play with your clit as I fuck your pussy."

I love it when she touches herself. Not as much as I love eating her pussy or fucking her, but it's pretty damn close. Just as she loves watching me jerk myself off.

"Are you close?" I groan. "Tell me you're close to coming on this hard cock."

"Yes." Her hand moves faster as she plays with her clit.

I lose myself, pounding into her until she's falling apart underneath me. Knowing her knees are about to buckle, I plant my hands on her waist, grinding into her. As I come inside her, I jerk my arm back and slap her ass. I shudder, my back straightening, and seconds later, I'm falling onto all fours. We catch our breath.

She's the first woman I've ever fucked without a condom. The first time, it was a spur-of-the-moment thing. Shower sex. It'd put a damper on the mood to walk into the freezing cold to put a condom on. She's on the pill, and so far, we haven't had any issues.

———————

"I MISSED HAVING you in my bed, baby," I whisper.

Georgia snuggles into my arms. "I missed how comfortable your bed is."

"Really? That's what you missed?" I grind into her.

We had sex ten minutes ago, but I'm ready for round two.

"That, among other things."

It's been two weeks since I got my head out of my ass.

Two weeks of me proving to Georgia that I'm sorry.

Two weeks of being the happiest man I've ever been.

"What if you could do it every day?"

She winces, staring back at me. "What do you mean?"

"Move in with me." I nuzzle my face into her neck, planting kisses along her soft skin. "Wake up with me every morning. Sleep in my arms every night."

She falls onto her back, and I level my palm on the other side of her, staring down while meeting her eyes.

"That's a pretty big step … it'd make things serious."

"I want to prove to you that I'm serious about us, baby." I tip my head down to kiss her. "I want this. I want you." I slide my tongue along the seam of her lips. "What do you say?"

She opens her mouth, sucking on the tip of my tongue, and the conversation stops momentarily as I make love to her this time.

With each circle of my hips, each thrust inside her, I hope to prove myself.

Show her how comfortable life is with me, how she'd wake up every morning.

She comes. I come.

She shrieks my name. I moan out hers.

"I need to make sure Grace can find another roommate," she whispers.

"Lola?" I ask. "Cassidy mentioned looking for a place too."

"I'll talk to her about it. I can't just bail on her."

"She can't make rent on her own?"

"She can. It's just … complicated."

# CHAPTER FORTY-NINE

## Georgia

### Two Months Later

IT'S BABY TIME.

Not mine, I should clarify.

Nor am I trying to make a little mini me yet.

I'm practically dancing in my chair while in the hospital waiting room. Anticipation has consumed me since Cohen called last night and said Jamie was going into labor. He asked us to wait until the baby was born before coming to the hospital since it'd just be a waiting game. An hour ago, he called and said there's another Fox baby in the family.

I'm over the moon for them. Jamie gave my brother the happiness he'd thought he'd never have again. His trust in people was shit, especially with a woman related to the girl who'd not only turned her back on him, but also his son. Having a woman look you in the eye and ask you to give your unborn baby up can be soul-crushing. My brother was never the same after that.

This time, it's a different experience. He's not going in, unknowing if Jamie will want their baby girl. There will be no bittersweet day when he's excited to meet his son yet scared of the agony of uncertainty if his child will have a mother.

"You excited?" Archer asks.

"I can't wait to meet her," I tell him.

He chuckles, squeezing my knee. "You're going to spoil the shit out of her, aren't you?"

"Damn straight."

I'm already guilty of letting Noah sucker me into giving him extra cupcakes and sneaking him fruit snacks that have actual sugar in them.

Not only am I riding the excitement of a new baby in the fam, but next week, I'm also moving in with Archer.

Even though Archer asked a few months ago, I didn't want to jump straight into the idea. I waited, giving Archer time. We were fresh, and my trust in him was still iffy. No way would I risk being homeless if he ran again. Our relationship has grown stronger, and I'm ready to take the risk with him.

I agreed to move in with him, and Cassidy will be taking Grace's new roomie spot.

"Hey, guys," Cassidy says, walking in with Lincoln behind her.

I smile and wave to them before leaning into Archer and lowering my voice. "Something will happen between them. Twenty bucks and fifty orgasms, they bang by the end of the year."

When we're at the bar, Cassidy flirts with Lincoln like it's her part-time job. Lincoln tries to keep his distance, joking that she's too young. Cassidy has had an easy life. Lincoln just got out of prison. They're not exactly bread and butter.

But hey, look at Archer and me.

"I'll take you up on that bet," Archer whispers. "I'll give you the orgasms no matter what, though. She's too young for Lincoln's liking."

"She's not *that* much younger than him. Their age gap is similar to ours."

"Let's just say, Lincoln likes them older."

"Older? As in cougars? Like, is his type women who need to hit their Life Alert after he gives them the D?"

He shakes his head, laughing. "Jesus, what am I going to do with you?"

"Answer the question. Now, I'm curious."

Come to think of it, I've never seen Lincoln with a woman. I stay with Archer all the time, and Lincoln hasn't gotten his own place yet. Not that I mind him being there.

Lincoln is good for Archer. Not only has their relationship grown but so has Archer's relationship with his mother. He has dinner with her once a week, and she's a frequent visitor at their place. Archer is finally realizing he doesn't have to face his problems alone.

"He's going to kill me," Archer says, keeping an eye on Lincoln. "He had a thing with one of my mother's friends." He pauses. "Two of them actually."

"You're joking."

He shakes his head.

It's not that I have a thing against age gaps. Archer is my brother's age. It's just surprising, especially the whole *mother's friends* thing.

"He can change, though," I say, having hope for Cassidy.

The girl is fun. I'd love for both Callahan men to find love.

"I'm sure you didn't think you'd end up with someone like me," I add.

He raises a brow. "Someone like you?"

"Quirky. Voice of a Valley Girl. Fun."

He grins. "Sure, but little did I know, a quirky, Valley Girl-voiced woman is who I needed."

Silas and Lola join us, interrupting our conversation.

Silas uses his sucker to signal between Archer and me. "When you two have a baby, you'd better hope it has your personality, Georgia."

I grab Archer's chin and move it from side to side. "Why? You know he has a shining personality."

"Only for you, babe." Archer winks at me.

"I think our baby will have a combination of our personalities," Cassidy says, smacking Lincoln's thigh.

"Your baby?" Silas asks. "What did I miss?"

Cassidy nods vigorously. "Hypothetical baby."

"There will be no babies," Lincoln corrects, shaking his head.

"I mean, first comes marriage." Cassidy smiles eagerly while glancing at me. "You'll be such a good sister-in-law, Georgia."

I burst into laughter.

All talk ceases when Cohen steps into the waiting room.

He rubs his hands together, a radiant grin on his face. "You ready to meet my daughter?"

---

ISABELLA GEORGIA FOX IS ADORABLE.

The middle name was a surprise to me.

I hold the sleeping girl in my arms, running my thumb over the peach fuzz on her head, and brush a quick peck to her forehead.

"She's so beautiful," I say, peering over at Archer.

His eyes are unreadable, and he smiles at me.

"Do you want kids someday?" I wrinkle my brow at the realization that we've never had this conversation.

He gulps. "I'm not sure."

I turn quiet, fighting to stop my face from falling. My face muscles hurt at my phony smile.

"You do." It's a statement. Not a question.

"I do." My body turns rigid, and I focus my attention on Isabella.

Another speed bump.

There are so many pieces in relationships. So many choices that can make or break you. Sure, you can love each other, have great sex, be happy, but when it comes down to spending the rest of your life with someone, there are conversations that need to be had, choices to make.

Where you'll live. Marriage. Kids.

Cohen's first relationship ended because his ex had decided out of the blue that she didn't want to be a mother after getting pregnant.

"Georgia," Archer whispers.

I shake my head violently, not looking at him. "Now isn't the time to have the baby talk."

"Georgia." When I don't look at him, he uses the tip of his finger to drag my chin up. His eyes meet mine, and they're gentle, warm, honest. "Don't ever feel like you have to hold back from me."

I shut my eyes before focusing on Isabella. "Then yes, eventually—*not* anytime soon—I want kids."

I peek up when the nurse walks in and starts talking to Jamie and Cohen. When she asks for Isabella, I carefully hand her over.

When Cohen was a single father and I was living with him, I helped him with Noah. I can change diapers, clean up vomit, and handle situations without batting an eye. It's why I work with children.

"Georgia," Archer says, scooting in closer to me, "you know I'll always be open and honest with you. In the past, I wasn't sure if I was mentally ready for children, but with each day I spend with you, I think about how much I want a family with you."

I grin at the thought of a family with Archer—of him being my husband and us having children running around. I wouldn't want to have one with anyone else but him. We may not be ready yet, but when the day comes, Archer will be an amazing father. I'm sure of it.

CHAPTER FIFTY

# Archer

I PEEK over at Georgia in my passenger seat. "I have a surprise for you."

She smiles. "Oh, really? What?"

"If I told you, it'd ruin the surprise."

"You're not going to blindfold me and all that, are you?"

I shake my head. "Nah, that only happens in our bedroom."

She laughs, blushing as her eyes downcast. No doubt she's thinking of our *blind-fold bedroom* times.

I pull down a street a few miles from Cohen's house before parking in the drive of a home with a For Sale sign in the yard. It's a home we pass every time we visit him and is what Georgia said her dream home looked like. As soon as it was put on the market, I scheduled a showing. As much as I wanted to put in an offer and surprise her, this is a decision I want her to be involved in. We haven't seen the inside, and I want her to make this *her* home.

"What is this?" she asks.

"You said this is what your dream house would look like." I shift my car into park. "Let's take a look at it."

She blinks at me, her jaw dropping open. "You're selling the penthouse?"

"Nah, not yet. I can't kick Lincoln's ass out." I chuckle. "Plus, I'm not waiting to live with you. We'll live in the penthouse until we find something you love."

The penthouse is a bachelor pad. It doesn't have much character with its minimal decor. None of that is Georgia's style. She loves bright colors, patterns, macramé, and plants. I want her to have a place she can make hers—ours.

I almost turned my back on us.

Almost broke us.

I thank God every day that I pulled my head out of my ass.

Georgia is it for me. She's the only woman who can drag me out of the darkness, out of my self-pity, and into her light. I don't know how she does it, why she does it, but she will forever hold my heart. She took me by the hand and led me to happiness.

"Plus," I say, clearing my throat as she admires the home, "there's more room here for a family."

Her attention whips back to me. "Family?"

I nod. "The more I see you with Isabella, the more I see that love and compassion on your face, the more I want to have a family with you. I'm not saying let's knock you up tomorrow, but I want us to have a home for when we decide to start a family, when we're ready."

"You want me to have your baby?"

My heart thrashes against my chest, just thinking about it.

I nod, fighting back a laugh. "I definitely want you to be my baby momma."

---

THREE DAYS AGO, we flew to Belize for a weeklong vacation. We were due for some alone time, away from the bar, just the two of us. I rented an overwater bungalow, and I've never seen a sky and water so clear.

The bungalow was a surprise, and Georgia has been all smiles since we arrived. It's her first time vacationing out of the country. She claims I spoil her, but she deserves the spoiling.

The air is salty while we have dinner on the terrace overlooking the crystal-clear water. She's beautiful against the sun glowing in the horizon.

I set down my fork. "I have a question."

Georgia takes a sip of wine while focusing on me. "Sure, babe. What's up?"

My heart is a hammer beating against my chest, and I draw in a deep breath between my teeth. "Are you still worried I'll leave … go MIA?"

It takes her a moment to reply, and her eyes soften. "No. To be honest, with any relationship, you always run the risk of being left." She reaches across the table to grab my hand in hers. "You make me happy, so incredibly happy. I love you, love you in my life, love our relationship. You've proven to me that I can trust you with my heart, you've opened yours to me, and you've shown me that you're in for the long haul. I believe you. I see your heart, past that hard exterior, past everything you try to hide. I wouldn't be here with you if I thought you were going to leave me."

My heart rages harder at her response.

Everything she said is the truth.

I'm in it for the long haul. I want to be with this amazing spitfire of a woman for the rest of my life. Georgia is it for me.

"There's something I've been wanting to ask you."

She cocks her head to the side. "Yeah?"

I deposit my napkin on the table, scoot out my chair, and stand. She stares at me curiously as I circle the table.

"I've been waiting for the perfect time to do this."

"To do what?"

I shove my hand into my pocket and dig out a box before dropping to a knee.

"Holy crap." She grabs her wine and chugs it.

I display the box in my hand, begging my hands not to

shake, and clear my throat. "To tell you that you're my heart, Georgia."

A sob escapes her.

"Before you, I planned to live a lonely life. I blamed myself, made myself suffer, because there was nothing I had to look forward to. And then you came along and changed that thought … changed me. You shook the hurt out of me. You saved me, Georgia. You saved me, baby. I want to spend every day proving to you that it wasn't a waste of time."

I open the box, and she gasps at the glistening diamond ring.

"I love you, and I would be on top of the damn world if you agreed to be my wife."

As tears slip down her face, she nods violently. "Yes. Yes. Holy crap, yes!" She jumps up from her chair, pulls me to my feet, and hops into my arms.

Her lips crash into mine.

I keep my hold on her and the box while walking to the bedroom. As I settle her on the bed, I snap the box open, carefully pull out the ring, and slip it on her finger. The teardrop diamond ring with pink diamonds wrapped around the band was custom-made for her.

We make love, her naked and only wearing my ring.

My broken life led me to Georgia.

She's who I needed to face my demons, who was meant for me in the end.

She heals me.

I love her.

We may be different.

We may love different.

But together, we are perfect.

Never would I have thought that the woman who gave me shit over a parking spot and a fender bender would be the one who brought me to my knees and made me fall in love.

# KEEP UP WITH THE TWISTED FOX SERIES

*All books can be read as standalones*

**Stirred**
(Cohen & Jamie's story)

**Shaken**
(Archer & Georgia's story)

**Straight Up**
(Lincoln & Cassidy's story)

**Chaser**
(Finn & Grace's story)

**Last Round**
(Silas and Lola's story)

# ALSO BY CHARITY FERRELL

# RISKY DUET

Risky

Worth The Risk

# ACKNOWLEDGMENTS

I want to start with **you,** the reader. Thank you so much. There are so many books out there, and you chose to spend hours of your time reading mine. I am forever grateful for you—for giving me this opportunity to write stories that I love and believe in.

**Mark.** I can be an emotional writer and sometimes take my frustrations out in the real world when my fictional one is giving me a hard time. Thank you for accepting that I'm a crappy housewife and having no problem with takeout being ninety-percent of our meals.

**Brooke.** If there's anyone that pushes me to get my shit together, it's you. Your guidance and advice has helped me so much in this career, and I'm so grateful that we're friends. Thank you for giving me motivation, answering my questions, and being a listening ear to my rambling voice messages.

**Jill.** For almost two years, you've been at my side in this journey—through writer's block, stressing over stories, and helping me plot until I'm a thousand percent happy with everything. Thank you for accepting the anxiety-riddled writer/friend that I am.

**Jen.** No matter what, I know I can count on you for advice and to read a chapter even when it's last minute. You're not only my publicist, but I'm so happy to call you a friend too. Thank you for believing in me and my stories.

**Wildfire PR.** Thank you for doing what I hate doing—marketing, and doing an absolute amazing job at it.

**Jovana.** Thank you for your patience with missing deadlines and always getting me in. Your eye for detail is impeccable, and I know my book is in good hands when you're editing.

**Jenny.** Thank you for being that extra-pair of eyes. You go above and beyond proofreading.

**Zoe and Paris.** My fur-babies who never fail to put a smile on my face even when I'm having the worst of days.

# ABOUT THE AUTHOR

Charity Ferrell resides in Indianapolis, Indiana with her future hubby and two fur babies. She loves writing about broken people finding love with a dash of humor and heartbreak, and angst is her happy place.

When she's not writing, she's making a Starbucks run, shopping online, or spending time with her family.

www.charityferrell.com